MIDKNIGHT RIDERS!

Thunder boomed!

Suddenly *they* were upon us, come to do their bloody business in the light of the moons, riding us down from the sweaty backs of tall beasts whose screams mingled with those of our helpless crewmen.

His mouth agape with terror, the lieutenant ran toward me, but a rider in tarnished armor cut him down with a single vicious blow.

In a stride, I was standing over the lieutenant as someone galloped toward me, a huge plume bobbing atop his helmet. He stopped his mount a half-dozen meters away, dipped his lance, kicked the animal's sides.

I shot him in the belly.

Also by L. Neil Smith

Published by Ballantine Books:

TOM PAINE MARU

L. NEIL SMITH

A Del Rey Book

BALLANTINE BOOKS • NEW YORK

For Cathy, my Butterfly Princess

CONTENTS

PART THREE *The Lamviin*

Prologue

A soft, fragrant wind heralded the coming of darkness. It brought with it the distant murmur of thunder.

"*Asperance* Reentry Command to *Lifeshell Four*, come in?"

Silence.

"ARC to *Lifeshell Five*, come in?" The radio operator's pleas were rewarded only with an empty static crackle. Eyes streaming, he backed away from the flames as the breeze shifted suddenly.

Beside him, standing over the smoky fire, the lieutenant shivered, thrust his hands into the pockets of his uniform, demanding impatiently, "Any luck at all?"

Still coughing, the operator looked up from where he squatted, trying to coax a signal from the unit in his hand while heating a can of rations at the same time. The expedition's cook—with most of our supplies—had been aboard the missing *Lifeshell Four*.

"Not a whisper, sir. They might be having problems with their own communicators."

"Both units?" The thunder was louder this time, forcing the lieutenant to repeat himself. "Both units?"

"Then again"—the operator held up his own radio—"it might be this one. I would not have any way of knowing, sir."

ix

That made a certain sense; the officer squatting by the fire was a botanist. Our regular communications expert was aboard the missing *Lifeshell Five*. Things would begin to get really interesting when it came time to erect the microwave array for sending a message home. That gear *was* aboard one of the four globes that had . . . no, it was not quite time to say "survived," in either sense of the word. We did not know whether the other two had perished, nor were we certain yet that we had succeeded at surviving.

The lieutenant shook his head, silently mouthing unprintable words.

The blurry government manual had ordained a landing at dawn, allowing us one full daylight period to establish ourselves on alien, possibly hostile territory. The planet's searing primary decreed that we rewrite the mimeographed pages. Even the scant few hours spent in orbit behind nearly opaque photo-responsive plastic had blackened the hardiest of us, covering some in weeping blisters. Thus we had chosen a landing site in the high northern latitudes, prayed, triggered the retroigniters.

The landing had not been as bad as the scientists had said it would be. I fractured a bone in my foot in two places. Four lifeshells had grounded violently within a few klicks of one another. We had not as yet located the other pair, although there was a fresh crater nearby. Where eighteen intrepid Starmen should have been—select of nation-state, pride of an entire planet—now trembled a dozen frightened, homesick souls, variously shattered, unanimously bewildered.

Again came the low mutter of thunder toward the horizon.

I checked my splint before attending to the other wounded. The aluminum pistol-cleaning rod kept slipping off the instep to a position beside the arch where it could not prevent the flexing of my broken foot. It was growing dark rapidly. Thunder boomed with increasing regularity until it threatened to become a continuous, intimidating roll. Soon I would have to break out the expedition's arsenal. So many wounded needed help—our medical officer, his supplies were in *Lifeshell Five*—there had not been time to think about my regular duties.

Dazzled, shaken though we were, the surface of the planet seemed like heaven: rich, moist; even in this winter hemisphere the soil was warm, darkly aromatic. Four small moons blazed overhead, their reflected glory unbearable to look upon directly. It was a place to build a new beginning, to love a woman, raise a family.

No square centimeter was not covered by green growing things. Ordinary birds, extraordinary in their numbers, filled the trees with music. Pale, day-bleached grasses whispered with the hasty passage of furry, four-legged creatures, or sparkled with half-hidden multicolor scaly life. Insects swarmed in myriads. Even as we cursed them, we laughed with astonished gratitude while they pricked away at us.

Not a hundred meters from the landing site was a brook, a small pond backed behind a barrier of mud-caked branches by some broad-tailed swimming mammal. For a solid hour, earlier in the day, I had sat on its edge, dangling my ruined foot, more running water trickling between my bare toes than my family had used throughout my lifetime.

Now the thought gave me a feeling of guilty apprehension.

As a precaution, I crawled back into *Lifeshell One*, fumbling through the litter at the bottom. I began uncrating hand-weapons—eight-millimeter Darrick automatic revolvers—getting them loaded, ready in their racks. Even through the thick walls I could hear the thunder now. Our telescopic survey from orbit had betrayed sparse signs of primitive settlement. On the one-problem-at-a-time principle, we had chosen to land as far from those as possible. Still . . . Finding two oblong packages, I stripped off the foil wrapping, exposing a pair of reloaders, tipped one of them into the port of a weapon, thumbed the triangular plastic cartridges into its grip-magazine. Repeating the procedure, I then fastened two issue holsters to my equipment belt. Now, if something unexpected happened, at least one pistol would be ready for each of the mission commanders.

Carrying another half-dozen Darricks, still in their corrosion-proof sealant, I crawled out of the globe toward the rack I had erected beside the fire. Already the uninjured men were trying, under the direction of the lieutenant, to inflate the microwave dish, spreading limp plastic in a circle safely distant from the sparks being whisked into the air by the twilight breeze. Like one of those sparks, our home star would drift across the sky tonight. Our signals would take two years to get from here to there.

No time like the present to start.

Thunder boomed!

This time it did not die. Suddenly, *they were upon us*, twilit figures of horror, night raiders, come to do their bloody business in the broad light of the moons, riding us down from the sweat-foamed backs of tall, long-legged beasts whose disminded screams mingled with those of the helpless men they helped to murder.

At the edge of the encampment, I saw a pair of officers lifted with a lance point, tossed away like refuse, smashed against the hard earth. The frail plastic of the microwave dish, our only link with home, was shredded beneath the monsters' hooves. Beside the fire, the botanist/radioman went down before a crushing sword slash.

The sun had not been down an hour.

His mouth agape with terror, the lieutenant ran toward me. I struggled with a holster flap, freed the gun, stretched it out to him. He never touched it. A rider, firelight reflecting blood-red off tarnished armor, overrode him, cutting him down with a single vicious sword swipe.

The lieutenant stumbled, grunting with surprise as much as pain. The rider swept past him, aimed his weapon at me. Before I realized what was happening, the Darrick's sights were on the grill-slotted front of his helmet. I pulled the trigger. Bloody flesh exploded through the helmet's seams. The beast went on without its rider.

In a stride, unconscious of my wounded foot, I was standing over the lieutenant. Over the bellowing clamor of armor, hooves, men possessed by the exultation of killing, the terror of dying, the blast of the Darrick had seized the attention of our attackers. Someone galloped toward me, a huge plume bobbing atop his helmet. He stopped his mount half a dozen meters from me, dipped his lance, kicked the animal's sides.

I shot him in the belly. The empty plastic cartridge fell at my feet to join the first.

As he toppled, spilling his life over the animal's neck, I heard a war cry close beside me. For the first time I was aware I had the other pistol out. My front sight found its own way to the mark. Another skull exploded within its steel jacket.

My right-hand Darrick spoke again. Another alien fell, dashing his pulped insides on the ground. A red haze formed before my eyes as the universe became the sound of my guns, the shadow of both front sights against firelit body-steel, the clash of edged metal, the flashes of my pistol muzzles in the dark. Men fell, shouting with surprised anger, screaming with agony, gibbering with fear.

What seemed to take hours must actually have been over in seconds. Ten star-traversing "heroes" lay mangled, everything that they had been gone to feed the warm rich soil. Almost unopposed, the enemy had hacked us to pieces.

I glanced down at the litter of white plastic cartridges between my feet. The lieutenant's arm was nearly severed from his body. Standing over him, I found myself with a pair of slowly cooling empty-handled pistols.

With a merciless *swoosh!* the nicked flat of a carbonless iron swordblade slammed me from behind. It did not take away my consciousness all together, only a certain amount of interest. Sullen, pockmarked faces swam around me under dented helmets, gabbling words I almost understood.

Rolling me aside, they stopped the lieutenant's bleeding with a rough clot of manure, twists of something resembling burlap, divided our few belongings quarrelsomely, stripping what was left of the lifeshells. They hauled us away on a wood-wheeled cart drawn by animals different, stockier than those the metal-suited warriors had ridden.

My last sight of the encampment was a tower of greasy, roiling smoke.

I would never return to Vespucci, my home planet.

I would never see my fair Eleva again.

PART ONE

The
Starmen

1

Dungeon Fire
and Sword

Three whole weeks for my eyes to adjust.

You would think I could have seen better by now, even in what little torchlight squeezed through the tiny, barred window in the rusty iron door of our cell.

Just as well: the gloom made it a whole lot easier, eating from the crock of half-frozen slush they pushed in at us whenever they remembered. You could ignore the fuzzy stuff growing on its surface, hold your nose, pretend some of the lumps did not squirm as they thawed in your mouth.

Darkness got to be a kindly friend.

Where I sat, I did not need any floodlight to smell the lieutenant's arm rotting off. Why he was not dead—maybe I should have thanked our preflight immunizations, but the shots simply let his nightmare, mine too, stretch out that much further.

Eleva would have called that *defeatism.*

It could have been that my perspective was all screwed up. In the last month it had shrunk, by abrupt increments,

3

from the sun-filled universe—perhaps too *much* room, too
many hard chips of starlight pressing in on us—to this
underground kennel, hip high, two meters square, lit by
the leavings from a jailer's passageway.

The lieutenant, *my* lieutenant, Third-Rater Enson Sermander, sprawled unconscious in one corner, gradually
surrendering to gangrene. Provided hypothermia did not
claim him first. He had not been much to look at, even
in the best of times: tall enough that his scalp had crested
through his hairline; about a year's eating ahead of his
calorie quota. His face was a brown plastic sack full of
stale pastries. He inevitably dressed like an unmade Army
cot. Incarceration with infection were not improving him
any.

Another corner was mine.

A third I had crawled to a couple of times every day,
in the beginning, back when I had cared. It still smelled
worse than either one of us. At least that helped attract
the scavengers away.

I wondered what Eleva would have said to that.

I kept thinking that the fourth corner would have been
perfect for a table-model ColorCom, but reception was
probably terrible down here, even if they had invented
CC—or electric lighting—on this putrescent alien mudball
the natives called Sca. At that, I would have gratefully
settled for my mandolar to play myself to death with, but
it had burned, with everything else from the *Asperance*.
Idiots who believe that olden times were swell ought to
try living in the real thing for a while. A place for everything—with everyone in his place.

Each midday, somehow, when the nastiness seeping
frozenly down the rough stone walls began to drip, mark-
ing high noon, I would summon up the energy to belly
over to the lieutenant, to check him out. Aside from shivering all the time, it was the only exercise I got. I was
not strong enough to stand up any more, but the Scavians
had taken care of that: there was not room to do it in. If
the torch outside was fresh, I would try picking some of

the blind, white, writhing things out of his decay-blackened arm to squash on the already slimy floor. He would moan at the attention, out of his head, struggling feebly. I was careful not to drop any of my own load of vermin into the wound. It took real character to move away from him afterward. His rotting infection was the only source of warmth in the place.

He would lie there, breathing raggedly, leaving me alone again with my thoughts, dreams of home, of fair Eleva, which were a subtle torture in themselves.

As thoughts go, they were not much, a stagnant, circular trickle of regret. Three horror-attenuated weeks *still* had not been enough to accommodate me to my probable fate. A day from now, a week—*never*, if they had really forgotten us down here in the dark—His Excellency the Bishop, His Grace the local Baron, would finally settle between themselves who got to dispose of us.

Lieutenant Sermander was lucky. He likely would not last that long.

Me, they would either drag to a secular gibbet in the "town"—a thatchy pile of animal droppings rucked up against the soiled skirts of this castle—or to a more highly sanctified burning-stake in the greater filth heap that passed for a metropolis, seventy-odd klicks north of here.

Either way it ended, back home on dear old Vespucci they would never find out what had happened to their eighteen intrepid Starmen, flower of the Naval Reserve. With sufficient encouragement, not to mention distraction, the citizenry would forget.

Everyone but Eleva.

The bureaucrats would breathe a discreet (but hardly unanticipated) sigh of relief. It would have been nice, they would tell themselves, to have found a paradise world, ripe for exploration. Even so, they would remind each other, now there would be seventeen fewer obsolete heroes to worry about. Never mind that it had been the most expensive liquidation, per capita, in the history of Vespucci, simply raise the tax on protein, or on birth or death

or water. The warriors who had recently helped to batter
our entire beloved planet into political submission—pardon, make that "solidarity"—presently figured in officials' minds as nothing more than the likeliest source of
counterrevolution, once-convenient nuisances to find a
place for, of honorable exile, dryrot.

The eighteenth?

No hero, certainly, obsolete or otherwise. Just a person who was good with certain kinds of necessary machinery. I guess you could say I was the single real
volunteer aboard, the sole enlisted man, the only one with
dirt under his fingernails, therefore, in the scheme of things,
a sort of machine himself. My reasons are none of your
business, but—well, she wanted to marry an officer. They
promised me ...

The only other individuals neither forgetful nor re-
lieved would be the scientists. But they would be *quiet*.
Their expertise had landed us here. Unless they contained
their angry curiosity, they would make perfect scapegoats
for our failure. Modern Vespuccian methods are more
technically certain (read: considerably slower) than any
medieval hanging-tree or pyre.

Eleva, beloved, where were you now? Were you thinking of me? Would you find an officer to marry, after all?

2

The lieutenant groaned, stirring fitfully.

With what amounted to a moral effort, I managed to
lift my good foot, bring it down at the rat nibbling on his
fire-streaked fingers.

I missed, of course.

The jar of my boot on the muck-coated stones sent
shock through my sick, stiff body. The dirty creature
scrambled back to its hole to chitter away displaced frustration among its less venturesome but equally greedy
companions.

They could afford to be patient.

Rats were only one surprising familiarity awaiting the Vespuccian expedition to Sca. Since the founding of our (then) Republic, some two centuries before, natural philosophers had been accumulating evidence that humankind had originated elsewhere. There was not enough air to breathe, except at the lowest altitudes. There was not enough water to drink. There was not enough food to eat, never enough light to see clearly by. Animal species on the planet were divided sharply: those like us, oxygen-invigorated, bilaterally symmetrical; those constructed on a radial, seven-lobed architecture, who extracted chlorine from the lowland salt-sinks. The latter predominated, perhaps because they did not lose three out of five newborn at every generation.

Each was thoroughly poisonous to the other, something that made the competition for environmental niches interestingly deadly.

Republican emphasis on reasonable individual liberty, a stable peace unprecedented in the fifteen hundred years of written planetary history, had allowed the leisure time, among other resources, to dig up—quite literally—astonishing confirmation of a thousand ancient, bitter tales.

We did not belong.

How else could we have realized, from the remotest prehistoric past, that Vespucci was a dried husk of a world, circling a dull-amber clinker of a star, never much of a home to anyone, totally without a future? That is what folk wisdom maintained. That is what science corroborated. If Vespucci had been our natural place in the cosmos, we would have fit, like the seven-legged crawlies of the marshes.

Vespucci would have fit us.

As the planet's shifting sands were probed, it began to appear that we—some of us, anyway—might try our luck elsewhere. Maybe that bright blue-white star, "merely" two light-years away. For the dessicated books, the incredibly preserved artifacts the explorers found revealed that there was an abandoned starship, orbiting Vespucci overhead, fashioned by the hands of men, our ancestors, who had known more than we, who had nevertheless marooned their helpless unhappy posterity in this waste.

Yet we scarcely expected to find human beings on Sca, nor ordinary rats. Nor powerful barons ruling a degenerate barbarism, nor the Bishops of the Holy Order of the Teeth of God, who, in an uneasy alliance with the feudal aristocracy, held their sun-bleached world in a double fist: faith, brutality.

Something slithered from between the mortarless stones behind my neck. I had been hearing it, with its bristly sound of stiff hairs or countless legs, for the past several days, halfway hoping it was large enough to eat—the rats were too fast for me—or poisonous enough to bring this insanity to an end. Perhaps I would have time to use it on the lieutenant, as well.

I moved; it gave a dampish bubbling squeal, then vanished, leaving silence.

3

Folks back home had seen us off grandly. Eleva commed me at the skyport quarantine. Military bands blared loudly over every channel as our clumsy shuttles one by one grumbled aloft toward the new, half-completed vespucciostationary satellite, assembled around the remains of an older technology. Fully finished nearby lay the *Asperance*, product of our two most important sciences: physics, archaelogy.

The World State (no longer a republic) called her a "starclipper."

Eighteen Starmen bound themselves in position along the flimsy framing, where they would work, eat, sleep, exercising grimly in place for months. Fireworks followed the speeches; interviews were ColorCommed to a grudgingly united world below. The ranks of heavily armed peace-forcers were not shown on camera in the crowd scenes. We floated free of the station, powered up the field generator, spread our sails.

Mankind was free of Vespucci for the first time in recorded history.

Technically sophisticated as they may have been, practicing scientific arts long lost to their grandchildren, our ancestors, we have learned, had arrived upon Vespucci by desperate accident.

Their lifeless vessel lay in orbit, lifeslip stations gaping. Within, in addition to their records, was discovered the Thorens Broach with which they had ducked *around* the laws of physics, hemstitching through an unreal continuum where all points in distance-duration are geometrically common—one's destination uncontrollably random. They had had a destination in mind. They had not reached it. The electronic log held stories of a dozen panic-stricken random leaps until, at last, a marginally habitable planet had been stumbled upon.

It was *still* only marginally habitable, which was why we were leaving.

I wondered at the time we read the papers, saw the unfolding story on the ColorCom: what had they fled to take such a chance? What horrors had they willingly traded for the parched nubbin they named Vespucci? I did not want to know. Neither did anybody else. We looked for *new* worlds, a future for ourselves, our children.

Generations of desperate hard figuring, plus a leg up from what had been rediscovered amidst buried shards, orbital trash, propelled *Asperance* starward on a newer principle, one that made us feel we had won a certain superiority over our unlucky forebears. Her half-meter-diameter core was an enormous paragravitic "antenna" spinning out a field rendering everything within her billowing plastic folds *inertialess*, no longer subject to the normal laws of accelerated mass. She would not *evade* the speed limit, as folktales held that those before us had been "punished" for doing; she would remain in normal space, to *ignore* the theoretical speed limit.

Half that capability we had achieved by the time I was born. Vespuccians—in this case meaning citizens of the single most advanced nation-state that had ultimately forced its country's name upon an entire planet—were old hands at navigating the local system, pushed by sails a kilometer wide, a single molecule thick. We had explored a dozen lifeless, hopeless balls of baked or frozen rock, often taking months just to travel a few astronomical units, discovering nothing for the effort.

A solar system, a planet, a nation-state, all named Vespucci. It betrayed, I thought even as a child, a certain narrowness of perspective. It was not the sort of insight I could talk about, even with Eleva. By the time of Consolidation, there were even those who wanted to rename the capital city, Volta Mellis, Vespucci. It was easy to understand: our options were as limited as the imaginations of our geographers. Not particularly coincidentally.

Asperance might make all the difference. Less substantial than the photon winds she sailed, she could traverse such local distances in seconds. Two light-years to the nearest star, a little over ten trillion kilometers, would require something under nine weeks.

4

Grimly, we hung on.

We forced down inedible rations. Dully, we exerted our bodies every day against elastic cradles to keep the Void from devouring our bones. Under its merciless cold pinpoints of light, we slept only fitfully. Scarcely crawling from the racks we had been assigned, we tried to forget— or at least not to remind one another—that we would have to find some haven in which to survive the years it would take for our puny signals to carry home the news of whatever we had found. Eventually we would be followed by those others like the *Asperance*, even possibly get back home someday ourselves.

Home.

Eleva.

If.

So, the officers played CC games, watched our meager stock of entertainment tapes until the brown oxide wore off the plastic. I chorded the button frets of the mandolar, wondering what was to become of us, seeing pale-blue eyes, coppery hair, the delicate red bow of a mouth, where they had no right to be, against the ebon canopy of space.

Sixty two days after our departure we orbited a promising cloud-swirled marble hanging before its overwhelming primary. It was green down there, even to the naked eye, heartbreakingly blessed with water, so inviting it seemed to stir a primordial caution deep within a company accustomed to less charitable handling by nature. Yet, with a little finagling, perhaps, this paradise was—*ours*.

We were prepared to pay.

Asperance shut down her paragrav, shed her filmy wings in free-fall. We eighteen huddled in six tough, spherical lifeshells of carbon filamentized polyresin she had carried at her stern. During the all-but-endless journey, they had served as our only refuge from the pale frozen stars.

Or one another.

Now, under the blinding blue-white brilliance of a foreign star, Sca's thick mantle of atmosphere began to abrade their skins, filling their bottoms with human sweat. Each armored lander became shrouded, isolated from the others in its own tortured curtain of ionization. We cowered inside, isolated equally, despite the inhuman crowding, each man alone with his thoughts. Our homeworld, niggardly as it may have been, was out of touch, perhaps forever, lost to us.

5

The baron, as heavily scarred by disease as the merest of his vassals, enjoyed a virtual ignorance of the geography of his own planet. He would not believe the "superstitious nonsense" I managed to communicate to him: that we were from that bright light in the sky, right there where I was pointing. We were invaders, he decided, foreign vandals, breakers of his benevolent peace.

He wanted to hang us.

The bishop, through a live-in delegation at the baron's castle, was all too ready to believe, naming us sorcerers, nonhuman demons, unnatural purveyors of some weird (but, it appeared, not very potent) magic.

He wanted to burn us.

The bailiff, a squat, evil-eyed old ruffian with a short axe in his belt, did not much appreciate being caught between two absolute powers. I recognized his type immediately: a retired head-trooper, the kind of battered career noncom who has seen it all, still does not believe a word of it. He was enthusiastic about my daily interrogation, however. That did not call for divided loyalties, no sir, not at all. He soon discovered my shattered instep, along with the fact that I screamed quite satisfactorily when he ordered it twisted. Given such "incentives," I found learning a new language ridiculously easy. It seemed to follow familiar rules, varied from my own more in pronunciation than vocabulary. I began to wonder whether Sca might be the hell-hole my ancestors had fled. Yet how could these savages have constructed even the absurdly unreliable drives we had discovered abandoned in orbit above Vespucci?

I became more fluent—also less curious—when they began using tongs, pincers, obscenely shaped irons thrust into glowing coals. For the most part, however, the bailiff preferred having my foot exercised. It was much less expensive than good charcoal.

I told them everything I knew, plenty I did not *know* I knew. I remember at one point offering to go back home to find out more. None of it seems very real, somehow, although some of the scars, inside or out, I will carry to the end of my days. I passed out frequently during those sessions. With no memory of the intervening period of relief, I would sometimes wake the next day to find a poxy minion wrenching my ruined foot again. Eleva's eyes, her smile, began to be elusive, deserting me when I needed their recollection to sustain me.

Naturally, most of what I had to tell them did not make sense. Even sane, physically whole, how do you explain air power or overlapping fields of machine-gunnery to a primitive in knitted-iron underwear whose notion of martial arts is to poke at his enemies with a metal-shod stick? At last they gave up, dragged me away until some agreement could be reached about what to do with us. The bailiff personally saw me bolted into a hole in the dungeon wall.

The lieutenant had remained unconscious during the eternity—perhaps a week—I had been put to question. That had not stopped them torturing him. The forms must be followed.

They had not invented locks on Sca. The door, a crudely hammered meter square of iron sheet, was fastened at its hingelike hasps with soft metal rivets a centimeter in diameter, quite beyond reach of the palm-size grating in its center or the slop-slot below. These were the lower-class accommodations, the literal bottom of the heap. The walls dripped constantly, when they were not frozen solid, with seepage from the luxury dungeons above. We were fed occasionally. Someone came to replace the torches in the passageway.

I estimated three weeks' time by making small tears in the edge of my flight jacket every time I awoke to the drip, drip, drip of the polluted stone around me. Very rapidly I became too weak to keep such a calendar, except that my uniform jacket obliged by getting easier to tear. Twenty-two short rips in the rotted fabric later, the Hooded People came.

2

Farewell to Eleva

The heavy woven-synthetic restrainers cut painfully where they rode across my midsection. Hardly noticable after the grandly hollow send-off, the crushing four-gee eternity from the dessicated surface of Vespucci to stationary orbit.

Nighttime reigned in this position. To the right, several kilometers away, the new space station lay, still under construction, a wild hodge-podge of beams, containers fastened to the hull of the ancient colonial ship that had brought our ancestors here. Between the interstices in the new construction, she could still be seen, a pitted dull-metal sphere, dozens of meters in diameter, dead, cold, empty for fifteen hundred years—until lately rediscovered by her creators' children.

Already copies of her fusion powerplant were being installed in Vespuccian cities all over the planet.

Reflexively, I smoothed the creases from the trousers of my special, fancy, useless uniform. Tailored just for that occasion, they were a violent shade of lavender to photograph well on CC, tricked out with silver braid, a deep maroon stripe running down the pants leg, a short, waist-length jacket that kept riding up, exposing the place where the shirt crept out of the beltless waistband of the trousers. The knee-length silver boots were clumsy, would have to be jettisoned for weight's sake before the *Asperance* shipped out.

At least I sat unburdened with the awkward matching pistol belt. The sole enlisted man among the crew, I was not entitled to carry a sidearm, merely charged with keeping them all in good repair, making sure the officers did not shoot themselves before I could stow the ordnance aboard ship. I carried my mandolar in its collapsible fabric case; it used up every gram of my personal freight allowance—I do not grow beard enough to need a razor desperately—but I counted on the mandolar to keep me sane during nine weeks' voyage.

I shifted the safety straps once more, trying vainly for comfort, peered forward to the end of the long, cylindrical transfer-cannister where they were projecting the festivities on a large ColorCom screen. At least they were interrupting the blaring military bands, the posturing politicians, long enough to give us a first clear view of the *Asperance* where she lay a few klicks off the new space station. She looked like nothing else in Vespuccian history, not like any kind of vehicle at all—certainly not like the stubby, heavy-winged orbiter that had lifted us earlier this morning into the purple sky above the capital, Volta Mellis.

From some vantage point, probably another shuttle, we could even see ourselves approaching the starclipper, the shuttle's bay doors opened already, exposing the tube that temporarily, uncomfortably, housed seventeen officers and their single general-purpose flunky.

No, the *Asperance* resembled a huge VHF *antenna*, a single long, extruded titanium mast no larger in diameter than a big man's thigh crossed perpendicularly at intervals with complex, tightly guyed spars. At her forward end were the shackles for her photon sails, kilometers-wide umbrellas she would unfurl to catch the solar winds that would sweep us to our destination. Aft, she bulged with a half-dozen multi-purpose spheres, heavily armored for the landing, stuffed full of consumable supplies for the voyage.

The *Asperance* gleamed dully in the reflected light of the sun. The entire fragile assemblage resembled a child's toy draped in transparent plastic tenting. At the end of every cross-spar clung either a skeletal one-man seating-rack or a cluster of instrumentation. Her titanium core housed the inertia-canceling field coils, the reentry spheres concealed the field generator/power plant. Thirty meters long, not counting her sails, she would prove far more uncomfortable than the shuttle we now occupied.

Four more exactly like her were under construction. We could see the torches flaring, the spacesuited figures swarming over them to our left.

2

"I just do not know, Corporal O'Thraight, three years is a long time..."

I watched Eleva Dethri through the smeared transparency, hating the quarantine procedures at the base, wishing I were on the other side of the plastic where her voice would not come to me through an electronic filter, yet, deep inside, a little grateful for the regulations that saved me from potential humiliation.

I never touched her; I never knew if she would want me to.

Behind her on the corrugated metal wall of the shed, garish posters proclaimed the glory of our coming leap to the stars, informed visitors of the many rules governing their brief stays, exhorted them to tell their friends, their coworkers, their families, how their voluntary tax contributions were building a magnificent future for unborn generations of Vespuccians.

"Yes, I know, Eleva, darling, if you could only... besides, when I come back, I will be an officer."

Dim red sunlight trickled through the windows on her side of the barrier. The shed stretched forty or fifty meters. At the door, a heavily armed Army guardsman stood at parade rest, watching each conversing couple closely. At a dozen similar stations we Starmen could have short, unsatisfactory glimpses of those we loved, of the lives we were leaving behind.

She was right, of course. Women generally are about these things. Three years *is* a long time, a lifetime, almost the same amount of time I had loved her, since an Officer's Club dance where she arrived on the arm of a slavering lieutenant. Since I had last played the mandolar in public, on a temporary assignment that was an unexpected break in my regular duties.

Changing my life.

"An officer?" Her pale-blue eyes brightened a little, she licked her lips uncertainly. "Why, Corporal, how wonderful! As astronaut, one of the first eighteen... but three years?"

Eleva the beautiful: fair, lightly freckled skin, tightly curled copper-color hair, taller than I by a centimeter or so, unless I stood up *very* straight. I sat up very straight. Combat boots helped, except when she wore high heels. I suppose, as the only offspring of a warrant officer—worse yet, descended from an upper-class family whose demotion, after a lost battle, had been the scandal of the previous century—she never fitted, either among the enlisted class of my beginnings or the officer class she desperately aspired to rejoin.

I shifted uncomfortably on the tractor seat bolted before the plastic partition. We eighteen, and our alternates, would spend two weeks in quarantine until we proved to carry no diseases that might compromise the mission. Air pressure measured slightly higher inside the buildings to insure our isolation. We communicated with the outside world by wire.

Eleva looked unhappy. "Corporal..." She glanced around to see whether anyone listened, a futile gesture, as our conversation was monitored by the psychiatric staff. "... Whitey, I—I do not know what to say. I, well, I had my plans, my life sort of laid out in front of me. Now you..."

Now I... I had thrown her an unpinned grenade by promising to become the officer she wanted. What else could I do? Did I want a commission for its own sake, for *my* own sake? I knew I wanted Eleva. Like most individuals of my class, I had learned not to want much of anything else.

"Say you will wait for me, Eleva," I answered, trying hard to cover the anger, the frustration I felt. "Or say you will not. Either way. You will not say you love me. We have never... But let me know, *now*."

"Please do not force the issue, I do not *know* what to say! Whitey, I do not know what I feel. Three years? Why, by then, I will be—"

"Three years older. Eleva, go marry a captain. I will learn not to care. Anyhow, it is too late. I am stuck here with this mission, all on account of—"

"Do not *dare* blame me!" She pouted. The door guardsman looked our way, raised eyebrows under his titanium helmet. "I never asked you to volunteer for the *Asperance*, did I? I did not ask you to do anything at all—except let me alone!"

This was turning out all wrong, not at all as planned, as dreamed about. Saying good-bye to the only woman I ever loved, I had expected something different from her, something warm to take with me to the cruel stars. Now I heard myself say all the wrong things, helpless to stop myself saying them.

"Then what the Ham are you *doing* here, Eleva Dethri? Why did you come?"

"I do not know!" she cried, flinging herself off the stool.

She ran out of the room while I could think of nothing to say.

"*Eleva!* I love you! Please do not go like this!"

But of course she could not hear me. The press-to-talk switch popped up the moment she released it.

3

Three years earlier, I stood before the battered desk of my CO/conductor, Colonel Gencom, trying hard to understand what they were doing to me. The office walls were lined with photographs of the band over two generations, half a thousand men in uniforms of varying obsolescence, half a dozen wars of varying unbearability. On the windowsill behind his desk lay a tarnished trumpoon with a bullethole through its bell; the unit colorcords hanging from it were stained with something that matted the braids together. Something dark, nearly black.

"Whitey"—the colonel shuffled through the sheaf of paperwork as if he, too, could not comprehend the reasoning behind this order—"you are the best damned mandolar player in the band. I hate to see this happen; you know how it is: 'Ours not to reason why...'"

Never mind that, in an orchestra, nobody hears the mandolar except the other musicians who rely upon it for harmony, chord progression, rhythm even the percussionist depends on.

Never mind that the papers on the colonel's desk were reassigning me to training as a field armorer, a sort of meatball gunsmith—something I knew nothing about, possessed no background for. There was a war on; there was always a war on; war imposes its own reasons, its own demented logic. There existed a greater need, in the eyes of the State, for field armorers than for mandolar players no one except the other musicians could hear.

Never mind that I had been trained to play the mandolar, by edict of the same government, since the age of seven.

I doubled as company supply clerk, meaning in the first place that I was in charge of spare reeds, mouthpiece covers, mutes, assorted junk like triangles, ceram blocks, train whistles, sand whistles, slide whistles. In the second, it meant I billeted with what I was in charge of, spending my days—except for rehearsals, performances—among endless shelves of odd-shaped semimusical detritus, inventory forms, storeroom dust of a hundred military years.

In the third place, I was de-facto repair officer: if a thumb key broke off a picconet, if the bass saxonel got dented, if the xylotron threw burnt insulation all over the xylotronist, they brought it to me, for soldering, hammering, emergency rewiring—even a little first aid. I got to be pretty good—undoubtedly the reason I had been chosen for retraining.

"It is not all so bad," the colonel shattered me of my reverie, although I thought he spoke more to himself than to me. "While you are in training you will be available should we need you. I suspect there will be no replacement, not in a hurry, anyway."

I nodded. Nothing he said required—or justified—a reply.

"There may be other opportunities, even after you are rotated out into the field. I shall try to see there are if it would please you, Whitey."

"I would like it very much, sir."

"Good. Also, you will always have your musical talent to fall back on, as a comfort to yourself, your comrades. It could be worse, could it not, Corporal?"

I saluted, snapped my heels. "Yes, sir, Colonel, sir, it could be worse, sir."

He gave me a very unmilitary grin, shook his head ruefully. If one thing the Navy—or the Army, for that matter—could arrange, it was for things to be worse. He knew it. I knew it.

I turned smartly, started out of his office.

"Whitey?"

I turned again, curious. He removed his spectacles, rubbed his eyes, looked back up at me. "Since we will not be receiving a replacement, take your mandolar with you. You will need to stay in practice, anyway."

"Yes, sir. Thank you, sir."

"Do not thank me, son, I am not authorized to give away Navy property. I do not know what happened to Corporal O'Thraight's mandolar just before he was reassigned. Thank the Navy, boy. I do it every day. You could never print the words I use to do it."

4

The voice in the corridor outside said, "Here it is: YD-038."

Nobody knocked. The door opened. Miss Sixte, ninth-floor mother for the local Navy Reserve creche, stepped inside.

I snapped to attention.

It was a gray room, three meters by three, with a gray door, six little gray bunks, YD-036 through YD-041 inclusive, smoothly tucked to regulation tautness. Miss Sixte kept pretty much to herself. Sometimes you could hear her sobbing in her own room after lights-out. None of the kids ever managed to discover why.

Everybody else had gone to calisthenics that morning; I had been told to wait. It made me nervous. I had never spent much time here in the daylight. Behind Miss Sixte, a tall, thin man carried an odd-shaped plastic box by the handle. "Whitey, this is Sergeant Tenner of the Twenty-third Aerofleet Band. He is going to be your teacher."

I had teachers, plenty. Tenner looked okay, though, if kind of weird: cadaverous, with slicked-down hair, olive skin, a good smile. Good hands, with long, thin fingers. "Whitey?" He offered me one of the hands.

"Sergeant," I answered, gravely adult as I could be. "What is that you are carrying, sir?"

"Not 'sir,' 'Sarge.' Take a look." He handed me the case.

I fumbled with the spring latches. Inside, in a tight-fitting bed of bright yellow plush, lay the most beautiful object I had ever seen.

About the length of my forearm, it had a long tapered neck on the flat face of which six inlaid columns of square brightly colored buttons touched each other at the edges, like mosaic tiles, each about the size of a thumbnail. They marched down the neck in twenty-four rows, until it blended with the body: not much larger than the neck, very slightly ovoid. At its bottom was a cluster of tiny knobs. Six long plastic vanes stuck out from the face, a centimeter high, six centimeters long.

Tenner took the beautiful thing from my reluctant hands, arranged the fingers of his left on the neck-buttons, *just so*, fluttered his right thumb down across the hinge-springed vanes.

A chord more wonderful than anything I had ever heard. E-minor-seventh.

"What do you think, Whitey?" Nobody had ever asked me that.

"What *is* it, Sarge?"

"A mandolar. From now on, it will be your life."

3

The Sky Demons

Slop, I remember thinking, is a bit early today.

I had heard the barred doors slamming open along the length of the hallway. The shadow eclipsed the only light in my severely atrophied universe. To my surprise, a heavy mallet rose, fell, rose, fell—exactly as it had done when we were sealed into this purgatory, this time miraculously splitting the soft rivets in the hasp.

The rust door grated open. Forms moved erratically side to side, throwing bizarre shadows into my world. I cringed backward, partly in terror of renewed torture, partly because my eyes were painfully blinded by the raw, unfiltered glory of a smoky torch in the sconce across the passage.

"Ye're of a certes as these be the ones ye're wanting?"

His harsh voice seared forever into my memory, the bailiff stood before the door, visible from the waist down. I recognized his boots, the hem of his mailed shirt over its padded vest. Hammer with chisel dangled from one calloused hand. A hatchet hung from his belt. Other fig-

24

ures, muffled in floor-length hooded robes, bent nearly double to examine us, each averting its hidden face as it did so, from the sight, the stench of two human beings slowly turning into piles of putrescence.

Rats skittered back into their niches.

The last of the apparitions, in a Scavian dialect almost unintelligible to me, spoke in a low sibilant crackle betraying not a hint of personality or gender, even of humanity.

"You are the sky demons?"

Backlighted by the torch outside, the vapor of its breath hung menacingly before my face in the frigid cell. I tried to look it straight in the face. Firelit shadows gave the impression of a brown-robed man, arms folded into opposing sleeves, faceless, terrifying.

"What do you want from me now," I croaked a question in response, the first words I had spoken besides Eleva's name in what seemed like centuries, "another confession?"

"With the right truth, demon, yet may you live to see the moons rise."

"Yeah, I will see them, all right—just before you light the bonfire! Now get out of..."

The comparative fresh sweetness of the air outside the cell was suddenly cloying. I began coughing uncontrollably, tears streaming down my face. Fever, followed by a chill, passed through me in waves. I was ashamed of the filth that covered me—worse, of humiliation before my captors. What would she—

"Silence!" the whisper demanded. *"Or the truth! Hold you the reins of the star machines?"*

It was another full minute before I could speak. At this rate, I would not last very much longer. The figure bending low before me, after its brief tirade, remained mute. When my voice came again, it was a hoarse sobbing rasp.

"What are you asking me, priest?"

"Guide you the star machines?"

Burning, I reasoned dully, is probably better than being

hanged. Once the flame sears your nerve-endings, I am told, you can not feel a thing. It certainly beat outliving my inoculations, as I seemed now to be doing.

"Sure." I lied, "naturally, of course, also, 'of a certes.' I piloted one such here myself." I paused, adding, "But it will not now return to the sky. It was not ever intended to. It has been burned, the ashes scattered by warriors. I have explained this."

Queerly, the anonymous form squatted on its robe-draped haunches, froze for another long moment as if in deep meditation. Then one of its companions out in the passage approached the bailiff.

Coins clinked within the silence of stone walls.

The bailiff appeared to look both ways, then withdrew. Almost as if a switch had been thrown, the hooded figure halfway into our cell came to life again.

"Demon," it hissed, lower, even more threatening than before, "tell you how your thunder weapons are fashioned?"

So that was it.

In the furious one-sided battle at the landing site, I had somehow killed or wounded a handful of animal riders. Their thin metal plating was worse than no protection against my fast-moving eight millimeter slugs. Staging singlehanded gunfights with barbarians had not been in my job description when I had signed on board the Asperance; I was supposed to prepare one arsenal for the officers. Had I done so, perhaps we Vespuccians might have fared better.

Instead, I had paddled my toes in a brook, fiddling with music, daydreamed about my girl, watched two moons rise, while, all the time, the enemy was coming to kill us. As armorer, I had been more useful playing the mandolar.

In any event, my guns had been emptied, confiscated by the brawling killers, the rest of our ammunition surely destroyed. Back home, in the Final Vespuccian War, I had done what the field manuals told me, with a fancy kit of gauges, drift-punches, screwdrivers, confident in the knowledge that replacement parts were never farther away than the resupply depot. I might be able to make certain of the tools; screwdrivers are easy, even good ones. What I knew of *manufacturing* the Darrick 8-mm Revolving Magazine Pistol could have been engraved upon the needle tip of the bailiff's back-up dagger with the same cold chisel he had used to open the door.

Naturally, I said: "Of course I can tell you. There is nothing to it. I know all the proper incantations. Burn me, though, I cannot teach you a thing."

The hooded speaker froze again, its companions likewise ceasing all movement in the hallway. Praying, maybe. Or thinking about a New Improved Holy Order of God's Teeth, augmented with a little advanced military hardware.

The baron would not be very happy, I thought. Then again—I started trembling at the idea—perhaps these "thunder-weapons" of mine were religiously illegal. Perhaps the bishop merely wanted to assure himself that, by disposing of us, he was eradicating dangerous forbidden knowledge.

Well, either way, I would die *warm*. The vile dampness had seeped into my bones. The insides of my lungs felt coated with the same fine mildew that garnished the cuisine. I would not last very much longer at this rate, whatever I chose to say. When they discovered the true extent of my technical education...

The faceless figure came back to reality.

"The other demon"—it gestured with a long, empty sleeve—*"knows it these things as well, the making of thunder-weapons, the guiding of sky machines?"*

I coughed again, this time to give me time for thought. Lieutenant Enson Sermander, in these late, great days of the Vespuccian State, had the finest military career his family could buy him—one of the old Command Families, with a real name. Do him credit, though: he had spent another fat half-dozen years purchasing even more status on his own.

In the War, he had flown (so he said) a ram-fighter against the Shirker States. Certainly at the launch ceremony nine—no, *twelve*—weeks ago, his chest had been ablaze with ribbons. Five confirmed kills, three probables. A feat of arms performed against blimps, biplanes. He was in the dungeon only because he had not thought quite quickly enough to buy himself into favor with the current regime. Being slow on that kind of uptake clearly marks one as a threat to national security. So, he had been volunteered for the *Asperance* expedition.

As for flying the starclipper, even the lieutenant had admitted that the computer was the best pilot aboard.

Nevertheless, he had not been too bad a guy, for an officer. A cheerful cynic, the only one of seventeen crew members who spoke directly to me outside the line of duty. I had come to like him, in a way. Those who actually knew what they were doing, he left strictly alone to do it. That is what constitutes a good officer these days.

The lieutenant was a good officer.

"He is the great-grandfather of all sky demons!" I announced, with as much enthusiasm as my weakened body would let me muster. "I am only his humble apprentice— but he is sick. He needs help!"

A nod from beneath the hood, then the hackle-raising whisper again. *"This may be arranged. Able are you to stand?"*

"Not in here."

The hooded figure backed out, straightened.

Its companions reached in swiftly, dragged me forward by the armpits to my feet. Agony tore through my right leg as I set weight on the much-abused foot. I bit my lower lip, choking back nausea. Tears squeezed from between my tightly closed eyelids as the priests carried me across the narrow cellar corridor before propping me against a wall. Breathing heavily, I clung to a sconce, my heart hammering like a machine-gun.

They slid the lieutenant's body from the cell.

He moaned, fought them weakly, trying to speak. Restraining him with a surprising gentleness, one of them extracted a relatively clean swatch of burlap from its robe, dabbed at the lieutenant's huge pustulent wound until fresh blood broke through the crust. A new rag was wrapped around his arm. *"Nothing can be done for him . . ."* it whispered chillingly, *". . . here."*

Fighting dizziness, I croaked, "Then let us go where something *can*!"

They nodded. The upward trip through seemingly endless underground corridors was a hazy purgatorial nightmare, reminiscent of my daily torture sessions. My foot was three times its normal size, swollen to the knee. I was queasy, only half conscious, weak.

The castle seemed a busy place. Screaming issued from every cross-corridor, pitiable moaning, the rattle of chains in wall rings. The priests looked resolutely straight ahead. The endless march went on.

I did manage distantly to wonder whether it was day or night outside. This was no trivial matter on Sca, where all life was active during the well-lit nighttime hours but scurried from the dawn as if from an enemy horde. Already, in the higher-rent districts of the dungeons, my eyes smarted from the more numerous, better-trimmed torches. Outside, the naked blue-white sun would burn the optics out of my head, then start boring for the brain.

Suddenly we passed through a pointed stone arch to an outdoor court I recognized from our arrival here. Around the yard were railed places for the servants busy with shovels. Near the gate stood another of those wood-wheeled carts, hitched to four big pulling beasts.

It was nighttime.

Under the gentle light of one risen moon, armored soldiers loitered, a great many of them. The bailiff was among their number; he approached us as we slowly crossed the flagging. An old man for his culture, he was perhaps forty, white haired, his face the usual Scavian battlefield of smallpox scars, fleabites, the marks of hard-fought mortal duels. He coughed as he spoke, a nervous hand fingering the pommel of his two-edged hatchet.

"Where be ye taking these here captives?" he demanded loudly. "They be properly duly held for my lord the baron!"

He wore a breastplate over his mail shirt now, a crested helmet, both bearing the local symbol of authority, a gibbet—rampant or gules or whatever—on what looked like a field of bloodsoaked mud. The hooded people gently placed the lieutenant on the courtyard flagging. The priest I had been leaning on stepped out from under me; I swayed a little but managed to stay erect. Soldiers all around us lost a bit of their transparently artificial nonchalance.

"*Here our warrant and seal is!*"

My guide had answered in a stage-whisper, nearly as loud as the bailiff's bellowed challenge.

From the broad trailing sleeve of a hooded robe, a parchment appeared. With arthritic fingers, the bailiff laboriously untied the ribbon, unrolled the document, skipped over the writing—which he likely could not read anyway—to the heavy wax seal affixed at the bottom. He eyed us, a trickle of sweat escaping from under his dented iron cap. Then he decided:

"This be but yon *bishop's* seal! Where be that and the word of my lord the baron?"

From all quarters of the courtyard, his men began to saunter casually toward us.

"*Here, treacherous canine, is word enough for the baron!*" said another of the hooded people in a low, threatening whisper. Metal whispered from hidden leather. Something steely blue was thrust into the bailiff's undefended armpit as two of the priests picked the lieutenant up. We marched past the bewildered guardsmen to the animal cart near the open gateway. The bailiff waved his men away, beads of sweat decorating his unlovely cratered face.

"Th-the w-word of God be Law..." he stammered. "Thy Holy Order rightfully b-bows to no temporal authority."

"You learn canon law quickly, villain," whispered the priest. *"Now help us with the oxcart!"*

Abruptly one young guard stepped forward as if to block our progress, his fire-hardened wooden pike at the ready. The free hand of the priest lashed out. The guard took a stunned step backward with a ruined face, blood gushing onto the pavement. He collapsed, the pole falling to the flags with a clatter.

Tension in the courtyard turned to fury in a wave that swept around its walls. More guards took a step, lowered fire-hardened spearpoints. Swords, daggers, axes were loosened in their scabbards.

"No!" cried the bailiff, his shoulder rising several centimeters under the impetus of the upthrust steel in his armpit, "Stand where ye be! Have that man broken if he lives!" The bailiff pointed at the wounded guard, but his face had turned to that of the priest; a murderous hatred raged behind his small eyes.

Together they pulled at the harnessing of the animals, turning them toward the gate. With some difficulty they lined up the crude wheels of the cart to fit between the raised beam-edges of the narrow drawbridge. I nearly fainted on the spot, only the thought of how Eleva would despise such weakness sustaining me. They carried me to the cart, handed me up where I lay gratefully in clean straw. Remotely I felt them place the lieutenant beside me. Two robed figures took hold of the strapping on the animals' faces, pulled them through the gate onto the bridge. It groaned under the strain.

The other priest trudged close behind keeping an eye on the bailiff, who had perched on the rear end of the vehicle then jumped up beside the man.

"I yield for now," the bailiff hissed between clenched teeth, veins standing out on his forehead, his voice beginning to rise as we passed beneath a rusted portcullis, "but we shall see anon who bows to what authority!"

The outer walls of the castle were lined at their tops with soldiers, each with a sheet-bronze cap, a leather vest sewed with iron rings, a sharpened wooden pike, each pocked face peeking out over the collar of a thick batting of cotton underarmor.

"The baron," continued the bailiff, "shall hear of!—"

There was the briefest of motions under the man's arm, no noise at all. He stiffened momentarily, lost interest in what he had been about to say, then slumped, propped against the hooded figure beside him as we rumbled off the end of the bridge onto a rutted dirt roadway.

Gradually, miraculously, the castle grew small in the distance.

I struggled to an upright position on the swaying cart, looked at the priest. "Just what *are* you going to do with us?" I asked, almost surprised that I was beginning to care again. About anything.

We turned a corner, losing sight of that hateful pile of stones behind a line of trees. The priest was a long time answering.

"You teach us," the figure said at last in a loud crackling hiss.

It gave the bailiff a shove. The body tumbled off the side of the road into a ditch, vanished from sight.

"Then you *disappear, as well!"*

4

Escape to Creativity

Another thing Scavians never seem to have discovered is that wheels should be round.

The man-tall weathered pair on the cart might possibly have begun that way. They were constructed of heavy parallel timbers, bolted together carefully with iron strap. But the end grain had worn less quickly than the rest of the circumference; it had never occurred to the wheelwright to apply strapping to the rims, as tires. Ah well, perhaps in another thousands years...

The straw-covered bed lifted, dropped, lifted, dropped, with every half turn each wheel made, ninety degrees out of synch with its companion.

The lieutenant did not notice. He lay even more deeply unconscious than before, although he seemed to breathe more regularly. His uniform was as tattered as mine; in addition to his wounded arm he was covered with sores from our long confinement. I wondered what they had done to him, what tortures his unconscious body had endured. Whatever it was, it did not show—which made me shudder with grisly speculation.

Though nominally winter, only a few hundred kilometers from the northern pole, it was much warmer here, aboveground. My toes, my fingers started aching as they thawed. I itched furiously all over; the vermin I carried with me were stirring from their torpor.

Fellow escapees.

How long it would take the baron to catch on that his bailiff was not coming back from this excursion, I could not guess. The hooded people seemed altogether too relaxed about it to suit me. My "Pistols (Darrick), 8-mm, Magazine, Revolving, One each," were Vespuccian history's most sophisticated hand-weapons, fabricated directly from specimens found aboard the colony's abandoned starship. Even they, I had found, could not stand up to enough mounted men, primevally equipped but unafraid to die. I was half prepared to wake up in my cell again.

Or dead.

Despite such grim considerations, well shaken by the irregular rocking of the cart, I dropped off into an uneasy sleep at least a dozen times before we made our first stop. I would wake up, startled, remember where I was, assure myself that the lieutenant was okay, watch the hooded figures marching silently behind us . . . Then *wake* again, repeating the whole heart-pounding process until it seemed I had been doing this same idiotic thing for all of my life.

Two of the moons were high, painfully bright. Sca's star, its sun, is an unbearable blue-white fusion torch, the color of metal being welded in front of your face. All surface life seeks refuge from the full deadly light of day— animals in burrows, plants by bundling themselves in thick, reflecting, toughened leaves.

Nighttime calls forth life again, illuminated far more brilliantly by the satellites alone than the high-noon surface of my own world ever is. Birds sing, flowers bloom. Peasants stumble from caves or tightly shuttered huts to till their masters' fields. The rare desperate individual forced to travel abroad by daylight does so closely robed, just as the mysterious priests who carried us with them.

A thought struck painfully through the fog inside my head: mankind could *not* have originated here! Unless it was this sun they were escaping, just as we, in our own way, had tried escaping the ungenerous star of Vespucci. I could not picture human life evolving on this planet, the place was far too inimical. Then again, perhaps the star had changed, somewhere in the past. Perhaps it burned hotter now.

The cart lurched to a stop.

I very nearly slid off the slick yellow straw into the dirt track, but one of the hooded people steadied me. The one in front made clucking noises at the animals, wrestled them into a right-angle turn. We trundled into a narrow cavern between two great growths of shrubbery, several meters tall. As the pulling creatures fed themselves from bags of grain tied to their faces, the hooded ones directed their attention to the lieutenant, then to me.

Him they stripped naked, efficiently, dispassionately. They turned him, examining ugly infected cuts, sores, abrasions he had acquired in our short, eventful stay on Sca. They were gentle with his deeply injured arm, working in a monastic silence that was perhaps appropriate, generating an atmosphere of calculated haste, cutting away the crude bandage with its sickening cargo.

I had rolled over to watch, when a sudden lance of pain shot through my broken foot. I stared down with agony-gauzed eyes as a robed figure busied itself at my trouser leg, what was left of my stocking. When the mangled foot was exposed, I looked away. It was nearly as bad as the lieutenant's arm. Without question I was going to lose it, counting myself lucky if that was all I lost. In any event, I would never again—

—abruptly, everything froze.

As one, the three hooded people turned away from the cart. Two of them crossed the narrow road then crouched

behind a clump of slowly-opening brush to conceal themselves from the direction we had just come—the direction
of the castle, of the baron, of the baron's murderous riders. The remaining figure hid itself on the near side.

They waited.

Eventually, there was a noise, a cascade of hollow
sound quite unlike any other. It was terrifying, especially
since I had heard it for the first time when our camp at
the *Asperance* had been overwhelmed. It was the sound
of hard-shod animal feet, pounding in their hundreds on
the ground, audible through the soil itself. Gradually I
made out, too, the metallic jangle of the men they bore,
weapons, equipment, rough shouting, the peculiar hair-
stirring high-pitched screaming of the riding beasts themselves.

As the mounted warriors thundered into sight, the
hooded people casually stepped into the roadway with a
smooth silent motion. The column braked to a dusty,
disorganized stop. Archers twisted their arms over their
mailed backs for arrows. Axes were loosened in their belt
thongs.

Swords were drawn with a ringing whisper.

After a brief unpleasant exchange of words, the officer
heading the column happened to glance for a moment to
his right—straight at me. He began to shout a command.

At once, a broad fan of energy leaped from the burlap
sleeve-ends of the robed people, showering the column,
flaring into a wall of flame where it struck the mounted
men. In a single horrifying instant the entire troop was
engulfed, consumed where they stood, animals, men,
without so much as a final scream of terror or pain.

The heat of the thing baked itself onto my face.

When the flames died a scant few seconds later, as if
someone had turned off a gas valve, all that remained in
the road were a few blackened, irregular smoky lumps
that might once have been saddles. Even the bones had
burned.

Quickly as it had begun, it was over. The three robed

figures calmly returned to the cart without looking back. They gave me water, flat-tasting, mildly bitter. Drugged. I was not particularly surprised to awaken, swaying, bumping once again, with Sca's four moons about to set.

Daylight was about to arrive.

2

Daytime on Sca is just about twenty-five hours long, Vespuccian. What's unusual is that so are the nighttimes.

I had been unconscious quite some while, apparently, wrapped up in a robe like those worn by the people who had either captured or rescued us, but with the hood thrown back on my shoulders. My right foot was bound up to the knee in clean coarse-weave, concealing something else, some other dressing, comfortable, yet firm.

All right, then, what was missing? What bothered me?

Lying there on that pitching wagon, I discovered with a little shock that I had forgotten completely, somewhere in the past few nightmarish weeks, what it was like *not* to be in constant pain, waking, sleeping, floating dazedly suspended between the two states as I had done most of the time. It was an *odd* sensation, like being thrown out of a high window. Pain had come to be the hidden foundation of my existence.

The lieutenant, too, wore a robe. Its brown sleeve was slit open to reveal the same rough burlap bandaging where the crude alien sword had nearly cut him through. He was snoring.

It was contagious.

What felt like only moments later, I awoke again, the moons apparently still setting. This time, something felt *very* wrong, deeply disorienting. Perhaps it was a remnant of the drug. I twisted around, glancing reflexively at the lieutenant, but his color, if one could judge in the slant-ways light, was steadily returning to normal. He breathed easily, if a bit loudly. The hooded people marched onward, two behind us, stolidly, mutely, any faces they might have possessed hidden away deep within the shadows of their clothing. A third guided the pulling beasts, who could scarcely have been more stoically unresponsive.

Then I had it: those moons were *rising*! I had slept one entire hellish day-period through. To all appearances, our little company had simply kept marching, when I had half expected we would take shelter somewhere, wait for another night to travel. No wonder I was warm; I was feeling residual daytime heat. This—

—then another thought struck me: what had fooled me was that the moons were on my left. If they were rising, then they should be on my right. We were traveling south.

Not northward to the city of the bishop—or the burning-stake.

3

Another night passed.

In one of my mother's ancient folk songs, there is a passage about some place "where the dawn comes up like thunder." On Sca, it comes up like a fission-bomb explosion. At the first excruciatingly brilliant bead on the cluttered horizon, the hooded people halted the cart again. There had been a false dawn on the horizon for some hours, naturally. It is never dark on Sca. Now the strangers stopped to drape heavy fabric over the animals, snugging string-drawn coverings tightly over the beasts' placid eyes.

The air had an expectant smell to it, insects suddenly silent, birds nowhere to be seen.

The lieutenant's disheveled robe was bound closely about him now by gentle, competent hands, his limbs carefully covered, the hood slipped up around his ears. They closed the front with a draw-cord, fumbling deep inside the face for some time until they appeared satisfied. I got the same treatment, every square centimeter of exposed flesh cloaked, everything accomplished in total eerie silence. Once the hood came over my head, one of the robed figures reached in, pulled a dark interior netting across my eyes, reducing my point of view to a small, increasingly brilliant circle. Soon it was like peering out the mouth from deep within a darkened tunnel.

Creaking into motion once again, we plodded onward under the near-lethal sun, meeting no one, seeing no one, not a single living thing except trees, bushes, other foliage, their leaves circled tightly into little knots to resist the deadly glory overhead. Time after time, half dazed, I would move to loosen my heavy stifling robe—my body drenched in sweat that made the itching worse—only to have my hands pulled gently away from the fastenings. Then I would remember what the sunlight could do.

On Sca, in addition to the gibbet, in addition to the pyre, daylight was a third form of execution, reserved for miscreant nobility.

Within an hour, everything appeared washed out, lit only in shades of white, impenetrable black, like an overexposed photograph. The lieutenant mumbled, tossed, struggled with his smothering protection. They propped him up, gave him something to drink through a small plastic tube thrust into the face of his hood. He rested quietly. In my own sweltering discomfort, I began to yearn for a sip from the same potion, probably the one they had given me the day before, but it was never offered.

We continued southward.

Slowly, I began to have an idea about what might really be going on. Growing up, I had been warned never to jump to a conclusion in the absence of reliable data. This is good advice. However, the human mind—mine, at least—is *designed* to jump reflexively on partial information whether its owner wants it to or not. Mine was doing it right now; since nobody else would talk to me, I thought I would give it a chance to explain, at least.

Say these mysterious characters *were* from the Church. They dressed the part. They had the bishop's seal. I do not believe that anybody but a monk, accustomed to long years of suffering in silence, could have endured the journey thus far as these individuals had, without so much as a sneeze, a hiccup, or a lame joke. I knew less about religion than I had about the manufacturing of weapons, but I knew a little history. The Church of Vespucci, compulsory in the nation's schools, largely ignored by everyone in adulthood, was a transparent prop for the State. It had not always been so; in earlier times it had been active, powerful—divided into a half-dozen schisms.

These hooded people might be renegades, representative of some faction that wanted neither the bishop nor the baron to kill us. Perhaps they wanted our technology—not that they appeared to need it—perhaps they wanted to dispose of us themselves. This was not pleasant speculation, but it was the only conversation I had. Whenever it got boring, I drifted off to sleep.

Exactly as I had done during services in school.

Nighttime came at last, almost reluctantly, as if the cruel blazing star overhead enjoyed what it did to the land beneath its hammer-blows. The cart pulled off the road again, animals were fed, watered lavishly. The lieutenant was unbound, his wounds carefully tended. His eyes actually opened for a moment. He looked at me with what might have been recognition, perhaps the same mild astonishment I felt at still being alive, then he lapsed once more into oblivion.

Gratefully, I unfastened the face-netting before they got to me, undid the hood, spread the robe wide open down the front. It was still breathtakingly hot; it would be several hours yet before the outside temperature dropped appreciably—Sca is lucky that its atmosphere is not thicker. Getting rid of all that insulation helped a good deal.

I almost laughed at the memory of nearly freezing to death in a dungeon day before yesterday. Now sweat soaked my hair, ran into my eyes, dripped from the end of my nose.

Somewhere in the past several hours, I had somehow

regained a trace of self-respect, as well. Feeling painfully distended below the beltline, I rose stiffly from the bed of straw, began to slip off the end of the cart with the idea of limping over to one of the more inviting-looking shrubberies.

Firm hands restrained me.

"Look, friend, I have to go to the little boys' bush!"

The two stepped back, giving me room.

I slid the rest of the way, put weight onto my bad foot. It held without much pain, but I was weak, as if my entire body were made of warm gelatin. I hobbled dizzily over to do what a man had to do, trying to ignore three pairs of invisible eyes fastened upon my every move.

I could not help, however, noticing how careful they were to stand upwind of me. Well, I could not very well blame them for that. If I could have avoided standing downwind of myself, I would have.

This time, the cart had been brought to rest beside a shallow, sandy-bottomed stream. Reorganizing my clothes beneath the burlap robe, I had another idea. I decided to savor it; however crazy it might be, it was better than being burned at the stake by second-string inquisitioners.

Several yards away, now, two of the hooded figures were at the cart, fussing with the animals. The third seemed to have been delegated to watch me, staying within a few arms' lengths. I addressed this nearest one.

"Say, are we going to be here for a while?"

There was the very slightest of nods.

"Then how about letting me wash some of the prison out of my clothes?"

No response.

"Look, Your Reverence, I saw what you did to a hundred armored troopers. Believe me, I am as harmless as a man can get. I am not going any place you do not want me to go. I have been steeping in my own filth for a solid month. Consider it a last request: maybe it will help your box office at my witch-burning!"

The swaddled form turned toward the others at the far

end of the clearing. One of them nodded, although plainly it was much too far away for my voice to have carried. On the other hand, they had heard the late unlamented mounted company a long time before I had. In any case, the nod got passed along to me.

"Thanks, I will do the same for you sometime—in the next life."

I glanced around, making certain of my surroundings in a manner I had been taught since earliest childhood. Especially I made sure of the lieutenant's location. I had been pleased to see my personal hooded chaperone touch reflexively at its waist at the mention of the massacred troopers.

Nice of it to show me where the real power was.

I turned, stumping wearily over to the streambank, making an exaggerated production of my crippling weakness. Dropping the borrowed robe on the grassy bank, I removed my jacket, peeled off what remained of my uniform shirt, unfastened my pants. My shorts, underneath, were in worse shape than the shirt, I discovered. Both garments were scarcely indistinguishable from the filth and the unsloughed flesh that seemed to be all that was holding them together. They began coming apart in the blood-warm stream the instant I attempted to rinse them. I let the rotting fragments slip away in the current, started scrubbing at my body with clean yellow sand.

Also thinking.

Nakedness is a very odd thing. Different people certainly react to it differently. I had known another lieutenant once, back home on Vespucci when the Navy Reserve had been "temporarily" handling routine urban police work under martial law in one of the first Holdout Kingdoms we had taken. We had been sitting on the steps of a police station, waiting for shift change, talking about burglars.

Corporal, he had told me, if you hear a noise in the night, always take the time to grab your pants before you grab your crowbar or candlestick or whatever to confront the thief. Otherwise, he said, you will be at a severe psychological disadvantage. Nakedness equals helplessness. You will know it. So will the burglar. You will lose, he will win.

Or something like that.

Later on, my CPO had observed wryly that an attack by a stark-naked crowbar-wielding householder might just be the perfect burglar medicine. At the least, it would startle the dickens out of the intruder, maybe buy you a little extra time for maneuvering.

Personally, I had agreed with the chief. I had always thought that the lieutenant, like all lieutenants everywhere, was just a little prissy. "*College boys!*" the CPO had snorted with contempt. But I was willing to bet, on this oppressively religious planet, that these hooded folk would be likelier to side with the lieutenant than the chief.

I rinsed my pants, rinsed my jacket, enjoying the air on my freshly abraded skin. Like Lieutenant Sermander, I was covered with ugly lesions, but they were healing already. I thought about some more things, like what to do about him, looked around as unobtrusively as I could, mulling the tactical situation.

My guard was paying more attention to its comrades than to me. Its back was turned. Peripheral vision, I knew from experience, was completely blocked by those hooded robes. I stepped carefully toward the bank, avoiding telltale splashes or ripples, keeping an eye on the other figures at the cart, as well as the one nearest me.

If I could just get hold of whatever had blasted that armored column.

I put off trying to figure out where the Holy Order of the Teeth of God might have gotten such a thing. Perhaps there *had* been a higher civilization here once.

Surely I could overpower one small monk who seemed more interested in meditating than in me, even in the lousy condition I was in. I had the advantage—I was desperate. Surely they would hesitate to incinerate one of their own number, if only for the second or two I needed to puzzle out how the weapon worked.

I had to keep the lieutenant out of the line of fire.

My foot found the stream-edge where the grassy turf hung over. I glanced down. The sodden burlap on my leg had slipped. Beneath was something rubbery, almost alive in appearance, silvery-gray like the reflective undersides of Scavian leaves in the harsh moonlight.

I put the foot carefully up on the grass, my good limb tensed beneath my weight on a large rock just above the waterline. Crouching, I breathed in slowly, silenty, deeply, trusting to lifelong martial arts training I had suffered through from grade school to boot camp. I had been good at it, my only "sport," the only one they do not give letters for . . .

I *sprang*! charging along the freshly opened grass, threw myself into the air for a flying—

—*slammed*! to the ground, the breath blasting out of my lungs in shock. I shook my battered head, looked up at my hooded guard, crouched low in a tense combat stance, hands out, ready for more trouble any time I was foolish enough to start it.

No longer hooded.

I was looking straight into the anger-flaming eyes of the most beautiful pale-haired blonde I had ever seen.

Window on Infinity

"Had enough, asshole?"

The weirdly lovely creature circled warily, stepping sideways, one small fist extended, one drawn back like a coiled spring, ready at her waist. Her hair tossed wildly as she moved, enveloping her face, lashing at her shoulders like pale fire, golden highlights, glints of copper-red, struggling for dominance in the moon-reflected glare of Sca's harsh primary.

I sat on the grass in the dent I had made, keeping my mouth shut.

"Don't be too hard on him, Cilly," another of the priests shouted suddenly, throwing back his hood. "He must have thought we were going to—"

"Stow it, Coup!" she spat, not once taking her eyes off me. They were green with undertones of that deep bluish glow you find in the heart of a nuclear reactor. "Anybody who sneaks up behind Lucille Olson-Bear bet-

45

ter be prepared for what he gets! *And don't call me Cilly!*

"How about it, jerk, ready to behave?"

I blinked, trying to absorb everything that was happening. Without thinking, I braced myself to rise—when a light sweep from a small foot kicked my hand out from under me. I was down again, liking it less every minute.

The one she called Coup interrupted once more, coming toward us with long unmonklike strides, abandoning the bantering tone for one of warning, of command.

"Quit playing with him, Lucille. We're supposed to be on his side, he's a customer, remember?"

This Coup may have been the biggest man I have ever seen, with a close-cropped, nearly shaven head that might have been chiseled from a mountainside, a big ugly nose, ears that would have looked like cargo hatches on anybody else. One of his hands was the size of both of mine put together.

"Yeah," I added from flat on the back of my lap, some confidence having returned at the prospect of having such an ally. "The customer is always right. Can I get up now?"

I had deserved that second knocking down; even a white-belted boot knows better than to—

"Give us your parole!"

Lucille had not relaxed from her combat stance, not by a fraction of a millimeter. She stood over me, breathing hard with meanness rather than exertion.

I could match it if I had to. "What the hell good would that do? You do not know me. Maybe I lie a lot." I was starting to get mad, all right—about a month's worth of mad, maybe a lifetime's. "You tell me what is going on, Goldilocks, then maybe I will give you my parole."

Perhaps.

A breeze stirred the trees around the clearing, lifting Lucille's hair softly. Her cheeks were flushed, tiny dampish curls stuck to the smooth curve of her forehead.

"Goldilocks, is it? Well, buddy, what's going on is a long, complicated—"

"You are not from Sca!" I interrupted suddenly. The

accent was different, more like mine. There was not a mark or blemish on her gorgeous face. "Nor from Vespucci, which means that there is a *third*—"

"Slow down, son." Coup loomed tall over Lucille. "Let's start with introductions—preferably vertical ones!" He leaned down, lifted me to my feet like a child.

"Whitey O'Thraight," I answered reflexively, giving it the formal pronunciation. "Armorer-Corporal, Vespuccian Naval Reserve."

At once I realized I was standing at attention without benefit of any command to do so. Also without benefit of my uniform or any other clothing. Well, the designations tattooed on my arms should be enough uniform for any *real* Vespuccian.

"Now there's a formula we've heard before," Lucille observed to our giant companion. "Name, function, rank. Buddy, the only thing you left out was your serial number. Or haven't they been reinvented yet where you come from?

"—and are you *ever* going to get dressed?"

She appealed to me. Embarrassingly, I was beginning to show it. Two months in space, another month in prison— if that is any excuse. Hastening to the riverbank where I had left my clothes, I called back over my bare shoulder, "Do you never ask one question at a time? That *was* my serial number."

"What?"

"Whitey O'Thraight; YD-038. Five digits. Almost a real name."

It *was* something to be proud of, after all.

Lucille whitened, muttered in a grim, low voice, "Sweet Lysander, what kind of a twisted, rotten—"

"Not in front of company, Cilly."

"Don't call me Cilly!"

He laughed hugely, patted her on the head, touseling her hair. "Corporal, I'm Geoffrey Couper, and this impolitic and violent young woman has already introduced herself, I believe. I take no responsibility, nor does anybody else, including herse—*whoops!*"

Good as she was, he was blindingly better, casually blocking her intended sidekick to the belly with an iron forearm, then seizing her extended foot. He held it for a moment as if contemplating twisting it off, then released her suddenly so that she had to hop for balance. Tension, a second's pause, then they both laughed. It was like watching desert predators at play.

Self-conscious, I gathered up the tatters of my uniform, along with what little of my dignity was left, put the pants on wet, then the jacket. While Couper continued sparring with Lucille on a verbal level, I hesitated with the robe they had given me, folding it over my arm. Then, changing my mind, I sought privacy behind a bush for some reason of irrational modesty, removed the sodden clothing.

It was my first real chance to examine the hooded garment. The coarse-weave outer shell was about right for the technology of Sca, but it was a deception. I should have noticed it at once: that rough fabric next to my much-abused skin would have *hurt*. But the robe was lined with the same odd material I had glimpsed wrapped around my game leg. It was silver-gray, buffed up into a velvety nap, the surface noticeably warmer than the night air.

As the front edge of the robe slipped between my exploring fingers, I felt a short cylindrical lump sewn into the hem. I squeezed one end, examining it. Instantly the lining cooled to the touch. Dew began to condense, running off in tiny diamond droplets. Frost began to form. It took several tries, twisting, pinching, before the lining was warm, had begun to dry again.

Who *were* these people?

2

"Who *are* you people?" I demanded, emerging from the privacy of my dressing shrub, uniform draped over my arm.

"*There* you are, Corporal." Couper was massaging the leg of one of the draft animals. "For a moment I thought you'd decided to go AWOL on us. Guess we didn't finish introductions after all, did we?"

Lucille was not in sight.

Couper turned to the last of his companions, a portly, gnomish individual with a broad face, black bushy sideburns that merged at the bottom of his chin. "Corporal, say hello to Owen Rogers, *our* weapons tech. Rog, this is Armorer-Corporal Whitey O'Thraight."

Rogers raised a skeptical eyebrow at my title, as if being introduced to a genuine flint-knapping savage. He nodded civilly enough, then went back to tinkering—with one of the group's incredibly small, impressively potent hand-weapons. *This* had wiped out a hundred cavalrymen? I opened my mouth to speak, but Couper went right on without me.

"I suppose that I should add that he's also our expedition praxeologist—a very busy citizen indeed, our Mr. Rogers."

"Don't call me a citizen, Coup," Rogers replied in a voice rather higher, more nasal, than I had expected. "I'm too tired to fight a duel tonight."

He took a paper packet from his robe, extracted what appeared to be a thin brown twig, flicked a small mechanical fire-starter, placed the twig in his mouth, lit the end, drawing smoke, puffing it out again. He peered critically at a part he had removed from the weapon, polished it on his robe, peered at it again.

"What is a praxeologist?" I asked for lack of better conversation. Lucille was still among the missing. "More importantly, who in Hamilton's Holy Name *are* you people? What kind of expedition is this?"

Both men stiffened slightly, as if at something I had said.

"We might ask the same of you, buddy—omitting the obscenity."

I whirled. Lucille was right behind me, coming from another section of the brook, her wet hair plastered down, bunched into a knot at the back of her neck. Even that way she looked good.

I was just about to ask *what* obscenity when Lieutenant Sermander began stirring on the cart. He groaned, tried to sit up against his good arm. Couper hurried over to him, gently pushed him down again, continued to address me as he examined my friend.

"Corporal, where we come from, there was once a primitive people who had time and distance somewhat confused in their cosmology." He glanced at Rogers. The praxeologist/gunsmith nodded professional confirmation. "They figured that, if you came from far away, you also came from the distant past. An odd point of view—"

"Which has its merits," Rogers interrupted, looking up from his work.

"In this instance, perhaps," acknowledged Couper.

He peeled off the burlap from the lieutenant's arm. Underneath was the same type of rubbery gray dressing I wore. Set into the resilient substance was a small rigid panel of the same color, two centimeters by five, decorated with tiny lights, miniature switches. One by one, as Couper labored over my friend, the little lamps blinked from red to yellow to green.

Then he returned his attention to me. "Where *you* come from, Corporal, there'll be legends." It was a statement, not a question. He gave me an evaluative squint that seemed to broadcast, even at its friendliest, that he was not a man to lie to. "There always are. Have you heard of a place called Earth?"

"'Earth'?" I rolled the unfamiliar syllable around in my mouth. "Is that where you people are from?"

Couper went back to the electronic panel in the lieutenant's dressing. Rogers' smile did not disguise a worried look that had accompanied his transformation from artisan to professional—what?

"In a manner of speaking, Whitey. Tell me, is this Vespucci of yours a nation-state, a planet, a planetary system, or a—"

"All three now, I guess. What do you mean, 'in a manner of speaking'? You are either from a planet, or you are—"

"Is that so, Corporal?" Lucille sat on the—what do you call it?—the wagonpart that connected with the animals, helping Rogers tend the weapons with an absentminded contentedness I have seen other women reserve for knitting. I looked down at the ground, suddenly self-conscious, for a variety of reasons.

"What if," she asked, "a child had been born aboard your ship while you were in transit to this mindforsaken place?"

"He would still be a Vespuccian, er...citizen." I glanced up at Rogers briefly, wondering if the word still offended him. Lucille answered for him.

"I see. Rog, hand me that orifice gauge, will you? This thing sprayed a little light against the cavalry out there, after I stopped it down for the torturer. Must be some play in the control ring."

She might have returned to her work without further comment, except that I spoke again. "I meant to ask you about that. You did not have *my* reasons for hating the bailiff. I know he was about to shout for help, but why did you—"

"I'd planned to fry him whether he made a peep or not!" Lucille said cheerfully, tightening an adjustment at her weapon's muzzle end, "That's standard policy with us—for *his* kind."

I must have goggled.

Rogers stepped in. "*Her* standard policy, she means. Still, there's something to be said for that, too. It's one reliable method of measuring how civilized an individual—or an entire planet—really is. Barbaric cultures encourage torturers. Merely primitive ones tolerate them, sometimes torture them back in revenge. A truly advanced culture—"

"Rehabilitates them?" I asked, beginning to feel I understood this fellow. Vespuccian education warns against the few like him at home, overrationalizing, sentimental—

"No, we simply *kill* them, as Lucille says, like any other vermin, swiftly and humanely."

"A plasma gun under the armpit," Lucille added, "does wonders for the local degree of cultural advancement."

Rogers chuckled. "Not to mention underarm odor!"

Suppressing a grin, Couper grunted, rewrapped the burlap around the arm of the sleeping lieutenant. He fiddled with the temperature-adjusting lump at the edge of Sermander's robe.

"Corporal, if I let this conversation go any further without ..." He stopped, started up again: "Son, bloodthirsty comments to the contrary, we're basically a scientific exploration team, assigned to study this garbage dump of a planet. Other questions—and *answers*, do I make myself clear, Lucille?—had better wait until we get where we're going."

Lucille stuck her tongue out but remained silent.

"Which is where?" As I watched, the girl reholstered her weapon somewhere under the robe. Rogers began putting his tools away in a canvas roll, took the feed bags from the animals, tossed them into the cart beside the lieutenant.

"That's a good example of a question that'll have to wait," Couper replied. "Anyway, doing something is better than being told about it. Saddle up, *scientists*, we've got miles to make!"

3

Thus it was back to the same plodding journey as before. Only this time there were differences.

I sat up on the end of the wagon, having had the little control panel on my own dressing examined, the burlap cover drawn back over it. All my lights had been green. Except for the negligible weight of the thing—the burlap on the outside weighed more—plus an occasional surprising deep twinge, my foot felt as good as new. The —Earthians?—did not discourage me from walking on it.

The subject of parole had not arisen again. They did not seem to care, now, whether I escaped or not. They simply assumed that I would come along with them meekly. They were *right*: wherever they were headed *had* to be better than where I had been.

But now, at least, they talked to me, also to one another, arguing, joking, even answering more questions I sneaked in from time to time, alsmost as if trying to catch up for their earlier stoic silence, whose purpose remained unexplained. We ate ration bars not altogether different from those I had enjoyed on the way from Vespucci. Theirs actually tasted like something. Chalk, I think.

Mostly, they asked *me* questions.

"We haven't any record of this planet of yours, Whitey, although the name Vespucci is familiar enough," Rogers said as he trudged behind the wagon with Couper while Lucille took her turn at guiding the animals up front. "It isn't too surprising. This is the farthest we've reached into your stellar neighborhood so far. How far is Vespucci from Sca?"

Was the query as innocent as the way it had been put? Or was there some deceit behind those open, questioning eyes? I looked at the unconscious lieutenant. "I am not sure I should answer that, sir. You must understand, I—"

"Don't call me sir, Whitey. And I understand your reluctance perfectly—for the sake of your home planet, you dare not take the chance of trusting me, no matter how you may feel about us personally."

I watched Lucille, her emerald eyes alert, golden hair

drying now, streaming behind her in the quadruple moon-light as she strode purposefully along.

"Something like that, sir—I mean..." Scientists were officer-caste to me. It was hard addressing him by his first name. I wondered what her body was like under that bulky— "What did you say, er, Rog?"

"I said okay, then tell me about the Navy, Whitey, your Vespuccian Navy."

"Naval *Reserve*. Mine—everybody else's, unless they are in the *Army* Reserve."

Rogers' forehead wrinkled. "You mean that *everybody* has to spend time in the—"

"I mean that I was *born* into the Navy, just like my father before me. That is why Vespucci—the nation-state, I mean, this time—was able to consolidate the entire planet so easily. Other countries were flabby, undisciplined. We are not."

A sour expression flashed over his face for an instant, then was carefully rearranged, although not without some visible effort. What is it about nosy strangers that makes you want to stand up for all those familiar things you hate the most?

"Meaning that the trains run on time? Well, that certainly explains the nature of your name, anyway."

"What is wrong with my name? I have the name my father left to me. We were a Gold Nova family, I will have you know. He died earning us two extra digits post-humously in the Battle of Kahl. You could not have a better name unless you were born into one of the original Command Families, like the lieutenant, here."

Couper, stalking beside Rogers, spoke, his narrowed eyes never leaving their suspicious search of the countryside around us. "And what would *his* name be?"

I realized that I had failed a little in the introductions department. "Enson Sermander, sir. He—"

Couper's forehead had wrinkled then he began to laugh. "One of the *upper* upper crust, huh? That's swell! Corporal, your lieutenant here doesn't have a *real* name, any more than you do!" He stopped a moment as we plodded onward, wiping tears from the corner of his eyes, then had to skip to catch up with the cart. "Great Albert's ghost, the things you run into out here!"

"I do not get it." I looked at Rogers; he maintained his hard-won neutral expression.

"Well, let's see: you're a corporal, right? In the *Navy*? Son, ensign is an old-time military rank where we come from, too—in the sea navy. About the equivalent of a shavetail, you savvy? Never mind. Does your friend here outrank an Army captain?"

"Army *Reserve*," I corrected automatically. "Yes, sir." I was puzzled. "Just below a Navy colonel."

"Death and taxes, what a world! Nonetheless, I'll wager a tall stack of chips that this 'Sermander' is nothing more than a corruption of the old-fashioned 'sir' and 'commander.'"

"I had never thought about that before," I replied, not wanting to think about it just then.

Rogers smiled his sad praxeologist's smile again, obviously wishing he were back repairing guns. "People seldom do, not about their own cultures. For example, at one time Coup's name was a title, too—'barrelmaker.' And there's an ancestor back in Cilly's family tree named after a huge furry animal. What do you know about the first settlers to reach your world, Whitey, the Hamiltonians?"

Who *were* these people? Who *were* these people? Who *were* these people?

"How in the name of Authority do you know about *that*? We have only recently discovered our past ... I *never* mentioned ..."

"Rog, do *you* know where all human beings originally came from?"

Embarrassed silence all around.

"The *stork* brought them!" Lucille snorted finally.

Rogers grimaced, picked up his pace, trudging forward to take his turn at coercing the animals. He never did explain what praexology was.

4

In the middle of that long bright night, we came to another clearing, indistinguishable from any other we had encountered. All evening we had been paralleling the stream I had bathed in. Since my first sketchy wash, my skin felt loose, as if it were about to fall off in ragged sheets. I *itched*. It was a form of torture in itself.

"Well," I said casually, presuming on my seemingly cordial acquaintance with these mysterious people, "if there are no objections, I am going for another scrub. That is, if we intend to be here that long." I slid off the straw-slick cart bed, marveling all over again how good my leg felt.

Couper helped Rogers guide the wagon under a low-hanging tree, began unhitching the animals. Searching through the straw, Lucille produced, unwrapped, unfolded a small machine resembling a portable electric fan. Rogers began sliding the lieutenant down with my enlisted help. We placed the unconscious man on the ground, propped against a boulder. The Lieutenant mumbled, eyelids fluttering, but went directly back to sleep.

"Only one objection, son." Couper drew his plasma gun. My heart skipped until I saw that he was glancing warily about the clearing. He reholstered his little weapon, began replacing the daytime shade fabric over the animal's backs. Using a section of flat harness, he slapped each of the beasts on the rump, driving them out of the clearing. "Some peasant is in for a profitable surprise," he said. "The objection, Corporal, is that we're *here*."

Lucille had set the odd device on the same rock that supported the lieutenant's slumbering head. She stared at it intently, glanced up suddenly at me, then, almost as if she had been caught at something naughty, threw a switch on its base. "Rapunzel, Rapunzel," she intoned, "let down your hair..."

I took it for some kind of code, like fighter pilots use. "...Rapunzel, Rapunzel, this is Lucy Bear!"

The machine spoke: *"Cute. You people ready? We're running late."* Involuntarily, my eyes lifted skyward, searching for some superadvanced starship come to pick us up. I almost began to cry, remembering how I had thought I was going to die in this miserable dirty place.

Couper's crew gathered around.

"Two guests, Ev," replied Lucille, "Nonhostile, more or less, and both wounded. They'll need special arrangements."

"Congratulations," the little communicator said, *"and a hearty well done—which is how I'll have 'em waiting, for you and your guests, unless you prefer yours rare. I've got the fix now...shouldn't be too long..."*

I found myself straining to hear rocket thunder, or the warbling whistle of some weird, wonderful alien drive.

"There it is!" Lucille cried. She pointed: a minuscule spark of brilliance, electric blue, appeared in front of us, about a meter from my nose. It quickly widened into a azure-edged hole right through the air in front of us! Through it, I could make out a complex metal-plastic interior where the light was softer.

One at a time, we stepped through the hole.

I helped Couper carry the lieutenant. Behind us, the circle shrank again, to a blinding dot, brighter than Sca's sun, disappeared with a *pop*! A plastic-upholstered bench fronted a circular wall. Above it windows reached to a domed ceiling. Through them glowed the stars undimmed by atmosphere. Below was the surface, deeply curved at this altitude, of the planet Sca.

We were in orbit!

"Welcome aboard the *Little Tom*," said a voice I recognized from Lucille's little radio. "Dinner is about to be served."

I turned—nearly fainted with surprise—to face my first genuine alien.

6

Little Tom

At least a couple of heads shorter than I am, man-shaped, but completely covered with fur, it nonetheless spoke with a deep, rumble-voiced authority, its voice seeming to emanate from a watch-size plastic instrument strapped to its hairy wrist.

Couper bundled the lieutenant off somewhere, mumbling about "medical stasis," "Basset coils," similar meaningless arcana. I continued staring helplessly at the nonhuman pilot, while Rogers, following Lucille's example, shucked off his monkish robes with every indication of relief.

Beneath, each wore a close-fitting overall of the familiar silvery-gray material, the sleeves equipped with an inset control panel like those on our bandages, only larger, sporting perhaps ten times as many tiny controls. Williamson—was that the alien's real name, or simply one adopted for the convenience of human tongues?—had on the "summer issue" version: shortened sleeves, abbre-

59

viated legs, the gadget panel situated where his belt buckle ought to have been. Each of my new acquaintances was armed with the ubiquitous small plasma gun slung in a highly unmilitary variety of manners: under the arm, at the waist, in separate holsters or in pockets integral with the suit.

As Rogers intently poked at his coverall's sleeve-buttons, a rainbow chased itself across the surface then stabilized, settling into a garish greenish-yellow check-erboard pattern. For some reason, the aesthetic outrage seemed to please him. He looked up, asked Williamson, "When do we eat?"

The pilot's stubby muzzle wrinkled, displaying an intimidating collection of long yellow fangs. "Very likely never, unless you tone down that vomitous tartan of yours. In any case, we'll wait for the boss." He flipped a furry thumb in my direction. "So who's the supernumerary?"

Thus spake the alien monster.

I kept wishing he would turn around so I could see whether he had a tail to go with the pelt, also if there was not perhaps a hole through his pants-seat for it, like a character in a cartoon. It did not seem polite to ask, however.

"One Corporal Whitey O'Thraight," Lucille answered before Rogers or I could do more than open our mouths. "An armorer, if we're to believe him, late of something called the Vespuccian Navy."

"Naval *Reserve*," I corrected stiffly, then, before I could stop myself, "A standing army is the age-old instrument of tyranny."

"No shit, Corporal-baby?" She yawned; before I could think of a suitably acid comeback, she added, "Well, this seminar's been fascinating, guys, but *I'm* headed for the showers. Ev, that mudball down there is more than any mere smartsuit can handle. The remotes don't tell the half of it. And you simply wouldn't *believe* that pile of garbage they call a castle. I'll be having nightmares for a week!"

Without waiting for a reply from the alien, she took a

step backward, almost seemed to melt into the floor. She vanished.

There was a chuckle. "Don't stand there rubber-necking, Admiral," Williamson seemed to be addressing me. "She treats everybody that way. Gonna be a fine human being someday—if we let her live. C'mon, park it somewhere. Can I get you a drink?" He turned slightly—no tail. I was disappointed.

I picked a spot on the continuous, well-upholstered sofa running completely around the room. Covered in some warm, supple plastic, it was the only article of furniture in sight, embossed with riding animals such as we had fought on Sca, men in broad-brimmed floppy hats twirling cables of some kind above their heads as they pursued creatures not unlike those that had pulled the cart. The plastic was a darkish tan, contrasting with the polished-metal window-framing, the deep, dark-colored carpeting that covered the entire circular floorspace from wall to wall.

"Thanks, er...say, do you mind my asking a nosy question?" On Vespucci, we are much given to ceremony, rituals where the masses mass, the officials officiate, everybody highly aware that something important is happening—such as the laying of a new section of sidewalk in a residential area, your tax dollars at work. All of this chit-chat seemed incredibly, almost scandalously informal, considering what was really transpiring. They seemed to take my presence for granted, as if they encountered evidence of heretofore unknown civilizations every day. It kept coming back to me, over again, that I was in an *alien starship*, beginning a perfectly polite, extremely trivial conversation with a *Creature from Outer Space*!

The Scavians *did not* count, somehow.

He turned back to face me, amusement in his large brown eyes, as a small section rose from the thickly carpeted floor behind him. "Depends on just how nosy you make it, Kilroy."

Kilroy?

Glasses, bottles, other universal alcoholic paraphernalia nestled in lined recesses in the side of the extruded column. A small deep-pile divot still rested on its upper surface. The furry bartender fumbled with the drinks.

"Well..." (Likewise, I fumbled—for an honorific, uncomfortably settling for a given name in its place.) "Geoffrey Couper tells me that he is from a—from some *place* called Earth. I am curious about where *you* are from, and, er, what sort of...*person* you are." How do you put a question like that courteously? What *species* are you, sir?

He paused, what might have been a grin on his face, stared out at the stars for a moment in contemplation. "I suppose you might say I'm from Ceres—take a right at Earth and keep going for another hundred megamiles. I'm a chimpanzee, which means my people are originally from Africa. Scotch okay, Kilroy?"

Rogers had done something to one of the windows. It had become a mirror in which he was critically examining the garish pattern of his suit. He glared resentfully over his shoulder at the pilot, then gave it up as an incomprehensible difference in tastes, slumped down on the sofa a few feet away from me with his arms folded across his chest.

"Chim-pan-zee," I muttered, trying to get a feel for the exotic word. All these planets I had never even *dreamed* existed: Earth, Ceres, Africa. "Scotch is fine—whatever it is. I will try anything once. What is a mile?"

"Five thousand of these." Williamson held his oddly shaped hands about twenty centimeters apart. "Rocks? Water? And what're you drinking, Rog?"

What did rocks have to do with anything—more importantly, who the devil was Kilroy? The gunsmith looked up from a contemplative study of the boots built into the legs of his—what had she called it—"smartsuit."

"Anything that burns, Ev. I'm gonna hit the showers when Annie Oakley's finished. She wasn't kidding about conditions planetside—no offense, Whitey."

"Listen, it is not *my* planet!"

Aside from an only partially psychosomatic surge of furious itching, this second mention of showers in five minutes made me realize that:

a) water falling downward; plus

b) rear ends adhering by themselves to sofas; must mean that

c) we were under acceleration.

A glance out the windows confirmed it spectacularly— Sca was slipping steadily away. I was not heartbroken. I looked at Williamson. The pilot handed me a glass of innocent-looking amber fluid.

I wondered who was driving.

I had been thinking all along, ever since I understood the nature of our location, of asking a question, even begun to frame it several times, but backed away, primarily for fear of the likeliest answer. Now, with trepidation: "Can you people take me—the lieutenant, also— *home* in this machine?" They gave each other odd, embarrassed looks. Williamson blinked. Rogers opened his mouth, then shut it. I did not much care for the long awkward pause that followed.

"Let's talk about that, *after* we've had something to eat." My head jerked around: Geoffrey Couper rose up through the carpet, stepped forward without leaving a hole behind him. His smartsuit, a dull, nonreflective gray, had the look of a uniform about it, abetted by a rank of tiny colorful campaign ribbons on his left breast. "How about it, Ev? Whitey's *lieutenant* is tucked away safely, and Lucille's right behind me."

So she was, oozing out of the floorboards just as Couper had done. I remembered the drink I had not touched, took a big gulp of the Scotch, gasped, wheezed, started coughing as I watched a sizable portion of the floor get taller, the carpet pile on the rising surface dwindling until there was a smooth, tablelike surface in its place. Then, up through the surface, dishes rose, silverware, substantial servings of food steaming in containers.

Who *were* these people?

2

More drinks were produced while the company waited through Rogers' turn to freshen up—also, it was loudly hoped, to reprogram his suit. We were five for dinner—if there were more crew aboard the *Little Tom*, they failed to manifest themselves. Couper paternally headed up the irregular shaped table, the Cerean/African/Chimpanzean pilot occupying a seat more or less at its opposite end. They honored me with a place on Couper's right, across from Lucille. With a thorough shampoo, some imaginative tinkering with the push-buttons of her suit (now a shade of violet with a single bright diagonal band of green), she looked exactly as she had before, a soldier of whatever kind she was, who happened also to be a remarkably beautiful young woman. That is, if you could overlook the pistol slung cross-draw at her left hip. The women I had known all of my life carried babies there, not guns.

Rogers sat beside me. They heaped their plates as if it had been they, not I, who had been living on Scavian largesse for weeks; I surprised myself by not being very interested in food. The stars outside drifted like faraway cities glimpsed from a high-flying aircraft. What must our velocity be? This had never happened aboard the *Asperance*. I am not sure it is ever supposed to happen. "Uh, aren't the stars supposed to bunch up, turning blue, or something?"

"Or something, right enough." Williamson laughed. "What you're seeing isn't even a computer correction. It's a holomural, entitled . . . now, let me see—something historical or literary, I forget—oh yes! *Stardate*. Personally, I think it's silly, but the passengers seem to like it. Pass the radishes, please—*excuse* me—the little red things in that bowl there."

I took another sip. Wine: I certainly found it more to my taste than Scotch, although, compared to what potables were available to the enlisted classes back home, even that was smoothly agreeable to the palate. I wondered: were we eating alien food, or was Williamson politely dining Earthian tonight? Or was it some eclectic mixture? I had not heard of anything on the table before me; each bite was a new adventure (or a risk, as I discovered when I tried one of the little red things—embarrassing afterward, too).

There were thick sections of grainy-textured protein called beef, akin to the Scavian pulling animals, I gathered, only bred by Earthians for slaughter. The most highly valued varieties came from two planets, as I understood it, Alamo, some place called Newer Zealand. No one mentioned what had become of Older Zealand. There was something, too, in impossibly monumental slices—correctly pinkish orange in color—but... Well, if ham does *not* come from a hamster, where *does* it come from?

Several different vegetables, none recognizable, took the place of Vespuccian turnips, palmetto, or cabbage. Beside a gigantic bowl of sugar, double-fist sized, grand enough to grace a general's table, rested a second, delicious powdery-brown condiment that some of my companions stirred into coffee—a hot black bitter drink—along with enough milk to dry up the community hutches for a week.

3

I am not certain what I had been running on, thus far.

I had drifted through everything that happened to me rather, well, numbly. Matter-of-factly. Now reality seemed to be catching up, suddenly casting everything occurring at that table into a dreamlike mood, requiring concentrated effort to focus on any given object, any specific moment of time.

Conversation lapped around me, words, phrases, whole sentences making no more sense than the babbling waters.

Even my palate was overwhelmed. So many new things, so *much* of it. If these people were nothing else, they were fabulously rich. This holiday feast was nothing more to them than a hearty farmhand's supper. At home, for example, custom reserves milk for babies, toothless ancients. These people fairly *swam* in the stuff.

Having tried coffee without much satisfaction, I somewhat diffidently asked whether they might ever have heard of tea—they answered me with a list of thirty or forty variables, enumerated on a CC screen that oozed out of the table surface.

"Just *tea*," I pleaded, beginning to shake all over.

They gave me liptons, sweet, aromatic; I took the cup, then found I had drifted away somewhere again—when I went to sip it, the tea was already cold.

I do not believe that I will even *mention* dessert. Back home, they arrest people for things like that. Dishes, fine delicate porcelain embossed with the name of the ship we occupied, cleared themselves away somehow, along with the silver, when I was not looking. Couper, still resplendent in his quasimilitary garb, poured himself another glass of wine. Others had been passed around without my noticing. Then he selected a small white paper tube from the variety in a container on the table, placed it in his mouth, lit the free end, drawing smoke with obvious relish. The container was passed. Lucille, with the praxeologist—his suit still garish plaid, bushy hair parted formally down the middle—joined their commander in this weird ritual.

"Now, son," Couper began once these postprandial ceremonies were seen to, "you have a lot of questions. I know you're tired, but—well, we have questions, too."

"Yeah," Lucille chimed, "like what in the hell were you doing on that medieval scumball in the first place?" She flicked a cylinder of accumulated ash into a small glass dish. Her burning-tube smelled sweet.

I blinked. "Why, I had been planning to ask you the same thing!"

She inhaled another lungful, trying, for some peculiar reason, to speak while holding her breath. "We asked first!"

Couper gave a low, fatherly growl of admonition, then grinned, letting it fade. "She's right. If you don't mind, son."

So, to the accompaniment of faint, unfamiliar music drifting down from somewhere in the area of the ceiling, I told them about the voyage of the *Asperance*, the massacre. How we wound up in the cesspool, the only survivors, where they had found us. It did not take long. To my surprise, it was the first I had thought of the lieutenant in a couple of hours.

I caught a riffle of melody from the overhead speakers that might have been especially composed for the mandolar—it was the first time I had heard music of any kind, aside from my own demented humming in the dungeons, for what seemed an eternity.

Couper sipped his wine, a thick sticky liquid whose flavor seemed to crawl all over the tongue like lukewarm fire. "What surprises *me* is that they let you live, after what you did to—"

"But we never did *anything* to them! I told you, we tried to *avoid*—!"

"What he means"—Rogers laughed—"is that *you*—second person *non*plural—singlehandedly disposed of . . . what did it come to, boss? You did the field interviews for me."

Couper shook his head with what appeared to be rueful admiration. "It depends on which village the information came from. I make it seventeen heavily armored knights, with weapons not terribly more primitive than your own, Corporal—yes, no matter what you *or* the Scavians may think, not terribly more primitive at all. You know, administering steel by hand or lead via expanding chemical gases is largely a matter of aesthetic preference." He took—a sip?—of his smoking-tube, tapped ashes off its end into Lucille's little bowl. "You're something of a legend back there already, son, one I fear is going to prove trouble-some for us in the future."

There was a lapse in the conversation that lasted several heartbeats.

"How many projectiles," Rogers asked at last, "did those quasi-rotary slug chuckers of yours carry, any-way?"

I felt the temperature rising in my cheeks. "Er, fifteen apiece, in the magazine," I mumbled, keeping my eyes on the tabletop. "I had two of them, all I could manage to get loaded before we were attacked. If I had been more conscientious when we first landed, my people might..." I found it hard to choke back tears that threatened to humiliate me even further in front of these strangers.

Couper leaned over, placed a big hand on my shoulder. "Those fancy-britches with their boughten commissions wouldn't likely have been much help, even if you'd loaded a hundred weapons for them, son. You still don't realize, do you? Great Albert's ghost, boy—half the reason the Scavians tortured you was simply to reassure themselves that you were really human!" He crushed his smoking-tube in the ash bowl. "You'll be a legend all over again when we get back to the ship!"

"Get back?" I looked around: this spacecraft of theirs was twice the size of *Asperance*. All I had seen so far was the *upstairs*. "You are trying to tell me that this is not—"

"This is *Little Tom*, son, a private auxiliary—with some amazing capabilities, but an auxiliary nonetheless. Begging your pardon of course, Ev."

The furry alien lifted a negligent paw. "A small thing but mine own, as I told a young female acquaintance recently." He fumbled with the container on the table, extracted a very large green burning-tube. The smell, very different from either Couper's or Lucille's, was horrible.

"But how—" I began.

"Wait and see," Couper answered, not answering anything at all. "As to what *we* were doing on Sca..." He looked around the table; they all looked back at him. "In a manner of speaking we were—and still *are*, for that matter—conducting a preliminary survey of the planet and its many and—"

"—and not-very-diverse—"

"Thank you, Lucille, when I desire your help, I'll lift your rock and ask for it. Yes, its not-very-diverse cultures." As if his own smoke had not been enough pollution in his lungs, he took the smaller tube from Lucille's fingers, drew from it, closed his eyes, held it for a while before expelling it. "Not very damned diverse at all!"

I thought about that guilty-looking glance they had all shared. "Preliminary survey? Preliminary to what? With exactly what object in mind?"

Rogers spoke: "Need there be any *particular* purpose for scientific inquiry? Isn't knowledge valuable in and of itself?" He ground his burning-tube out, immediately lit another.

"So sayeth the guy who doesn't pay the bills!" Lucille retorted. "We're free-roving traders, Corporal-darling, privateers looking for a fast ounce any way we can get it, by hook or by..." She patted the weapon on her hip suggestively. "You can get more with a smile and a gun— than you can with just a smile."

"Arrgh!" agreed the gunsmith in a funny croaking voice. "An' I'm the Jolly Rogers hisself!" He covered one eye leered obscenely, folding his free hand into a fist except for the middle finger, which he crooked, clawing at the girl.

She giggled, looked suddenly startled, then peered suspiciously at the paper tube between her fingers.

Williamson: "Come on, Coup, set him straight before they have him thinking we're going to make him walk the plank. He isn't a bad guy for a Kilroy."

Kilroy again—I had to fight that drowsy, drifting feeling stealing back over me. In addition, I was becoming self-conscious about the fact that I was the only one there who had not bathed recently. I did not count the sketchy washup in the creek. What was so bad about walking on a plank? If Lucille was trying to make me think that they were all brigands of some kind, the fact that they had gone out of their way to rescue me and the lieutenant spoiled her story a little.

"They have a wine on Sca," Couper declaimed with sudden incongruity, holding his glass up to the light, "which is remarkably disgusting in every respect—except that it has peculiarly potent antibiotic properties against a disease which dolphins frequently contract on Ganymede."

I could see that. "What is a dolphin?"

This time they all blinked foolishly at one another. This conversation was making less sense all the time. I began to suspect the wine. Or possibly the burning-tubes.

"Another kind of nonhuman intelligent being," Rogers supplied finally, giving Williamson a courteous nod. "Good friends of ours, and for a long, long time."

"Yeah," said Lucille, "some of my best friends are dolphins." From some well-hidden pocket, she took what looked like a small flat stone, inserted the last two centimeters of her smoking-tube, drew heavily on the other end. There was a sharp *crack*! sparks flew from the object.

"Seed," said everybody at once.

"Bet you think I did that on porpoise." She winked.

Music continued playing. Unable to think of anything better to say, I asked, "This planet the dolphins are from, this Ganymede you mentioned?..."

Couper ignored me. "The point is, son, that we explore sinkholes like Sca, hoping to discover new materials, new ideas, even manufactured goods occasionally. We heard about you two 'sky demons' in marketplaces for two hundred miles' radius around that pile of incompetently chipped rock where they were keeping you. At first we thought you might be one of our own we'd somehow lost track of. There are quite a few of us out here. Later, when it developed that you couldn't be, it was even *more* important to pull you out in one piece."

"Why was that?"

More embarrassed silence, then: "Because," said Rogers, assuming his grim professional expression, "yours is the first independent star-traveling civilization we've ever discovered."

Williamson rose, excusing himself to attend to some technical matter. He took three paces, sank through the floor, disappearing.

"The first?"

None of them seemed particularly delighted at the prospect. Watching the pseudostars drift by "outside," gave me something else to think about; now seemed as good (or bad) a time as any. "Speaking of star-traveling, I . . . I mean I have sort of been wondering what your plans are. You see, I—"

"He wants to go home, Coup," Rogers interrupted. "A perfectly natural, easily understood request. We should have talked this over earlier. I *told* you—"

"Son, I have to admit, I've been putting this moment off as long as I could manage. There are reasons, all of them highly sensible, although I don't expect you to see it that way, why we can't just—"

"Orders," Lucille stated suddenly, flatly.

"Huh?" responded the older man, uncomprehending wrinkles furrowing the space between his eyebrows.

"The corporal is a *soldier*, Coup—or a sailor, I'm not sure I've gotten that straight yet. Anyway, he understands orders. Whitey, we're expected at a rendezvous. We simply *can't* take any unexpected sidetrips until we report." She paused, looking from me to Couper. "I don't think it'll hurt anything to tell you this much: the discovery of another culture with faster-than-light capabilities is a shock to us. And it's a matter of very serious concern. Policy has to be generated, dig?"

I nodded, long-familiar with being on the receiving end of policy. "What does that make me, then, a prisoner-of-war or something?"

"Hardly!" Lucille guffawed. It was a startling thing to

witness. "Old Coup here is right: what it makes you is a celebrity. Think you can stand that for a while? Cocktail parties, interviews, empty-headed newsies hanging on your every word, then distorting them beyond all recognition? I'm not sure *I* could."

"*I* might give it a try," offered Rogers, "just for the heck of it." He winked broadly at the girl—who returned a suspicious stare—licking his lips. "*Groupies.*"

"Groupies?" I echoed the alien-sounding word, perplexed. Good heavens, what planet were *they* from?

"It's simply a disgusting expression from perhaps the most alien civilization we've ever—"

"*Excuse us, folks*, is it too late to set another place at the table?" We all turned to see the Chimpanzean pilot rising slowly through the wall-to-wall carpeting. Beside him, grinning in apparent perfect health, stood my lieutenant, Enson Sermander.

7

Rendezvous in Space

"I am somewhat fatigued, Corporal, since you are kind enough to inquire." He was dressed from collar to shoe soles in the fashion of our hosts (or captors) except that his wounded arm was sealed inside the silvery-gray suit, folded across his chest. "Nor shall I be using this"—he indicated the missing sleeve—"for quite some time, I gather. Aside from that, well, consider the *alternative*."

His skin tone was good; there was a healthy sparkle in his eyes—especially once he caught sight of Lucille.

"Well, well! Pardon me, Corporal—you were through with that chair, anyway, were you not—what have we here, a cactus blossom among the thorns?" Rosy fingers brushed along Lucille's graceful neck into her cheeks. She stared down with apparent shyness at the tabletop, nervously fingering a napkin. I must have eaten too much at dinner; I wanted to regurgitate.

"More likely just another thorn, Lieutenant," Geoffrey Couper answered before the girl could speak, "a more decorative one than most, admittedly. Sir, allow me to introduce my colleagues. Owen Rogers; I believe your term is 'armorer,' also Sc.D., Praxeology, Mekstrom University Limited, Titan. Captain Williamson you've met. I'm Geoffrey Couper, Mission Supervisor. This is Lucille Olson-Bear, Security and Defense—our *principal* thorn, in fact. And now I think that's *quite* enough of titles for the moment."

Lieutenant Sermander bowed low over the table, scooped up Lucille's hand, kissed it as he clicked his heels. "Miss Olson-Bear, gentlemen: you have my deepest gratitude. My life is yours, for you have preserved it in the face of the bleakest—"

"Thank Whitey, here," Rogers interrupted. "He kept you in one piece long enough for us to find you."

"Why, yes, er...well done, Corporal. It shall be so entered in my report when we return to Vespucci." He straightened, turned to face Couper with a shrewd expression. "We *are* returning to Vespucci, are we not?"

Suddenly I could understand all the previous embarrassed pauses I had encountered. Nor was there anything I wanted to say, either.

"Um, *directly*, Lieutenant," Couper answered.

"Um, *indirectly*," Lucille corrected. "Lieutenant, we were just explaining to the corporal, here, that our orders call for checking in with our primary vessel. Until that's accomplished..."

The lieutenant spread the palm of his good hand outward. "Say no more, dear lady, you have my understanding—my sincerest sympathy. I, too, have impatient superiors to whom I must make an account of myself. I would impose that much further upon your gracious hospitality: have you a microwave capable of—"

"*Microwave!*" Couper was amused.

"Not even for cooking," answered Williamson, "and even then, it wouldn't—"

"He's talking about *radio*," Rogers said. "Lieutenant, I'm sorry to tell you that it would take—what, Ev?"

Williamson rolled his eyes back in thought. His muzzle twitched slightly. "Four point two-three years."

"It would take four point two-three years for an electromagnetic message to reach Sca, let alone Vespucci, even if we had the equipment, and even if—well, your corporal's been pretty closed-mouthed about telling us where the planet is."

"Four...*light-years!*" It took superhuman effort not to scream it. "We have come that far in only—"

"Steady, son," said Couper. "We don't communicate by radio waves, Lieutenant, and, without belittling its considerable accomplishments, I doubt whether your civilization could make much sense of any paratronic transmissions we sent them. Even so, the time lag would be lessened by a factor of only...let's see: a whisker under e-squared times pi..."

"Sixty days," supplied Williamson, who seemed to be an instant mental calculator in addition to being the underworked pilot of this machine. "It would take two months, and, long before then, you'll be at rendezvous. Face it: there's nothing faster in the known universe for transportation *or* communication than a spaceship. Sorry."

2

"Look," Owen Rogers said impatiently, "it's simple: I've keyed the colors so you'll understand, okay?"

"Okay nothing," I objected truthfully. "What do *colors* have to do with sinking through the floor?"

Dinner was long over. Couper, Williamson, the lieutenant were conferring. Lucille had gone below, which is where I would be going if I could ever get the hang of it. I, alone among the company, was still unshowered, unshaven, also extremely *unslept* ; that fact was being brought home to me now as I struggled to comprehend what my fellow armorer was "explaining."

"Look, the ship isn't keyed to your...call it *brain-*

waves, I guess you'd say. There's no point in correcting that now, since we'll be at rendezvous pretty soon. So I've adjusted this section of the floor—right over your quarters—to let you through."

I puzzled over this. "Thoughtful of you or the ship. What keeps me from breaking both ankles when I hit the floor below?"

He snorted. "That's what I'm trying to explain! The marked section's yellow, the deck below is blue. You step on the yellow bit, the ship senses that it's you— never mind how it knows, it *knows*."

"Great. Then what?"

"Well, you saw how the dinner table came up? The molecules the floor's composed of simply expanded, read-justing themselves to take up a little more room, and *viola*, a table!"

"That's *voilà*," Williamson commented from across the room. The alien had incredibly sharp hearing, I thought to myself.

"Whatever. Where was I? You step on this yellow section, a piece of floor downstairs expands until it hits the ceiling. Its blue molecules interlace with the yellow ones, and you'll get green!"

"I am getting that way already. You mean the mole-cules of the two floors actually intermingle?"

"Sure. There isn't a cubic inch of the whole ship that isn't smart that way. Then the upper-floor molecules get out of your way, while the blue ones contract again, low-ering you gently to the—"

"Hold it! That may be all right for carpets, but I am *not* mingling my molecules with any—"

"Of course not! They get completely out of your way, leaving a perfect, Whitey-shaped hole—actually the shape of your latitudinal cross-section—as you sink sedately through the floor."

I looked at the pentagonal yellow area Rogers had "ad-justed" for me, observing that his taste in interior decor matched his taste in clothing. The rest of the carpeting was maroon. "Sorry, Rog, it just seems like magic...."

"Right," he answered smugly. "Any sufficiently advanced technology will—"

"Resemble advanced technology," Couper finished for him as he approached, "And nothing more. The theory you're quoting, Rog, is a crock. Once a culture has the idea of technology per se, it eventually stops believing in magic at all."

"But Whitey just *stated* —"

"I heard him. He's tired and probably didn't mean it literally."

I opened my mouth to agree with him—also to comment that his hearing was fully as acute as that of the furry pilot—but yawned, instead.

"Obviously," said Couper, "this discussion is keeping our guest from a hot shower and a soft bed."

I shut my mouth, stepped onto the pentagon, not caring much what happened.

"Sweet dreams," said Rogers as I sank through the floor. "And whatever you do down there, *don't* push the button marked T.R. Cut it out, Coup, I was only kidd—!"

3

The ceiling closed over my head, depriving me of any further byplay from the two. I found myself descending into a small, neat cabin with a pair of single beds, connecting to a compact bathroom. Shaking off my robe, I peeked at the shower stall, expecting more magic. I was not disappointed. The curtain was a rigid elastic membrane, transparent, with no visible opening. On a hunch, I pushed a hand against it. The hand went through as I had expected, followed by the rest of me. Immediately the membrane changed from transparent to translucent, offering me privacy.

No faucets. Instead, a colored band, ranging gradually from blue to red, crossed the front wall at chest level. I

touched it in the middle; water began to flow. I mean
flow. The stinging ultrasonically propelled mist I was used
to at home was replaced here with a torrent that nearly
knocked me off my feet. I had touched the broad colored
band at its top edge—no savage, Whitey; Couper was
right about technology—now I placed a finger near the
button; the pressure slackened. Then I ran the finger up
again, enjoying the Vespuccian-bred reflexive guilty feeling as liter upon liter cascaded around me.

Soap: there was not any. I glanced around the stall.
Not so much as a tray. Well, I would scrub as well as
possible, as I had in the stream, learn the secret of the
missing soap tomorrow. Finishing up, I noticed that soap
was not the only amenity lacking. No towels hung in the
bathroom, I was certain. Possibly a cabinet outside. I
stepped through the curtain—

—coming through dry as the sands of my native planet!

Clean, as well. I recalled suddenly how my hair had
squeaked in the shower, how the flaking film of unsloughed skin had been blessedly absent. The shower was
a stall, all right. Purely for recreational relaxation purposes, I guessed. It was that membrane curtain that—
literally—did all the dirty work. I stepped back into the
bedroom—

Surprise. On the right-hand bed, rolled up in their Ves-
puccian-issue fabric belt, lay a pair of 8-mm Darrick pistols. My pair, it appeared, in the regulation holsters.
Unsnapping the flap of one, I checked the grip. Empty.
Well, either Earthian technology had its limits, or they
wanted me to have my weapons—but did not trust me
with live ammunition. Nevertheless, it was good to have
the pistols back. I wondered how they had been retrieved.
I would hate to be the Scavian noble holding them if
Lucille did the retrieving.

Turning, I noticed a bare spot in the blue carpeting.
The robe I had discarded was gone. Working my way
around the walls, pushing my hand against them as I had

done the shower curtain, I finally discovered a closet whose "door" vanished upon penetration. Sure enough, there was the robe, hanging beside the remnants of my uniform—also that of the lieutenant.

I was not fooled. All of this was fun, it was interesting, but Couper was right: magic it was not. I folded the blanket down, got into bed, cradling the double pistol belt in my arms. The lights started dimming. I was not afraid, of the darkness nor of the power of these people. I simply envied them their wealth, their knowledge, hoping that someday, *my* people . . .

4

I awoke from a dreamless sleep, better rested than I had felt in months. Beside me, in the other bed, Lieutenant Sermander lay snoring, still wearing what Lucille had called a smartsuit. Rogers had used a similar term, trying to explain the weirdly cooperative carpet of the *Little Tom*.

Untangling myself from the bedclothes, I quietly stumbled into the bathroom to discover no magical surprises where the rest of the plumbing was concerned except that it used a lot of water. I decided to test that gimmicky shower curtain again.

Into the stall, out again.

I definitely felt different—clean, but not refreshed. You need hot running water to wake you up, shake you out— not to mention doing something about what a good night's sleep does to your hair. I fiddled with the red-blue shower control, deciding to ask about toothbrushes later. Yes, if you are morbidly curious, there *is* a shower curtain–type membrane stretched across the toilet seat. They may have spent water like it was going out of style, but they certainly did not waste paper.

In the closet hung my tattered uniform, the burlap-veneer robe I was thoroughly tired of. Also a smartsuit.

Eyes wide, I took it off its hanger, began slipping my legs into the—

"Don't try that without help, Whitey, you might hurt yourself." I *jumped* at the voice above me. Owen Rogers' head protruded down through the ceiling like some ghastly trophy. He caught the startled look in my eyes, rolled his own backward until only the whites were visible, let his tongue hang out one corner of his mouth. "Hold on"—he laughed, finally breaking the pose—"I'll give you a hand."

He withdrew his head; there was a pause while a section of the bedroom floor grew up to meet him. Then his feet appeared, his horribly patterned suit legs (this morning purple was locked in mortal conflict with two shades of orange), then the rest of him. I signaled for him to be quiet on account of the lieutenant.

"Constitution, Whitey," he answered in a voice only slightly quieter than an orbital shuttle taking off, "I'm supposed to wake him up, too. Say, if you fit the catheters in that way, *you'll* wake him up—with your own screaming." He was referring to the suit's inner arrangements, very personal, very embarrassing. He brushed my hands aside, did what had to be done efficiently without fuss. "Now you'll know whether you're coming or going. Just pass your hand along the diagonal seam, that's right, hip to shoulder. You're done—all except selecting some real snazzy pattern."

"I think I will pass." I had noticed that the others preferred solid colors, or simply the natural hue of smart-suit material. Then, catching sight of my bedraggled uniform, I asked, "What could you do with that?"

"Fascist-modern," he said, appraisingly, then imitated Lucille by wrinkling his nose. "Oh well, you fish your side, I'll fish my side, and nobody fish in the middle. Is the color right, or has it faded? I assume that sleeve originally ended in a cuff, like the other one? . . ." Pressing buttons on my arm, he created a facsimile of my Navy Reserve uniform, complete to the chevrons. Campaign pips decorated the counterfeit pockets. On the collar were displayed the crossed pistols of the field armorer.

"Great," Rogers said standing back for a look. "Sure you won't have any jackboots? Sam Browne belt? We're having a special this week. How about your hoglegs, then? I cleaned 'em up the best I could. Sorry there isn't any ammo, the Dardick was a fine old design, and—*oops*! Forget I let that slip, Whitey, have mercy on a fellow peon."

I looked at him closely, then turned, retrieved my pistols from the bed, belted them around my waist, unaccustomed to the extra weight on the left side. "What are you talking about, 'a fine old design'? Where do *you* know Darricks from?" About a hundred extremely odd notions were flitting through my mind.

"Honest, Whitey, I can't—why, good morning, Lieutenant! Glad to see you slept well. We dock in about ninety minutes; I'm here to invite you to breakfast." News to me, too. Sermander blinked stupidly, hoisted himself upright, blinked stupidly again.

"I shall have rock-lizard eggs on toast, four strips of crisply grilled hamster, plenty of tea. Do not bother setting a place for me, the corporal will serve me in my quarters." Looking first up then down, his eyes settled on the pistol belt. "We shall discuss *those* later." He stretched, threw his legs over the edge of the bed, rose, waddled off to the bathroom. Behind him, the door dwindled, leaving a blank wall. I had not known it did that.

Rogers appeared to be in deep thought. Then he too blinked at me, focusing again. "Uppity son-of-a-bureaucrat, isn't he?"

Before I could reply, the carpet started doing odd little things again. Geoffrey Couper was descending into our midst—the little cabin was getting crowded. "You fellows go on upstairs," he suggested, "I'll straighten the lieutenant out. That arm of his needs looking at, anyway, and *nobody* gets waited on around here, especially by the man who saved his life. How's the leg, Whitey?"

"I had completely forgotten about it, sir."

"Then git—and don't call me sir!"

We *got*, me wondering how he had known to come straighten out the lieutenant.

5

Strange food, strange drink, strange conversation. Only I was awake now, fully rested. This morning Lucille smoked what everybody else did. No one said a word about my weapons. I felt conspicuous, although the others were carrying guns of one kind or another. Couper came with the lieutenant twenty minutes later, my fellow Vespuccian red in the face, not looking pleased. He changed all that for Lucille's sake, however. He was even mildly civil with me.

"You actually piloted that flimsy box-kite between stellar systems across two light-years? Nine weeks—how horrible!" She never looked at me, but smiled, flirting with the lieutenant, fascinated by everything he had to say. He glanced in my direction before answering, warning written on his face.

"We had a good computer system, my dear, not like in the old days when it was seat-of-the-pants flying against a determined foe."

"You're too modest, Lieutenant. Gosh, I've never known a real aeroplane fighter before!"

You *still* do not, I found myself thinking. Then I shut it off: it is an officer's world; there is nothing any NCO can do about it. I was mentally debating whether to be annoyed—the lieutenant had programmed his suit to duplicate his own, rather grander, uniform—when Williamson stopped in the middle of an unlikely fable he had resumed, about an old lady blowing up an entire planet, to make a philosophical point.

"Ammonium nitrate, she told me, soaked down with number three diesel fuel and—excuse me a moment, will you?" He generated an expression of mild concentration. Outside the computer mural faded suddenly, replaced by

a more accurate frozen starscape in the midst of which
blinked a solitary light. Abruptly, the brilliant point virtually exploded into a solid object, a blazing hemisphere
hanging in the void before us, occupying the entire field
of vision. It rotated until we approached from its flat
underside. There was nothing to give one a sense of scale,
but the thing was *huge*, possibly six or eight times larger
than the *Asperance*, three times greater in diameter than
the *Little Tom*, its curved upper surface featureless, lit
from within by an eerie, grainy scintillation. Underneath,
near the edge, a bowl-shaped opening yawned, only one
of seven, six deep cavities around a seventh in the center.
Each, save the empty one we closed on, was neatly filled
with a smaller craft, miniatures of the giant spaceship,
identical to the *Little Tom*. The joining seams were nearly
invisible, the lower contours of the small ships matched
those of the mother vessel, matched, too, its blue-white
brilliance.

"Last chick home to the nest!" Williamson relaxed
again as the great form closed over us. The original starry
display was restored. He pointed a broad-nailed finger
ceilingward. "In case you Vespuccian gentlemen are wondering, that baby up there is *big*. Eight hundred sixty-
nine feet across. Dunno what that would be by your reckoning." He rose. "Well, it's been fun; thanks for traveling
Little Tom. If something profitable ever comes from that
dark-age dustball Sca—which I misdoubt sincerely—let
me know. I've got three percent."

General laughter around the table.

I got up, started downstairs to collect my few belongings. Behind me, despite the finality of his words, the
pilot perched on a corner of the table as the conversation
continued. "You can be sure, Ev," Rogers mused, "that
whatever policy is decided on, we'll be doing the Confederacy—the entire galaxy, for that matter—a real favor.
Besides, there's *bound* to be something—organics, min-
erals, handicrafts—we can use."

Buried to my shoulders in the floor, I could not see

the pilot but could hear his scorn-laden reply. "Easy to say! Since when were you an expert on planetary exploitation *or* sterilization? Rog, I've seen dry planets before. Don't con a starship, I won't run herd on your pet savages!"

Savages?

My head sank below the carpet, my heart sinking deeper than the dungeon on Sca. So we Vespuccians were savages. No wonder this run-around about going home. I gathered my uniform, left the robe behind, rode the pillar of extruded floor back upstairs, knowing I would have to discuss this with the lieutenant as soon as possible. The dining-room table was gone when I returned. Couper, Lucille, and the "pet savage" expert stood together in the center of the room, a few small items of luggage scattered about their feet. The lieutenant, chatting with the girl, turned as I approached.

"Ah, Corporal O'Thraight. Enough is enough—time to hand those play-toys over. I *am* the ranking survivor, after all."

"Sir?" I knew perfectly well what he was talking about, but intended making him come out with it.

"The sidearms, Corporal, give them to me." I sighed, draped my tattered uniform over a travel case, reached for the quick-lock of the belt. Couper stepped between us.

"Wait, son. Lieutenant, we've a longstanding tradition where I come from: *we don't permit self-styled authorities to badger a man out of his rights.*" I would not have liked being on the receiving end of that scowl. The lieutenant, in turn, looked confused.

"Permit? Rights have nothing to do with it, sir. Those pistols are issued by a state of which I am the highest-ranking representative present. O'Thraight, give me that belt!"

I reached for the buckle. "As you were, son," Couper ordered. I dropped my hands. "Sermander, you're in my—what's the word, Rog?—*jurisdiction*, now. Whitey earned those rotary popguns preserving *your* carcass. Moreover, *no* state has the right to issue weapons *or* reclaim them— no, nor any rights at all, even to *exist*! The argument's over, unless you want everyone you meet from now on to know the true color of Vespuccian gratitude."

The lieutenant's face reddened then, abruptly, he relaxed with a shrug. I unclipped the left-hand scabbard from its eyelets on the belt, extended the holstered sidearm. "Take this one, sir, that way we will both—"

KLANGKLANGKLANGKLANGKLANG!!!!!

Abruptly, a blood-curdling alarm filled the ship. The lieutenant froze. I looked around, heart racing, wondering what it meant. The Earthians stood at alert attention, all eyes on Ev Williamson.

The individual, his own eyes closed momentarily, his head cocked as if listening to something, stood rigidly for a few seconds. When he opened his eyes, it was as if he were a different person. His deep voice rumbled:

"Rendezvous is aborted. Take your places. We're under attack."

8

Mysterious Strangers

Surprisingly little action filled the next few moments.

Lucille followed Couper, huddling with Williamson as if in conference. None of the three uttered a word, nor even seemed to be looking at the others. Each stood in eerie silence, eyes closed, consciousness directed inward. Owen Rogers glanced their way, then ordered, "Whitey! Lieutenant! Come with me—never mind your stuff, it'll be just fine where it is!"

Three steps, he dragged us, to the center of the room, the lieutenant emitting an indignant, "My good man!—"

"Lie down—right on the floor. There's gonna be some shooting, you'll be out from underfoot—I know, Lieutenant, you're Snoopy, Lando Calrissian, and the Red Baron rolled into one, you wanna be in on the action. Me, too—but as a praxeologist *or* an armorer, I'm a supernumerary in this flight, just like you." Without waiting for us, he threw his bulk flat on the carpet. I should not have been surprised: he began sinking, a cavity forming around his body, until all but his rounded belly lay flush with the surface. "Well, what are you waiting for?"

We followed his example, the lieutenant reluctantly. Lucille, Couper, Williamson the pilot, also lay on the floor—in it—as the ceiling showed the rendezvous ship spitting out vessels similar to *Little Tom*.

Our luggage, too, had become part of the deck.

Suddenly: *"Here they come!"* Ferocity rang in Lucille's voice. At an eyestraining distance, a cluster of dots showed infinitessimal against the starry background. We pulled away from the mother craft, other auxiliaries taking up their own positions in a loose sphere about the large vessel.

"Might as well let our passengers see what we're up against," observed Williamson, no excitement audible in his voice. The dots turned scarlet—more than had been immediately apparent. Hundreds of "stars" now stood revealed as an attacking fleet, growing as it approached, individual craft still too small to be discernible except as pin-pricks of blood-colored light.

"Lee, this is Tom-squared," a voice in the ceiling crackled. *"I've got 'em on instruments at twenty and closing."*

"Acknowledge, Tom-Tom, twenty-thousand and closing. Hold your position and engage at will."

The first voice was tinged with masculine excitement, the second serenely feminine. Rogers said, *"Tom-Tom*—another auxiliary. He's closest—these bandits don't show on radar—it's what makes them so—"

"Bandits?" squeaked the lieutenant, a beat ahead of me.

Blamm! The ship shook with impact, our makeshift acceleration nests cushioning what must have been titanic shock. "Where the state did *he* come from?" swore Williamson. The starscape reeled as *Little Tom* maneuvered sharply. In an instant, we could see the enemy, headed straight for us again.

Peculiarly, the object resembled *Asperance*, not streamlined like *Little Tom*, yet different from our Vespuccian ship, too. With nothing to give an idea of scale, it consisted of a central shaft, a lozenge shaped nodule at one end. Where shaft met presumed crew cabin, half a dozen hydraulic-looking landing jacks sprouted, angled slightly outward toward the stern. Our adversary had sustained collision damage, a couple of his legs bent, fuselage dented badly.

But he was persistent.

As the enemy loomed nearer, its shaft-end pointed menacingly toward us. What destruction had *Little Tom* suffered? Closer... closer... tension filled the room until it seemed the hull would burst. Lieutenant Sermander ground his teeth. His corporal suppressed a whimper.

"Right on, baby," growled our pilot from his own gravelike depression. "Come and get your medicine!" A brilliant flash washed out the sky display. The enemy fighter reappeared, damaged even worse, body charred, legs burned away to stumps. *"Got the son-of-a-bureaucrat!"*

Williamson's cheer was premature. Despite the punishment, our adversary swiveled until we saw it base-on, swelling as it bore unstoppably closer. The sky flashed again—an explosion, a shower of debris. "Just in time, too," the pilot observed. "Let's see how many of these vermin we can burn before they punch us full of holes!"

"Rogers," the lieutenant demanded—the tip of his nose just visible as he talked, "you said we Vespuccii were the only space-traversing—"

Flash!

He was cut off by a brilliant, frightening display. To the right, a saucer-shaped vessel, sister to our own, confronted two of the strange craft, each three times larger, shaft-end to lozenge-tip, than the diameter of the scout. The smaller vessel's underside pulsed blindingly. Energy spat from the entire surface, crashed against the alien antagonists. Both retreated, severely hurt. The saucer pursued, firing its peculiar keel batteries. One oddly shaped attacker dissolved in a greasy cloud of scattering scrap. We swerved again, blasting an unseen opponent, losing sight of the other ship, the outcome of its battle.

"In a way," offered Rogers from his dugout, "yes—and then again, no."

"What?" I beat the lieutenant to it, this time.

BLAMMM!!

The ship shook side to side as if hungry predators were tearing at it. "You guys sure have short attention spans," Rogers continued. "I meant, yes, you're the only space-traversing folks we've run into so far, but, looking at it another way, you're not, exactly."

"How informative," the lieutenant sneered. I paid attention to the praxeologist rather than our impending doom. Hideous ripping noises made this difficult. "What do you mean?"

"He's a social scientist," offered Williamson across the room. He should have been preoccupied, unable to hear our conversation. "It doesn't have to mean anything!" Light flared again. Another alien vanished in swarming wreckage. *"Gotcha, you hyperthyroid ant-grunt!"*

A lull, as if between strokes of heat-lightning. "Owen's referring to his Gunjj." Couper sighed. "Nobody believes a word of it, but—*Bandits, two o'clock low!* " The ship dipped, swerved; light flared blindingly. "—he still burdens helpless strangers with the story on occasion." A low shudder ran through *Little Tom*, threatening to shake my internal organs from their fastenings. Every centimeter of the vessel groaned—a pair of bristly jointed limbs lashed briefly across the view area.

"I actually meant these things—*ouch*! Take it easy, Ev—I've got a tender stomach!" For a moment it seemed we were hanging from the floor, looking down at the ceiling.

"Not with your taste in clothing."

This was insane, five-sided bantering while fending off a deadly enemy. At least Lucille kept silent. "What are they?" the lieutenant contributed. "Or is it another of your precious secrets?"

"Not at all, sir, they're *virus*."

"What?"

"Near as we can tell, they evolved in deep space out of clouds of interstellar—*Oh, boy!!* "

Miraculously retaining my stomach contents through another violent loop, I gulped, "Why do you call them—'gunge'?"

The praxeologist wrinkled his face, then shook his head. Even at this angle, I could see sweat beading on his somewhat greenish features. "We don't...call them...I mean...the Gunjj"—he spelled it out—"are an intelligent species."

"*M'aidez, m'aidez!*" the communicator crackled at the limit of intelligibility. Outside, a Confederate vessel struggled with six gigantic organisms; they worried it like desert scavengers. "*Tom Swift Maru to anybody listening! They've penetrated my hull—it's filling up with scat—I've set autodestruct, we're bailing out. Stand by on pickup!*"

Lucille spoke: "Got you, *TSM*, and relaying. We'll—" *Tom Swift Maru* exploded in a blinding ball of flame. "At least they took six of the bastards with them!" Lucille said grimly. Our ship swerved suddenly, its batteries snarled, another supervirus vanished.

More insanity: "Truth is, until recently we—the Confederacy—have never had full contact with another sapient species—nobody counts the Gunjj. We call them Gunjj because, when we first began exploring, we kept running across their calling cards: given a nice, clean, uninhabited planet, oxygen and greenery, sooner or later we'd find, carved in a tree, or painted on a rock, a characteristic inscription." He lifted an arm above the floor like some weird insect buried in the sand, used a rubber-

coated finger to trace a sign in the carpet; the pile oblig-
ingly turned contrasting blue.

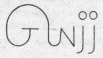

"Mind you, we never found it on any occupied planet.
Just what it indicated, no one had the slightest idea. Sometimes the symbol appears ancient, only half legible. Others are fresh, as if the grafittist had left only a minute ago.
It's often associated with artifacts—empty plastic containers, other refuse, occasionally a broken tool." Groan-
ing loudly again, the ship wheeled, blasting, pivoting once
more for another shot. The hull *clanged!* harshly. I wondered how Rogers could go on so calmly, after seeing a
sister ship destroyed with her entire complement. Then
I saw his eyes roll at the noise—this was his way of keeping his nerve.

I listened for the same reason.

"Some were tiny; they could hardly be read. Others,
gouged across entire continents, were naked-eye visible
from orbit. Each case was exactly like this, cursive styl-
ized emblems appearing to spell the word 'Gunjj'—of
course it had to mean something else in an alien language.
Except for showing up on planet after planet, it might
have implied no more intelligence than the dried slime
track of a snail—you know what a snail is?"

There was a screeching tearing noise; a section of the
viewing dome went black. I said nothing about snails; he
would not have heard me anyway. His voice rose half an
octave, increased pace fifty words a minute, but went on.
"It was as scientifically disreputable a mystery as the
Loch Ness monster or the lost planet Lucifer—and might
have gone on the same way, unsolved, if it hadn't been
for a near-disastrous practical joke.

"Gunjj resemble bunches of asparagus—well, all right,

a bundle of long, semiflexible tubes, bound in the middle by a bit of string. Only they're twelve feet tall, a sickly pale gray, and the string supports a belt pouch for personal effects. They don't stand their full double man-height, but drop the tops of their stalks like tentacles on a sea anemone—which I can see you don't know anything about, either."

The missing viewscreen sector flickered, lit again. It did not present a pretty picture: enemy virus were much reduced in number; so were Confederate ships. The ruins of a dozen littered the void, some with tiny figures escaping from them, some without. I looked at the lieutenant. Either he was more courageous than I had believed, choosing to catch up on his sack time, or he had fainted.

"There are a number of theories," Rogers continued, oblivious to the scene before us, "concerning extraconfederate life-forms..." He seemed to lose his place a moment—perhaps due to a catastrophic explosion on the rim of the mother ship, then went on: "One sees evolution as convergent, every intelligent species we find should resemble humans, simians, or cetaceans, because they'll inevitably occupy similar niches in the ecologies of their own planets..."

Again he tapered off. I was afraid that he had fainted, too. I could not bear the thought of his joining the lieutenant, leaving me alone to face this nightmare. "Yes, praxeologist," I imitated Sermander's peremptory tone. "The opposing theory?"

"—Yes, er, the other position... says evolution can never be *that* convergent, enough to make up for an isolated beginning, billions of years of independent development, on an entirely different planet. By this reasoning— which has so far been confirmed by the few glimpses we've had—the lowliest Terran slime mold is a vastly closer relative to us than any outsystem organism, and resembles us more nearly."

Terran? So I was a Terran—if Rogers had actually meant to include me in his "us." I thought about the obviously alien native organisms of Vespucci. No mistaking them for anything our ancestors had brought along. From Terra, it would appear.

"Most praxeologists agree intelligence can't vary much *psychologically*, the requirements are just too narrow. We'll be able to play chess, swap horses, tell dirty jokes, in any civilization we ever encounter. Semicontact with the Gunjj seems to confirm both theories—of physical difference and psychological similarity. They *look* weird, but they're no more alien in world view than, say, the Japanese seem to North Americans—lost you again, didn't I? But it's true. I know, I was there."

"It was a dark and stormy night . . ." interrupted Williamson—himself interrupted when a giant virus squadron zoomed toward the *Little Tom*, requiring rapid action. The attack seemed to be slacking off, but it was not over yet.

Rogers snorted. "Some people just don't appreciate a good story when they hear one. It was aboard the old *Tom Smothers Maru*, a small scout, not unlike this one. The pilot was Koko Featherstone-Haugh, before she ascended to a higher plane of existence, and I was fresh out of school myself. We were exploring the masked region between a pair of nebulae, not looking for anything in particular except a potential profit, when the long-distance rangefinders began squawking. Heavy metal ahead . . ."

2

Captain Featherstone-Haugh (Rogers pronounced it "Fanshaw") put the helm hard over. "Not one of ours—see what magnification the traffic will bear, will you, Rog?" Koko was an imposing individual, nearly two meters tall, almost as wide, heavily muscled. Not human. She *was* in charge. For a young man with the ink still wet on his diploma, even wetter on his commission, it was enough.

He obliged. In the overhead viewscreen, an apparently empty sector of space broadened suddenly, the spaces between stars widening, more stars becoming visible. Off to one side, the clouds of gas blanked out the stars, leaving only impenetrable blackness.

A tiny point of light appeared, swelled into a pair of closely associated points. Little more was visible; trailers from the gas limited visibility. "Captain, ma'am, any more and we'll be looking at microbes clinging to the roof instead of objects, er ... fifteen light-minutes away."

The floor dilated around the odd figure of a creature neither simian nor human. It stood—on all fours—approximately half a meter high at the shoulder, was perhaps a meter in length, sported sharply pointed ears, a matching nose, a thickly bushed tail. It answered to the name G. Howell Nahuatl.

Highly articulately.

"I say, fellow beings, why have my ablutions been interrupted? Aren't you distressed that I actually found a *flea* upon my person after our last planetside outing?" The animal sat on its haunches, scratched at one of its prominent ears with a hind foot.

"It wasn't a flea," answered Koko, "but some other form of bug—more like an isopod, I thought, and when it tasted your blood, it died. Look what we've got here."

Howell's eyes were not particularly good, yet he had a quick, analytical intelligence his companions valued. "Could it be, at long last?"

Rogers nodded vigorously. "One for the books—an alien spaceship."

"Or a pair of rogue asteroids fused together," replied Koko. Her simian heart beat rapidly, hoping, hoping—but, after all, she *was* the captain, if only of a tiny scout ship.

"Whatever it is, it's dead in the water," Rogers said, "no signs of powerplant emissions, life-support operations. With our luck, it's been here for half a billion years, and everyone aboard is a mummy."

"No jokes about motherhood, you two!" Koko warned. "Mummies or not, it would still be fascinating."

"For everybody but the mummies," Howell replied blandly.

"Well, we're never going to find out this way. I'm going in. You two want to settle into the floor, just in case?"

"I'm going to meet my first alien civilization stuck up to my navel in broadloom? You must be kidding." Rogers readjusted his smartsuit to what he considered its cheeriest design.

Even the colorblind coyote shuddered.

Nevertheless they approached the object cautiously. Soon it was unmistakable: an artifact, two large spheres fused together, the riveted seams plainly visible. No drive tubes were visible, no shackles for light-sails, no broad surface for the generation of propulsive photons or tachyons, such as their own ship employed. In short, it must be powered in some manner completely unfamiliar to the Confederate crew of the *Tom Smothers Maru*. Portholes followed a peculiarly skewed line about the equator of each globe.

Light showed in them.

Koko halted her command a thousand kilometers away. A thin mist from the nebula concealed nothing, but lent an eerie quality to the scene. She began transmitting every customary form of energy used for communications in known space.

"Here it is!" cried Rogers. He pointed to the image of the ship on the screen. Overlaying the picture—it was hard, sometimes, to remember you were seeing what the computers saw—was a bright reddish aura, pulsing, dancing, pulsing, dancing.

"What I should like to know," said the coyote, "is how we're expected to make sense of this without any referents? And don't give me any nonsense about counting up to ten—how do you ask for flashlight batteries, first-aid kits, or frostberry sodas with numbers?"

Half an hour later, Howell's question was answered.

Repeatedly, the alien vessel communicated: "529, 529...529, 529...529, 529..." It occurred to Koko this might mean they intended sending a picture, five hundred twenty-nine pixels high, by the same number wide. "Good thing," she muttered to herself in disgust, "they don't have triangular telecom screens—I'd never have figured it out!"

The Gunjj turned out to be harmless—as harmless as intelligent life ever gets. They, too, had been worried, more so than the crew of *Tom Smothers Maru*, since it developed the Gunjj were marooned—becalmed might have been a better word—right in the middle of nowhere. None of this became clear very quickly. Having pictures helped. So did actually traveling over to the alien ship for more direct communications. Slowly, a context was built up in which communications, cybernetically assisted, became possible.

The best translation of the Gunjj ship's name would be *The Disgruntled*. She was nominally a warship, long since decommissioned, presently used as a training vessel for several hundred young Gunjj on the equivalent of a midshipman cruise in the middle of their educational period. It was fairly easy to tell the relative ages of Gunjj: when they were "born," they were a single stalk or strand, fully as tall as their elders. In time, the stalk split—although not altogether away from the individual's body—resplitting again until the adult, in its prime, resembled the collection of vegetables Rogers had referred to.

The practical joke?

Midshipmen will be midshipmen: The Gunjj used a peculiar system to "drive" starships faster than light, based upon the mathematical/metaphysical principle of nonsimultaneity. Over interstellar distances—in theory, over any distances at all—it is nonsense to speak of two events happening at the same time. No method exists to synchronize the time scales. Or can exist. All right, reasoned the Gunjj, why not work it backward? There is no guarantee that a ship departing the Gunjj homeworld, headed for some destination, will arrive at any specifically given time. Such would *imply* a synchronicity which physics holds to be nonsense.

Suppose the voyage is supposed to take a hundred years. It makes as much sense, from this abstruse standpoint, for it to arrive a hundred *thousand* years after takeoff, or a hundred *million*. Likewise, a mere hundred seconds, or nanoseconds—accomplishing, in effect, travel vastly faster than the speed of light.

Gunjj ships have no actual velocity, yet, for practical purposes, their transition between points—*any* two points—is instantaneous. Thus the obvious, widespread traces of their planetary explorations, while at the same time no one encountered any of their ships in flight.

Until *Tom Smothers Maru*.

The Gunjj, no different from humans or chimps, liked to have their fun, particularly at the expense of nominal superiors. *Everyone* is nominally superior to a midshipman cadet.

Thus another principle of physics was brought into play. The Gunjj nonsimultaneity drive could not be used immediately upon leaving a planet—something about gravity fields. Neither was it actually instantaneous—although how anyone could testify to that with any certainty is questionable. As a joke, half the midshipman class arranged to calculate, to twenty-three decimal places, their *velocity* during transition. They did all the calculations but one, ready for the final readout at the tentacle-squish of a computer button.

Meanwhile, the other half of the class was equally prepared to state, very precisely, the ship's *location*.

Unfortunately, Heisenberg—along with his equivalent in the culture of the Gunjj—says you cannot do this. You can know, with great precision, either the velocity of a particle (or a ship) *or* its location. Not both at the same time. The ship took off, exceeded the necessary number of planetary diameters for transition across the galaxy, prepared to go hyper—then two buttons were pushed. The ship froze dead in space, where she was found, full of frightened midshipgunjj.

The Gunjj had been trapped there a decade when *TSM* discovered them—naturally, highly grateful to have been found. Koko puzzled over the problem, consulted with Rogers, with Howell. Learning the Gunjj language, they discovered the aliens were extremely shy, would never have contacted the Confederacy, left to themselves.

It was Howell—knowing nothing of physics, but plenty about logic—who discovered a solution. The Gunjj vessel was taken under tow—quite a strain for a little ship such as *TSM*—toward a random destination, at a carefully un-calculated velocity. The Gunjj vanished, resuming their instantaneous voyage to wherever it was they had been going.

3

"You expect us to believe this nonsense?" the lieuten-ant asked, when Rogers seemed finished.

"Oh, Lieutenant Sermander, you're with us again. No, I don't expect you to believe it—nobody else does."

"Excuse me," I said, beginning to notice the shooting was over. There were no more supervirus visible on the screen; ships had begun returning to the mother vessel, including ours. "I do not understand how this Howell's idea was a solution. Did it not simply render the Gunjj more lost than to begin with?"

Rogers laughed—I noticed the others, relaxing now from their battle posture, standing by to watch us take the punchline. "But Whitey, they were never lost. They were the least-lost travelers in history, which of course, was the problem. Howell's solution worked because it restored their Heisenbergian uncertainty. They were no longer trapped, caught on the horns of a metaphysical contradiction. Thus they were able to move, after ten years frozen."

I blinked. Then it occurred to me to ask: "Did you ever find out what this symbol—the 'Gunjj' mark—really meant?"

This was what the praxeologist had been waiting for. "Sure. It turned out to be not much of a mystery at all. It meant nothing, more or less, than 'Kilroy was here'!"

Kilroy again. Who was this Kilroy? The lieutenant, rising from the floor with a weary look, scratched his head, but said nothing.

I said nothing, scratched my head.

Couper grinned. "I never could decide, myself, about the story—though Howell backs it up—never known *him* to be a liar." He gave Rogers a dirty look. Then: "Hold on, elevator going up!" The floor began rising, taking us nearer the phony stars. It required courage not to hunch claustrophobically as the ceiling approached. Then we were through—presumably the hull of *Little Tom* as well, standing within the mother ship above the docking bay.

"Welcome aboard TPM3C—*informally known as* Tom Lehrer Maru*!"*

I stared, mouth agape. The source of this welcoming female voice was half animal, half machine, a man-sized legless lizard in a smartsuit, its own rubbery gray-black skin surrounding a pair of wise brown eyes above a roguish protuberant muzzle. The creature rested in the gleaming frame of a wheeled conveyance, mechanical hands responding to her wishes as she greeted us.

"Armorer-Corporal Whitey O'Thraight, Lieutenant Enson Sermander: I am Leelalee Eckickeck S'reen. Please consider yourself at home, landlings. We dock with our *own* mother vessel in approximately six and one-half hours."

PART TWO

The Privateers

9

The Garden
of Leelalee

In the salt marshes of the Vespuccian Low Desert live certain rare, minuscule creatures without legs, breathing water instead of air. A porpoise is like that, except it is bigger, uses lungs like human beings, pointedly claims possession of a mind, a nervous system more subtly complex than any human's—also considers itself the hottest pilot in the known galaxy.

I was not certain, in the beginning, which of these quirks was true of porpoises in general, which peculiar to Leelalee Eckickeck S'reen. She was the only porpoise I had ever met. It was equally true that six-plus hours were not going to be enough to get well acquainted, even if I had wanted to. It was not really time enough to absorb anything.

Around us, people (here I use the term as loosely as they did, taking into consideration the variety of finned or furry folk within eye's reach) were busily rising or sinking through the floor of what appeared to be a broad green shallow valley. The virus attack seemed to have generated some urgency or excitement among them, which was natural enough. I recalled the damage I had seen being done to this ship, wondered what its condition was.

Difficult to say. From wall to unseen wall, a thick carpet of vegetation lay randomly punctuated with trees, sometimes sparsely, often in thick copses interwoven with a complicated network of brightly colored rubber footpaths. Also fin-paths, as I was to discover. If there was appreciable battle damage, it was not in these quarters.

Lost to everything, to everybody else, the lieutenant stood where the deck had extruded him, deep in thought. Or culture shock. By default, the task of carrying his luggage with my own was delegated to the lowest-ranking representative of the Vespuccian State then present.

Geoffrey Couper smothered my hand in his own giant paw. "I got chores waiting. Have a good time, son, take a sightseeing tour. We'll round you up when it's time to transship again, right, Rog?"

The praxeologist hiked a shoulder bag closer to his chest, shook my hand when Couper had released it, clapped me on the back. "Hoist a couple for me. We'll see you in a few."

They turned their polite attention to my superior, all but Lucille. She looked at me as if seeing me for the first time, a puzzled expression on her pretty face. Then she shrugged, shook her head ironically, took a step in my direction. I barely avoided the reflex to shrink away from the tense ferocity she always carried with her. She stood briefly on tiptoe, brushed her lips across mine. "That oughta hold you for a few hours, Corporal, till we get the fire put out." There was a nip at the end of that semikiss, painful on the lower lip. It throbbed for a long time afterward.

It was not the only thing that throbbed.

As the company from the *Little Tom* dispersed, we Vespuccii followed the porpoise Leelalee, at her suggestion, walking briskly behind her shiny mechanical trundler. I did not even think to ask her where we were going, being a bit worried about the lieutenant, who had not yet said a word. He had to be nudged before he started moving.

"What? Oh...yes...let us go, by all means. There is a good fellow." Immediately he fell silent again. I was more than a little dazed myself, but this had more to do with the tiny blood blister forming on my mouth than with any scenic wonders the *Tom Lehrer Maru* might have offered. Lucille was a girl who believed in fighting fire by starting others elsewhere. Nonetheless, I made admiring noises at what seemed to be the right places. It seemed the polite thing to do.

"How gratifying, young landling." The porpoise pointed her spindly manipulator at some object of interest. "I am fond of the vessel myself—and do not much like having her attacked—albeit she is merely the material consequence of gross human/simian manipulatory capabilities. Evolution seems to have bestowed them in lieu of adequate cognitive faculties.

"However, in plain truth, if you're interested, you must wait until you see the ship we're due to meet!"

Her wheeled contrivance slowed near the bank of a narrow canal that paralleled the footpath. I stopped, then had to take the lieutenant by the elbow until he halted, as well. He looked up at me blankly, blinked at the swift current he had nearly stepped into, then returned to his thoughts.

In one respect, I *was* impressed: unlike the *Little Tom*, no one was rising or sinking through the ceiling here; it might have been fifty or a hundred meters high, difficult to tell in the mist-diffused glare. Leelalee steered her gleaming contraption down into the water. With a gleeful *splash!* she left it, continued by swimming along beside us.

Occasionally the path would dip or the canal would rise, then her sleek form would be visible through transparent retaining walls. In several such places, usually encompassed by privacy-creating leafy bowers, there would be a table with chairs set on the synthetic flagging before the water-windows. People conversed with porpoises through the glass, the inevitable topic being the combat action that had just occurred. There did not seem to be much concern for the safety of the ship or its complement, rather the atmosphere resembled a break in the routine, a holiday of sorts. I would try to remember that, the next time I found myself cowering in a foxhole in the carpet.

Some distance ahead, I could make out a complicated double loop figure-eight, where several converging footpaths vaulted the water and a transparent aqueduct arched over them, in turn. Meanwhile, sharing overhead with the birds, many chimpanzees, humans, other bipedal sentients less clearly discernable hung from fabric-covered wings, swooping, soaring, kicking at the treetops with laughter. Occasionally a land dweller, plastic extensions on his hands or feet, a large lens on his face, would meet Leelalee in the canal, nod, pass her by. This seemed equitable: not every marine being we observed had abandoned its wheels. I had to dodge several on the footpath, pulling the lieutenant out of harm's way before he was run down.

Finally we reached the rim of the vast parklike chamber, almost needing the reminder of oval-doorwayed bulkheads that we were inside a gigantic starship, moving at incomprehensible velocities.

I said something about this to Leelalee.

"You'd remember, my fine shore-grubber, were we *not* moving!" the captain observed as she swam into a waiting set of wheels to join us on the walk. "Each precious drop of water, every clod of carefully cultured soil, would be swirling in a muddy maelstrom. Instead, we allow a calculated inefficiency in the inertialess field, enough uncorrected acceleration to give us one-half standard gee, if that means anything."

Ranged around the garden perimeter were shops, storefronts, cafes, with fancy, interesting window displays.

Was this a spacecraft or a shopping center? I bounced a little, experimentally, on the balls of my smartsuit-shod feet. "It feels about right to me, Captain." Among its other virtues, dense-cored Sca was a great place for the development of fallen arches. "Which would be closer to your standard," I said without thinking, "Sca or Vespucci?"

"How would she *know?"*

The lieutenant's sudden derisive snort caught me by surprise. "She has not been anywhere near *either* planet," He gave the porpoise a look of apologetic embarrassment. "Enlisted people!"

Leelalee's wire wheels rolled nearer, leaving diamond-pattern tracks on the tile that dried quickly in the warm atmosphere. "On the contrary, pompous one, this Sca where you were found falls within three decimals of Earth-like gravity. Your—Vespucci? Do you actually call it that?—appears a rather small, tired world, approximately eleven-tenths standard."

He stared at her in astonishment. "How could you possibly—"

"I, er, make it my business to know these things, Lieutenant." She fell silent, then: "After all, I *am* the captain."

Now there was an answer that made sense to Lieutenant Enson Sermander. He shut up again; we continued along the esplanade, looking in shop windows.

2

"How are we supposed to pay for this?"

Leelalee had left us at a colorful open-front restaurant nestled in a shop cluster at the margin of the park. Where we were seated, we could gaze out over the landscaping or into a rippling blue-green tunnel courtesy of a transparent canal wall passing directly through the cafe. Both thoroughfares bustled with passers-by of a half a dozen species.

The waiter, a short, wiry, bald-headed human male

attired in a dark-green two-tone pinstriped smartsuit that
might have nauseated even Owen Rogers, rolled his eyes
ceilingward a moment as if for divine inspiration. "Says
here it's on a survey-service account. Funny, you ginks
don't look like no survey-rowdies. Where'd y'get them
fancy suit patterns?" He indicated our Vespuccian Navy
Reserve markings.

I opened my mouth, but the lieutenant held up a hand.
"I believe, sir, that we are *specimens*. Now tell me: does
one choose a white wine with this repast, or a red?" I had
wanted to ask the waiter how he suddenly knew that two
strangers who had just walked into his establishment were
on an account of *any* kind. Also, who was *he* to talk about
funny suit patterns?

He goggled at the lieutenant's inquiry. "With lobster-
burgers? How 'bout a Coke? It's the real thing. Fresh
shipment, and a *very* good month. Specimens, huh?
Thought *those* came in a bottle, too."

"Please, not at luncheon! We shall, with certain self-
explicable trepidations, accept your recommendation.
Now leave us, if you please." The lieutenant eyed the
food before us with suspicion, then looked up at me with
much the same expression on his face. "Corporal, I would
be interested in your impressions thus far."

"Um, well, I cannot tell whether these little things on
the bread are insects or seeds of some kind. I do not think
I am going to eat them."

Outside, an enormous dark chimpanzeelike animal
knuckled past, gliding on tiny wheels attached to its feet.
One of its massive arms was in a silvery rubber sling.
Abruptly, a bright pink balloon blossomed from its face,
swelled nearly to the diameter of the creature's head, then
collapsed, leaving sticky remains across the leathery skin.
The monster blinked, cleared its eyes, its nostrils, looked
around to see if anyone else had witnessed the accident,
stuffed the substance back into its jaws, hitched up its
heavy gunbelt, rolled onward on its little wheels.

"No, you dimwit! I refer to our situation—to our experiences—to our putative hosts, their society, their technology. I realize that you are scarcely the trained observer I am, but—what are *your* reactions?"

I thought about it, sipping at the bubbly brown wine the waiter had brought us. So far, I had been too busy gawking to do very much processing. "Well, sir, I do not much care for the cavalier manner in which they are shuffling us around. Oh, they are polite enough about it, but just the same . . . another thing—" I was beginning to warm up now—"I do not like the disrespectful way Couper treated you. About the guns, I mean, I could have—"

"Nonsense, my dear boy!" He waved a hand negligently. "I understood entirely. Chain of command, et cetera, et cetera. Come to speak of it, I rather *liked* his keen, decisive manner. Beneath the facade of sloppy—one might almost say *civilian*—casuality we see around us, there is a core of steel, unembarrassed in the exercise of power. Confidence. Discipline. Combinations not often enough in evidence in *our* military, let me tell you!" He took a large bite from his sandwich, got a very odd expression on his face.

"Lieutenant!" I said, glancing wildly around. "You must never say things like that!"

"Come now, Corporal," he replied around the bite of food. "Have you never entertained such thoughts yourself?" He gave me a knowing, cynical look.

Keeping my eyes on the tabletop, I replied, "Well, sir, if I had, I would not voice them out loud, certainly not in public." I made a gesture that, for generations in Vespuccian enlisted society, has meant "The walls have ears."

"Wise precaution, Corporal—Whitey, there is something profoundly wonderful about these people, reaching further than bland explanations concerning scientific research." He lowered his voice, with it, his head until he resembled a Vespuccian carrion bird. "Obviously our expedition—what is left of it—has accidentally stumbled across the cutting edge of a vast, wealthy empire. They are ultracautious at their frontier, or follow a velvet-glove policy in general, but the power is there, mark my word. They make the Vespuccian World State look like—how do the ranks have it? Like 'tiny turnips.'"

"Lieutenant!"

"Hush! I am going to get to the bottom of this. When I do..."

"Yes, sir?"

"Well, *now* is scarcely the time for making irrevocable decisions, is it? Are you with me, Corporal?"

"*With* you, Lieutenant?"

"Are you prepared to follow my leadership in this?"

"You are the lieutenant, I am only a corporal, sir." Which was as noncommittal an answer as I could think of with a second's notice. The lieutenant was either an acute judge of political realities, or verging into paranoia. In either case, it did not sound as though he were all that anxious to return home immediately. I fingered my bruised lip, agreeing with him mentally that now was no time at all to make irrevocable decisions.

Then I thought of Eleva.

"*Whitey?*"

Suddenly, beneath my sandwich plate, the tabletop lit up to speak my name. I jumped, nearly upsetting the lieutenant's drink, then cleared away the dishes. The image of Owen Rogers, in three-dimensional color, was staring back at me.

"I finally got out of that federated staff meeting! Our little miniwar has made trash of every schedule we had. Thank Lysander's intransigent shade that armorers don't make policy, otherwise I'd be stuck until rendezvous-after-next. You got any plans right now?"

I looked up at the lieutenant, chin resting in his palm. He gave me an irritated glance of dismissal, went right back to his thoughts.

"No, Owen, apparently not."

"Well, then, follow the edge of the park around about a quarter-circumference to a place called Chuck's—I'll meet you there. Oh yes, and bring your boss along. Got a surprise for you."

The image faded behind its sprinkling of breadcrumbs, salt shakings, the little seed-bugs I had scraped off the food. I glanced at the lieutenant again, raising inquiring eyebrows.

"Oh, very well, Corporal, by all means! Let us go see what the fellow wants." He rose. I realized then that Rogers had not mentioned which direction we should turn, leaving the restaurant. I interrupted the waiter who was clearing off a table in obvious ill humor. He flapped his dampened cloth, refolded it, smeared it around the plastic a little.

"Atmosphere they want, huh? Antique electric light bulbs right outa the Fission Age, and dumb appliances! Which means *I* gotta do medieval chores like this! Too bad the dadblamed virus didn't eat the whole place up! What I wouldn't give for a modern, sanitary, self-serving, self-cleaning—what? Chuck's, is it? Well, turn right, and it's more like a *third* of the way around." He snapped the cloth at the floor, folded it again, began to return to his task, then took a good look at my gunbelt with its double burden. "Shucks, don't look like you *need* t'do business at that place—but, Constitution, the customer's always right. Or so they tell me."

Except when he is confused.

Nonetheless, we followed the waiter's instructions out around the colored sidewalks, dodging trees, canals, pedestrians, wheeled fish-types, until we came upon a broad plaza with a fountain in the middle. Imitation sunlight poured down over the scene, several dozen people strolling, standing, talking, dangling their feet in the water. The emergency seemed to be over. I wondered when or if they ever worked for a living.

Strange what you will not notice in unfamiliar surroundings. Now, when I was looking for something specific, I realized all the shops lacked an important commonplace feature—not a single written word was displayed on any of them. Often there was something resembling a sign, a more or less self-explanatory graphic. Otherwise, empty space where there should have been a company ident, the name of a proprietor. I filed this with other odd-shaped data—the fact that Leelalee had known all about Sca, even Vespucci, without contacting the returning survey from *Little Tom*. Or that the waiter, after a moment of conspicuous cogitation, suddenly knew whose cuff we were eating on—but neither who nor what we were.

Rogers met us at the fountain. "It's right over here. Come on."

The sign bore the holographic image of an unfamiliar handgun but did not say Chuck's. The entity behind the counter was a squat, broad-shouldered, powerful-looking being with a dark shaggy pelt, much the same as I had seen a while earlier on tiny foot-wheels. It wore a strange hat, two part-hemispheres of different sizes, canvas tan, the smaller atop the larger. Some sort of sun helmet, I guessed.

"*Jambo, B'wana!* Long time no *ungawa!* What can I do you for?"

"Can the Swahooie, Chuckles. Got a couple customers for you. This is Whitey O'Thraight and Enson Sermander, both late of the planet Vespucci. Gentlemen, Charles C. Charles, O.D., a professional colleague and the hairiest, if not the hugest, gunsmith in the known galaxy. He's an eccentric genius, in his safari mood just now. Be sure not to step in the *usunga*."

Charles took the Darrick I unholstered for him, examining it minutely, his huge black fingers surprisingly dextrous. "Vaguely familiar. Looks like an old-fashioned soldering gun. Pretty anemic—what is it, about thirty-two?"

"Eight millimeter Darrick."

"A thinly veiled alias, in both senses. That's *Dardick*,

with a second 'd.'" He glanced significantly at Rogers. "Something lost in the translation?"

"About fifteen hundred years," the praxeologist replied.

The gunsmith whistled, then got back to business. "Let's see: plastic casings, I'd guess, triangular in cross—"

"Trochoidal."

"Same difference. Something with a polymeric memory, most likely, for obturation and extraction. Feeds in here with a stripper—fourteen, fifteen, sixteen of them. The rotor lifts when you cock the hammer or cycle the trigger, forming two sides of the chamber. Topstrap forms the third. *Bang!*—and out this little slot comes the empty, no deposit, no return. An automatic revolver, by Albert, or a revolving automatic. Handy thing for mystery writers who can't tell the difference."

I nodded enthusiastically, enjoying the first conversation I had fully understood in days. "Surely you do not have ammunition for it, though."

"Don't call me Shirley. I can order it fabricated."

He paused, that same look of deep thought on his face that the waiter, along with many others, had displayed.

"There. I'll take measurements, signal them on ahead to the rendezvous, and they'll be waiting for us at the mother ship with any luck. Five hundred rounds do you?"

"I, er . . ."

Owen Rogers stepped in. "Put it on my survey-service account, and make it a thousand. The corporal's a bit out of practice."

"There is an over-powder wad." I gulped, unable to frame a suitable reply on several counts. "A disc made of the same plastic as the cases."

"Gotcha. Make yourself to home while I'm out back."

He disappeared behind a curtain. I wondered whether it laundered him as he passed through it. He looked pretty clean for a gunsmith, though a bit singed around the edges of his fur. Probably from tinkering with plasma guns. Meanwhile, Rogers thumped a broad finger jovially on the transparent display case he was leaning against. Once again I noticed the lack of signs, posters, tags, around the shop. It was as if writing had never been invented in this culture.

"What's your pleasure, Lieutenant? Can't go around socially naked like that. Pick out a roscoe, it's on the house—or the ship, if you prefer."

Enson Sermander blinked, suspicion wrestling with amazement across his jowled countenance. The walls of the place were lined with racked pistols; there were five more big display counters full of weapons in bewildering variety. Only about a quarter of the machinery was immediately recognizable as firearms, the rest unfamiliar technology. Some were obvious projectile throwers, but with what energy source? Others apparently shot pure energy like the guns I had seen used to grisly effect on Sca. Not a single long-arm-rifle or shotgun—was visible. Like writing, these Earthians did not seem to have stumbled across the concept, although they had a couple of unique notions of their own.

The lieutenant cleared his throat. "I appreciate the gesture, praxeologist, truly. However, a sidearm is merely insignia, a badge of authority. It serves no other practical purpose; no one can hit anything with a handgun. Thus, in circumstances where just *anyone* is free to purchase, possess, to actually *carry* one of the things..."

He let the implication go unstated.

Rogers did not. "An officer and a gentlebeing might be mistaken for one of the peasants? Okay, Lieutenant, it's your life and a Free System—just keep in mind that in the Solar Confederacy such officers as we permit don't have any flunkies to do their killing for them. You may want to reconsider."

The lieutenant's face began turning an alarming shade of purple red. He opened his mouth to blast Owen Rogers into some netherworld when Charles C. Charles reappeared just in time to prevent the catastrophe.

"Okay, Whitey, here's your piece. We'll hold the chamber pressure on the first lot at twenty-five K, just to be on the safe side, but if you ever feel the need for more power, the weapon's structural metal can be treated—and there are better plastics available."

He tapped a broad nail on the Darrick–Dardick's upper receiver as he said this. Rogers waggled his eyebrows, rolled his eyes, as if restraining himself mightily from asking what is the point in gilding a cactus blossom.

"Uh, thanks. Where... when can I—"

"Right here, after rendezvous..." The furry giant stood still a moment, his attention elsewhere. Then: "... which should be coming up a little ahead of schedule, I think. We got into trouble, and Mama came a-running."

We walked out of the shop just as darkness fell.

It took a moment to recall that we were *not* outside on a planet's surface. Occurring overhead was a display such as I had seen aboard the *Little Tom*, although certainly on a greater scale. As soft lights came on across the wooded park, the real stars glittered down at us for the first time. Two of them swelled, grew into perfect replicas of the *Tom Lehrer Maru* or its small auxiliaries: glowing white inverted bowls, featureless, smoothly contoured, yet seeming to vibrate with pent-up power.

"... see Chuck when he's being Nanook of the North," Rogers was saying as we watched the events overhead. It must be an old story to him, I thought, he scarcely seemed to notice it. "A gorilla with *two* fur coats is overdoing things a little."

Outside, the paired ships grew again! One of the vessels came nearer—or we approached it, these things being relative. Just as *Little Tom* had nestled in a recess beneath the vastly greater *Tom Lehrer Maru*, so now the ship we occupied was dwarfed almost to insignificance as it maneuvered toward one of seven docking bays on the lower surface of a monstrously larger vessel. I estimated that this "mother ship" everybody had been talking about had to be somewhere three to four thousand meters in diameter. Three or four *kilometers*! Why, monstrous was hardly the—

"Two point one zero Jeffersonian metric miles," Rogers observed as if he could read my mind—a possibility I was beginning to take into serious consideration. The second ship, mate to the first, stood off as we manuevered into place. I wondered why it was here, what it was waiting for.

"But wait," said the gunsmith-praxeologist, "you ain't seen *nothing* yet!"

The stars dimmed briefly, blotted out as we docked, then reappeared as if we were seeing through the mother ship—as if we were now a *part* of the mother ship, seeing things from its point of view.

Ahead still lay that second vessel, swelling every moment, expanding, growing, engulfing the universe from rim to rim.

I gulped as my battered sense of scale underwent another dizzying reorientation. *Beneath the ship, seven giant docking bays awaited!* The first ship had been only intermediary. Now we were preparing to rendezvous with *its* mother ship, riding up into a vast bowl, featureless, brilliant white; the stars went out again, stayed out this time. Daylight was reinstated, motion returned to the garden—the tiny backyard garden—of Leelalee.

"Tom Paine Maru," Owen Rogers exclaimed, grinning so hard I believed he would crack his face in half if it went any further. "Seven and one-half miles in diameter—a little better than twelve of your kilometers, if I understand right.

"This is where we get off!"

10

Pool of Information

G. Howell Nahuatl called at my assigned quarters first
thing the next "morning." I was already up. The door
became transparent, revealing a furry, four-legged creature in the companionway outside, one hind foot scratch-
ing absently in the vicinity of his brightly multicolored
collar.

"Do you have any idea what time it is?" I called as,
freshly showered, I entered the main compartment from
the bathroom.

I needed to ask someone about shaving; my beard itched
although it did not look terribly bad—somewhat unmilitary, but so was the pattern I hastily programmed into
my suit: eight or nine subtle shades of gray-brown hairy-
textured illusion, matching the natural coloration of my
visitor.

The coyote considered. "Why, yes," he answered over
the door communicator, "It's just six. Oh six hundred, to
you, Corporal. I thought you'd appreciate the opportunity

to have some of your questions answered."

Pleading urgent business, Rogers had introduced me to the remarkable creature from his remarkable story—quite unlike the simians or cetaceans I had met thus far—almost immediately upon our arrival the night before. But I had scarcely had the energy to do more than be guided to my billet, fall into an exhausted unconsciousness. Dimly, I recalled something about the lieutenant's being seen to. Also a promise, issued by the canine, of more guide service the next day.

He—the canine, not the lieutenant—nipped suddenly at the base of his tail, then turned back with sedate dignity to wait. Thinking that my foremost question—when would we go home?—*never* seemed to get answered, I wrapped my pistol belt around my middle, checked each magazine. Sealing the final suit seam, I asked, "Can we have some coffee first? What is the drill this morning, Howell?"

The door dilated. Howell sat, exactly as before, no sharper or apparently real than he had been courtesy of sophisticated imaging electronics.

"The drill?" I could not tell whether he was confused by the question, or by my smartsuit pattern, which was supposed to be a joke. "*Ah, yes!*" he replied at last. "You mean, 'what are we about to do?' Well, we shall obtain the coffee to which you have become so rapidly habituated—very shortly after we meet your comrade-in-arms. I shall conduct both of you to *school*—for your first formal lesson in privateering for fun and profit."

He blinked, scratched at an ear. "You know, either the vermin are growing immune to my shower curtain, or I must have my circuits examined for an altogether different sort of bug."

2

We walked down the corridor a few meters to a transport patch. I was still a bit dizzy at the casually mixed color in the decor, the absence of written signs. I hitched at my gunbelt, fastened it a notch looser. Life aboard the Confederacy's ships was already having as unmilitary an effect on my waistline as it was on my grooming habits.

"Privateering?"

"A small joke. Wait a moment before you follow me."

He hesitated himself, then trotted onto the scarlet carpet covering a two-meter square. An area the same size covered the wall behind. He walked directly toward this, as if it did not exist, then was gone. Even in the full light of morning, I did not believe I would ever get used to that particular sight. Howell's head popped back out of the wall.

"Well, Whitey, are you coming?"

"No, but my eyes are glazing."

I stepped into the wall as Howell had done. There was no sensation. Blackness, silence surrounded me, then we were both on a mustard-colored patch, facing the opposite direction, away from a wall, Hamilton knows how far from where we had started.

The coyote looked at me with what my unpracticed eye took for sympathy. "It requires getting used to, being squirted around like the contents of a small intestine. If it's any comfort, I had to be *carried* through the first time, drugged and semicomatose, while the electronic portion of my consciousness decided the walls weren't *really* eating me." He sighed. "It would appear some of my canine instincts are more difficult to suppress than others. Count yourself lucky in this regard."

He blinked, gave a cheerful flip of his tail, trotted to a door not far along the corridor.

"*. . . what do you want?*" bellowed a familiar voice as I caught up. This side, the door remained opaque, preserving the lieutenant's privacy. "Oh, it is only you. Wait while I get something on."

Sermander had not yet learned to sleep comfortably in his smartsuit. The door vanished, he stood before us, arrayed in the Naval Reserve pattern, employing his usual vice-regal tone. "Do you two have any idea what *time* it is?"

"Everyone thinks I'm a chronometer this morning— what d'you think I have, ticks?" He glanced at me to see if I appreciated the joke, gave a desultory scratch. "It's precisely six seventeen, Lieutenant, of a beautiful dawning in the season of your choice. Will you have some coffee, or will you just eat us here?"

The lieutenant shot a look of hatred at the little canine, then gained control. "Coffee—yes, something to eat. What is the agenda today, Nahuatl, another round of profitless philosophizing?" We left the compartment, walked back toward the transport patch.

"Profitless? Scarcely, lieutenant, as I am explaining to the corporal. At last, you're going to *begin* to grasp the function of ship...."

Sermander's eyes lit, but he kept his peace, as he stepped into the wall.

Blackness, silence.

"Coffee and breakfast for two," Howell requested as we stepped through the carpet onto another patch. The chimp who met us nodded, began turning away. Howell called, "And a brace of tender lamb cutlets, rare, while you're about it, will you, with a glass of chilled rosé? Gentlemen?"

I blinked. We were surrounded by junglelike foliage, the bustle of multispecies traffic somewhere in the background beyond.

The resilient lavender walk skirted the edge of a wide meadow. At its other end, looking small as insects, teams of individuals, ropes strung between them, descended a rocky cliff face. A faint shimmer glimmered in the air between us. The area had been partitioned somehow, forming its own climatic zone. On the other side, dust was blowing, a brisk wind fanned sand into a wispy pompadour at the top of the cliff. It almost resembled home.

Howell noted my interest. "For Sodde Lydfe," he observed. "A difficult place. These conditions duplicate the equatorial wet season. Not my idea of recreation."

We stopped to peer at the cliff base, where a pair of figures fired at an enraged orange multilegged beast charging them. Its furious screams were audible this side of the barrier. As the plasma hit, the hair thing gave a cough, rippled, vanished.

"Holo," Howell explained. "Keeps them on their toes. Shall we move on?"

The sidewalk plunged back into the forest, through a clearing where a dozen chimpanzees threw flat steel knives at a mark between the trees. The weapons stuck with a *thump!* Chatting gaily, the nonhumans walked forward to recover their hardware.

"Also Sodde Lydfe," Howell offered, "They really ought to be practicing in burnooses with a sandstorm howling. Elsewhere you'll find others diving in hot water or controlling ultralights in a dust-filled tornado. Now that the captain has returned, the training will double its pace, I'm afraid. Not my lid of tea. Let's betake ourselves to moister climes, whatsay?"

The lieutenant scratched his scalp, offered not a word. He was impressed. Discipline was apparent here, a purposeful order both of us could admire. Nonetheless, I continued worrying over Howell's remark about doubling the pace—rather, the lack of clocks it had reminded me of. Not a single book or sign, any labels or products or artifacts. No thermometers, barometers. No one, at least in my sight, had consulted any written reference, or written anything down.

People on the ship simply seemed to *know*, without effort, without any source for the knowledge. I wondered what the lieutenant thought of it, but had not yet had a chance to ask. Now might be the opportunity: Howell had continued along the walk, while Sermander hung back, preoccupied.

"Discipline, you say?" He almost whispered. "Try asking someone about it. Its existence will be denied promptly! I have small patience with this affected leaderlessness—

there is an imperial iron fist hidden somewhere in the Confederate velvet glove. I want to know who wields it— whom they plan to wield it for them on Vespucci!"

"Lieutenant! You do not think!—"

"Be obedient to orders, Corporal—if only for lack of a more substantial course. Accept my lead, refraining from comment or expressed opinion. I know you are as curious as I about this 'Sodde Lydfe,' all the careful preparations. Still, I caution you: accept only answers that are volunteered. Ask nothing yourself. That way we both may live to understand what is going on."

3

We caught up with Howell along the purple walk, just as the sound of carefree laughter came splashing at us.

"Nahuatl, if this community of yours operates so equitably upon your goodwill,"—the lieutenant gave my pistol belt a contemptuous look—"tell me what purpose is served by all these warlike preparations."

"You couldn't possibly be more mistaken, Lieutenant!" Howell laughed, an eerie sound in the mouth of a dog-creature. "Goodwill hasn't a thing to do with it, and— what did you say, equitability?—that's utterly irrelevant. Self-serving behavior of the productive, benevolent variety is simply more *marketable* than the aggressive or self-sacrificial kind. Why, we run on nothing more than common—but here, gentlemen. Won't you be seated so they may bring our food?"

The rubbery sidewalk had merged with a red-brick court centered about an enormous blue-tinted pool. Sprawled on the tiles everywhere, sitting at a dozen tables, lolling indolently in the water, was a collection of sentients that made the place look like the revolutionary committee at a zoo.

My first *orca*, an imposing individual, lay at anchor in the pool, magnificent in black-white freeform. He rolled

majestically, keeping his sensitive hide moist, exposing
himself evenly to the warm rays of the light-source. The
pool was a miniature lake; he was not at all crowded by
the horde of porpoises who enjoyed the water with him.
A salty tang hung in the air. Humans, chimpanzees, the
larger simians I had learned to call gorillas, lounged about,
having their own breakfasts (lunches, dinners—you could
never tell what "shift" someone was on), conversing quietly, doing any one of a dozen other things, none of which
seemed connected with going to school.

Across the water, I glimpsed Lucille. My heart jumped
inexplicably; I had trouble breathing. She scowled, then
turned back to the tall bronzed male sitting at her table,
laid an affectionate hand on his arm. It was clear by now
she did not like me very much. The compliment was heart-
ily returned. Which made the twinge of—jealousy?—I felt
toward the bronzed muscle man very annoying. Whenever we conversed, discussion invariably ended at high
volume. Just as well we were on opposite sides of the
pool just now; we were on opposite sides of everything
else.

"On Earth, the development of speech from simple
pack-hunting calls," a small chimpanzee began abruptly—
she stood away from a whitewashed table under a gaudy
umbrella, "initiated a period of catastrophic physical evolution among prehumans that has left a contradictory
legacy to this day. The question before us is whether this
pattern is inevitable elsewhere."

Taking a few steps toward the pool, she looked dis-
dainfully at the water, fingered her bracelet speech syn-
thesizer, the only article of clothing she wore, as the
background noise died.

"We are speaking here of hyperrapid changes, for the
first time under control of the evolving species—yet only
partially. Therein lies the tragedy: those involved had no
idea whatever what was happening to them."

The killer whale pivoted on his tail, ribboned around
to face the chimp, regarding her with a docile brown eye

that belied the ferocity of his teeth. Waves splashed over
the edge, darkening the brick flooring. The fastidious chimp
hopped backward, fearing dampened feet.

"Can this be?" demanded the *orca* in a ridiculous shrill
voice. "Can something, under control, as you say, be yet
out of control?"

"Friend waterlog," interrupted a naked human dangling his toes at the pool's margin. His neatly rolled up
pistol belt lay on the tiles beside him. "They *thought* they
were doing something else!"

Laughter all around. I did not see anything funny.

Our table was near the water. An ear cocked to the
conversation, Howell hopped onto a chair; the lieutenant
dug into breakfast without a word, ignoring what was
going on. I sat down absently, trying to make sense of
things. I thought of Eleva, wondering if whatever I learned
might help get us home. Next to us, a gorilla played back-
gammon with an unfamiliar orange-furred alien draped in
swollen purple rolls of fat.

"Correct," this unattractive person offered through her
wrist-talker. "Ms. Lakebones simply felt Mr. Flintchip
told funnier stories than his rivals, which, from the typically human viewpoint, made him better husband material. Unless he demonstrated his virility by raping her
first, of course."

"Cynic. Maybe he just whispered sweeter nothings."
A woman lounging in a suit adjusted to conceal everything
but her skin grinned. A huge pair of tinted spectacles
perched atop her nose. Her fingers were laced together
across her middle, a dozen centimeters too high (or low)
to salvage anything resembling modesty. She was beginning to burn a bit or was of a naturally red-pigmented
subspecies. "The fact we evolved language at all refutes
the image of our species—its males, anyway—as inher-
ently brutal, that rape is instinctive or even particularly
widespread! We wouldn't be sitting here discussing it—
none of us would carry the genes to make it possible!"

At her feet, two black-haired children braided colored

string complexly through their fingers. One gave a double flip of the wrists—the pattern changed completely, at which the other child giggled delightedly. Children were present everywhere, human, nonhuman, many paying rapt attention, others—in this respect they did not differ from their elders—variously eating, drinking from tall, frosted glasses, dozing in the increasingly hot sun, knitting, cleaning weapons, tanning, playing games alone or with companions. A blond-bearded individual mercilessly stropped a huge curve-edged knife on a peculiar stone as he listened, periodically testing its edge on the fine gold hairs of his heavily muscled forearms.

Utter chaos.

Worse, I could not tell who was who: the chimpanzee I had taken to be the lecturer, who had begun the session in what seemed its middle, had returned to her table to ponder a chess problem, uttering not another word throughout the morning. Three meters away sat a blond, blue-eyed girl-child on the warm brick tiling who could not have been more than nine. In one hand, she held a loop-ended stick, in the other, a container of some liquid, foamy at the top. She wet the loop, extracted it, blew through it, releasing dozens of glistening bubbles that wafted on the still air over the pool, shimmering with iridescent colors.

"The point is," the child lectured, dipping into the liquid again, "that previously, nature had conducted evolution through random mutations, winnowed for viability by environmental stresses—a rather slow but thorough procedure...." The adult words sounded odd, delivered across a soft palate, through the beginnings of her second set of teeth. She blew again, making more bubbles. "Then, suddenly, people began selecting *themselves*—rather, each other—for a narrow list of attributes, without any idea what they were doing, or of the likely consequences." Producing another impressive stream of bubbles, she subsided to let someone else talk.

This someone was a large gray dolphin sloshing in the

slanted shallows, nibbling a rack of freshly grilled fish.

"Quite so," it whistled through its blowhole while it ate, "yet before we speak to the disastrous consequences of overly selective processes, it is vital to realize that language, during this period and afterward—only secondarily a medium of communication—was and is vastly more important as the substance of thought, the software of the mind. This will be the case whenever we—"

"There he goes again!" A chimpanzee laughed behind me. He waved a long cigarette holder at the porpoise. "Belaboring the obvious!"

It was not obvious: if speech is *not* primarily a means of communication, what is it? I leaned to whisper this to Howell; before I could, the lieutenant grumbled, "So *this* is what you dragged me out of bed for—a freshman squat-session at six in the morning!"

The fellow sharpening the knife strode to the pool's edge. He was younger than I had taken him for, angrier: "Norris," he growled a sketchy introduction, "just off *Peter LaNague*, fresh from Obsidia!" He pointed the blade at his ankle, thickly bound in gray-silver. "I'll be disabled two weeks because speech on *that* rotten mudball is neither communication *nor* thought!" He stood, the huge double-edged dagger in one hand, the odd Y-shaped stone in the other, feet spread in a combat stance.

A gorilla with her arm in a familiar-looking sling lounged beside the pool across from young Norris. "I got this day before yesterday, just *practicing* for Sodde Lydfe."

For some reason, laughter rippled through the crowd again. Somebody at a nearby table murmured about "roller skates, clumsy!"

"I heard that!" The injured simian would have stamped her foot, had she not been sitting down already. "Ever rappel down a cactus-covered sand mountain? The whole place is like that, and the operations planned are a lot more complicated than anything we'll be doing off Obsidia. It's a primitive planet—so what? There are lots of them—because almost *none* have discovered the 'obvious' facts this class is supposed to cover."

Norris nodded grudgingly, turned to sit where he had been, but never stopped honing the knife. I wondered what would be left of it by the time we reached the Obsidia he had so bitterly spoken of. Now it had been called to my attention, quite a few of those present were recovering in various stages from injury or disease. One person, a dark-brown man with black, tight-knitted hair I had first taken for a cap, was covered with the greenish blotches of some exotic infection. He lay in the "sun," soaking energy as if it were a cure. In addition to casts or splints on every kind of limb possessed by these highly varied beings, some wore flat bandages, eyepatches, backpacks, all of the basic smartsuit material. I wondered about this last—then made myself stop. It would be a place to carry an artificial heart or liver.

The lieutenant paid no attention to any of this, but went back to his breakfast as mine grew cold while I gawked.

There was plenty to gawk at.

"Howell," I whispered, "I thought all your Confederate ships were named 'Tom' or 'Bob' something . . . 'Maru.' Someone told me it means ship. Now this Norris says he is from 'Peter LaNague'—"

"Japanese," supplied the coyote, "one of many ancient languages of Earth. Our universe is vaster than most people know, young friend; not only is space infinite, you see, but so, too, is time—in more ways than one. I cannot explain all at once, friend Whitey, but we've three fleets, altogether. Tom Paine Maru, Tom Edison Maru, others of what we term Tomfleet, operate in one sort of space. Bob Shea Maru, the other Bobs, operate, nearly identical, but separated from the first by time—a different kind of time than—well, you lack the basic vocabulary, I'm afraid. Peter LaNague's part of a third fleet, ranger vessels that traverse the distance—or rather, the difference between the two."

"I see," I lied.

"No, you don't," Howell corrected cheerfully, "but you shall, with due effort, I guarantee it." He returned attention to the larger conversation, still going strong.

Everywhere small knots of individuals spoke quietly among themselves, seeming not to disturb others. In a corner near the pool, on a stretch of thick grass, a pair of human males sparred—some sort of karate—trading blows, grappling, stopping to contribute to the class discussion.

Madness.

"Right!" spoke Lucille's all-too-familiar voice, replying to the injured gorilla's comment about "obvious" facts. "We're wandering off the subject. I was *born* on Earth, where this problem started. My mother was one of the Healers who had to deal with it when cross-time immigration began. My dad was an immigrant, fleeing a government fully as nasty as our Vespuccian guests over there represent, sort of a pragmatic praxeologist who, for some reason was never afflicted—"

"It's *you* who're wandering now, my dear," Howell said politely. "And I believe I, of all beings here, may speak to the subject of genetic predisposition with some authority. I have borrowed civilization from the human race, as have all you simians, without paying the evolutionary price. The origins of cetacean culture are lost in the mists of an antiquity so ancient as to be irrevocably untraceable.

"The real conundrum is this: will a different evolutionary history, that of the Sodde Lydfans, produce a different attitude toward authority? Will a different physical placement of the generative organs—at the opposite end of the body from those of elimination—have a salutory effect? How will a broader birth channel affect their psychology? Not to speak of their rather novel number of genders..."

4

It went on a full six hours, until noon, people arguing, debating points I could not comprehend. Finally, the session began to break—well, perhaps melt away is a better term. Increasingly fewer sat around the pool, were interested in the talk.

Abruptly, the blue-eyed girl-child with the bubble pipe jumped up, ran in our direction. Without prelude, she threw both arms around Howell's neck, unhesitatingly kissed him on the muzzle.

"Gotta go now! Koko promised t'show me some American video flatties of Carl Sagan for the History of Xenopsych lecture I hafta give tomorrow morning."

The coyote nodded, once he had been released, used his right front paw to poke a lock of the young girl's golden hair back into place. "That should be amusing. I believe I've seen those old tapes myself. I needn't caution you not to take the man too seriously, Mowgli?"

"Aw, Daddy, don't call me that!" She blushed. "Anyway, he was practically a Kilroy himself, wasn't he?"

Howell gave his odd laugh. "A few decades before the fact, and in a galaxy far, far away. It's a state of mind, sweetheart. See you at dinner."

She picked up her toys, said good-bye, ran full pitch away from the pool. He turned to us, pride in his artificial voice. "My daughter Elsie, gentlemen. The only xenopsychology student on the entire praxeological staff. Until very recently, it was a discipline largely in search of subject matter. Now she finds herself the resident expert at a time of crisis, I'm afraid." He nipped at a knot in his fur. "Well, would you like to see something else, stir up the circulation a bit, perhaps think about lunch?"

"About the only thing I shall have gained from a wasted morning," complained the lieutenant, but he rose, following the little girl down the path with a confused expression.

"Howell," I asked, as we left the brick-floored clearing for the woods again, "there is one thing you could explain..."

"Surely not that Elsie is adopted?"

"No." I admitted how little of the morning I had understood. He assured me again that, in time, all would become crystal clear—I had not believed that the *first* time he had said it.

"But—I am embarrassed to confess—I do not even know who the *teacher* was supposed to have been!"

The coyote stopped on the path, looked up at me.

"Whitey, the principle focus of this morning's session was *you*—and the lieutenant, of course.

"And you did perfectly splendidly, take my word for it!"

11

Nobody Hears
the Mandolar

It is one thing to look at water, appreciate the miracle of it, sit on a bank dangling your feet luxuriously as it slips between your toes. It is quite another to ride on top of huge amounts of the stuff, grimly pretending to enjoy yourself. In that respect, I shared the prejudices of a chimpanzee.

"Wahoo!" a voice from somewhere shouted, as a curved glistening wall threw itself against the boat, threatening to overturn it. A big white bird flew overhead, making noises like a rusty hinge.

"Yippee! I knew you'd like this, Whitey!"

"Ulp!" I answered, giving the voice a sickly smile.

The wave passed—the water wave, not the wave of nausea it provoked—depositing cold spray down the neck of my jacket. Koko Featherstone-Haugh, a strapping-big girl who wore pink ribbons in her dark curly hair, my sailing companion for the afternoon, worked mysteries upon a bunch of ropes, hollered at me to *duck!* The spar

131

at the bottom of the sail swung around, brushing the top of my head with only a hint of its potential for destruction. The boat pitched over in the opposite direction.

As did my stomach. I threw up.

Somewhere below-decks in this mobile torture instrument, Koko kept a small four-stringed "ukelele" in a waterproofed suit-fabric case. At her waist, she lugged a monstrous reciprocating bullet-gun, fifty-caliber Gabbet-Fairfax—about twelve millimeters—she told me a gift from "a dear and trusted friend."

Oh, yes: Koko was also a gorilla, the one with the sling on her arm that morning beside the pool. And because she was an alien she quickly became one of the few people I felt sure about aboard the big star-traversing ship. With nothing but Vespuccian experience to guide me, never having met people like the humans, I was uncertain how to read them. Couper: a man you could lean on, big, tough, ugly—on Vespucci, officers like him routinely ordered other men to certain death, all the while assuring them everything was just fine. Owen Rogers: a fellow artisan, but with a distinctly Confederate attitude—whatever that ultimately implied. Howell, like Koko, not at all human, I liked.

I trusted that little witch Lucille no farther than I could throw her. Not far at all, the way she was trained.

Earlier that terror-filled morning, I spoke again with the lieutenant. He was fascinated with this great ship, with everything aboard it, with its obvious dedication to a cause. He seemed avid to possess what Rogers called "a piece of the action." How could a mere corporal insist his superior consider more carefully what little we actually *knew* about this action?

2

"Corporal, do not be a fool."

We were in the lieutenant's quarters—a four-compartment suite with broad windows overlooking *Tom Paine Maru*'s answer to an ocean. Up to my ankles already, in sandy-color wall-to-wall carpeting, I looked down several dizzying stories, onto that dangerous, foam-flecked mirror, shining under an artificial sun. I anticipated the morning's new experience with dread.

Even this early, I had come across groups of people taking language lessons under the brilliant sky, seen peculiar equipment being made in rooms I passed, being fitted, tried out. Repeatedly I had been told "Oh, that's just for Sodde Lydfe—" Followed by a change of subject.

I needed to compare notes with my boss, learn what he had discovered.

Lacking an artistic bent of his own, Sermander—whose talents lay more in persuading others to do things—had badgered Howell's little girl into selecting a 360-degree holo of some less deadly desert, from a lengthy Confederate catalog of such images, a planet called Wyoming. Three walls had been given over to it, creating an illusion of furniture grouped amidst sandy scrub. They had dimmed the sun, shriveled visible vegetation, until it was indeed like the Central Oasis at what passed for springtime on Vespucci. I cannot say it made me feel homesick: I had seen a battle fought in this place, during the Final War. Ten thousand dead.

Koko I had met formally last evening at a "dinner theater" my praxeologist friend had insisted on attending, *TPM*'s amateur musical production of *Loose Lips*, based, I gathered, on an ancient classic about a young mutant, the physician who taught her to capitalize upon her peculiarity, the many men whose problems her unique talents helped solve. I blushed through the entire performance.

Recognizing Koko, I made the mistake of telling her how much I had liked the swimming pool. Her broken limb was fine now, in just a few days' time, thanks to the Confederacy's medical technology; she intended to celebrate by risking its integrity again, on the high seas.

Distracted by the play, I found myself conscripted into going along. Before keeping my dubious appointment with the ocean-going gorilla this morning, I was determined to convey my doubts to the lieutenant, ask what he thought.

He told me.

"Corporal, this vessel is over twelve kilometers—*twelve kilometers!*—in diameter. These people—if thus we must call them—are part of something even more enormous...imagine the industrial establishment capable of such construction! Imagine the energy source! The place names we hear, the products we sample, betray an empire vaster than Vespucci ever dreamed!"

He strode to a cabinet beside the door, poured himself a drink, tossed it back, poured another. "This is larger than your petty misgivings, O'Thraight, larger than you are—but *not*, I assure you, larger than Enson Sermander!"

For some reason, he seemed uncomfortable on the glass-fronted side of the room. The view was somewhat daunting: far across the water, cloaked in haze, nearly at the horizon, there appeared to be a city, tall buildings gleaming. He paced the carpet in front of a sofa near the claustrophobic safety of the hallway door, one hand thrust into his pants pocket, the other locked around his drink. He seemed to mutter at the floor, rather than at me: "Yes, yes, I know what it must sound like. But let us face facts, Corporal, let us be realistic."

"Yes, sir," I answered, my gaze distracted momentarily. Outside several individuals, wearing huge multicolor triangular wings, soared above the pounding waves. "That is what I am trying to do, sir. I am not comfortable, being friends with people I do not understand. I wish to know if you believe they can be trusted."

"Immaterial, Corporal—Whitey—they can be trusted to be whatever they are, to do what they have already done, create a stellar hegemony with unimaginable resources to draw upon. Think, man: when they confront *our* puny world-state, Vespucci will not last a microsecond!"

"I was thinking much the same, sir, but is that not scandalous, disloyal, unpatri?—"

"But *think*!" demanded the lieutenant again. "What does *true* loyalty demand? We must survive, learn what we can, return upon the day of confrontation with an understanding of these people, an ability to negotiate, to intercede, to...."

To rule, he was thinking, I was certain. The lieutenant imagined himself Confederate viceroy on Vespucci, destroying our independence in order to save it.

"But, sir!"

"But *nothing*, Corporal!" He sighed dramatically. "Oh dear, how true it is: the underclasses invariably defend the system most vehemently. Corporal, I am attempting to make an appointment with the *captain* of this vessel, whoever he may be. I await his call at any moment. I shall *offer* my knowledge of our planet, offer my *wisdom* in promoting peaceful contact between the two civilizations. Vespucci needs her strongest minds at this moment, her strongest hands, her strongest resolve"—

Her strongest stomachs. I had first heard this speech at the age of five, when they were announcing a reduction in the milk ration. I told myself he could not help it; he was an officer, after all.

—"in order to survive! Trust them? In the long run, it will be an investment. Work with them, eat with them— sleep with them, if such is your inclination. I shall see you are awarded a medal for duty beyond the call, once we get home."

Once we get home.

Already, it was beginning to sound like an unattainable fantasy. The lieutenant was correct about one thing: we were helpless, dependent on the Confederates for our return to Vespucci, for day-to-day survival, even for the clothes we wore.

"If you say so, sir." A year ago, a month, I would have found Sermander's attitude quite normal. He scowled at me, then winced when his line of sight took in the faraway horizon, the vast agoraphobic chasm just outside the floor-to-ceiling windows.

"Sir," I offered, "you can shut these things down, if you want—just turn this knob at the base."

I demonstrated. The windows faded to opaque. Just as quickly, the desert landscape wrapped around, enclosing us securely in the pseudofamiliar. Sermander seemed to breathe easier. He finished off his drink, poured himself another.

"Get out of here, Whitey, go—what did you call it?— sailing. Think upon what part *you* might play in a Confederate-Vespuccian order. Perhaps it will take the starch out of that overly stiff collar of yours."

I got.

3

For days sitting around, I am waiting for your call,
*　　Hope my face won't fall—off the wall.*
And the daisies in the ground are around ten feet tall,
*　　Though they started pretty small, half-past*
Fall . . .
Butterfly, how come why I never see ya?
*　　Have your fun; when you're done, I wouldn't*
*　　wanna be ya*
'Cause I'm through sitting around, getting rusty on the
*　　shelf—*
*　　I can be lonely, by myself, without your help . . ."*

Koko started over at the bridge, "*Butterfly . . .*" repeating the final line. By the finish, I had figured out the chording—you mashed your fingers down on the strings between the inset wires, just as if they were buttons. I was eager to try.

She passed me the little box, a remarkably primitive artifact for so advanced a culture. I found I could omit the finger positions for the last two mandolar columns, play a creditable C, F, G7. I strummed the strings where they passed an acoustic aperture in the body, just as if they were control vanes. The sound was crude, yet somehow wistfully appealing. Koko promised to show me a tune called "Ukelele Lady." Meanwhile as I experimented with *her* ukelele, the lady extracted a cigar from a pocket on her gunbelt, lit it, lay back in the sand, watching the waves roll in.

We sat on a dune at the margin of the water—her little boat hauled up, the brightly colored sail furled. In the "west," the artificial sun was setting, as spectacularly as any ever did—except, perhaps, on Sca.

We were not alone on the beach although Confederates give each other lots of elbow room unless otherwise invited. Others sat, watched the sunset; several were assembling scraps of water-worn wood. A larger number stretched a net between poles thrust into the sand, batted a ball over it, using hands, heads—even feet.

One of these impressive kickers proved to be the injured Norris from yesterday's "class." Blond, bearded, stocky, he was also short—almost tiny. Despite the dressing on his leg, he gave a good account of himself, spinning, twisting. His good foot was a lethal instrument.

I turned to Koko. "Tell me about Obsidia."

"Zzzzz—*what?*" She started awake just in time to avoid a cigar burn to her pelt. "Where'd you hear about Obsidia? Oh, yes . . . it's another primitive planet, Whitey, our next stop, according to the scientific types. The name is just one we assigned it, appropriate to the tech-level; there's about a zillion tribes, nations, empires, all of which call the place "Dirt" in their native languages. Conditions there are your standard nasty, brutish, and short, thanks to widespread sentient sacrifice and a ruling priesthood in what we laughingly regard as the leading culture, similar to the ancient Aztecs—if that means anything."

It did not.

"It's our final visit there for a while, then on to Sodde—hold on, isn't this Howell coming?"

Koko must have had fantastically sensitive hearing. It was a good many seconds before I heard their voices myself, coming from the other side of the dune behind us, even more until they were in sight. I heard Elsie first, chattering gaily, skipping barefoot alongside the coyote. Then I could not help but notice Lucille. Her costume may have begun as a smartsuit; in terms of material, it was economical, if not downright penurious. A little while later, I remembered, with some annoyance at myself, to breathe.

They stopped, Koko exchanging greetings with the females. Elsie ran off to play in the water. The gorilla scratched the coyote behind one ear, careful not to disturb the dark glasses he wore. He extended me a paw. "Well, old fellow, how d'you like sailboating?"

I reddened. "The porpoises would thank me if I gave it up." I did not think to ask myself until later how it was he knew what we had been doing.

Koko laughed, not without sympathy. Howell admitted he felt much the same about the sport. Lucille sat gracefully on the sand beside them, as far from me as possible, took a lit cigarette from a small case, looked out over its orange-glowing coal at the darkening water. A dozen yards away, someone set the head-high heap of wood afire. I felt its radiation on my face almost immediately.

Or maybe it was just imagination.

"Something to offend everyone, Corporal?" Lucille peered around the gorilla's impressive bulk, the lesser obstruction of the coyote, gave me a malicious grin. "It may surprise you to learn there are people on this ship—two-legged and otherwise—with the same instinctive reaction to your kind as you have to sailing."

She expelled smoke as if it were a bad memory.

I was getting tired of this. "Precisely what *is* my kind, Miss Olson-Bear?"

"Lucille is always prepared to be specific," Howell offered blandly, "though less often to be polite."

"Your kind, since you ask, Corporal, is the uniformed, goose-stepping soldier-boy kind, who want to 'fight and bleed and kill and die,' in the words of the poet, for an institution that hasn't any more right to exist than *he* has!"

Koko watched, her eyes mild, as fingers of heat felt their way up my face. Howell shook his head.

"No right to exist?" I repeated. "I understand now how you could slaughter a company of men in the name of some stupid abstraction. On Vespucci this would make you a great politician."

Lucille snapped into a combat stance. "Get up to say that, storm trooper!"

"Why? You would only hit me for expressing my opinion."

"Oho!" Howell exclaimed. "Hoist by her own petulance! Have we suspended free speech when I wasn't looking, Lucille, or is somebody simply being unethical and rude?"

"Sit down, Cilly." Koko drew on her cigar, patted the ground with a hand large as both of mine placed side to side. "You're getting sand in my ukelele."

The furious girl glared sharply when called "Cilly." "All right, Koko—for now! But *somebody*'s got to give this Kilroy an education!"

"And aversive conditioning," the coyote replied sarcastically, "is such an effective means!" Koko offered Howell a drag on the cigar. He took it, blew out smoke.

"Howell, don't be mad," Lucille said. "Can't you see— these Vespuccians are *military*—they represent a *government!*" She thumped back to the sand, this time only one space away, to the left of the coyote.

Howell grinned. "I'm not angry, Cilly. Say you're sorry, that'll make it square."

He laid his muzzle on her lap, sighed.

Tears were in her voice, rather than her eyes, "I'm sorry, Howell..."

"No, dear, to the corporal. He's the one you're riding. My back wouldn't have stood it this long. I'd have to've done something about it." He gave me a significant look.

"I'd rather die!" Her voice was almost a whisper.

"Somebody may arrange it," I growled. "I will not feel ashamed of my country. If everyone was like Howell or Koko—rational—this *system* of yours might work. But if even *one* is like you, Lucille, everybody needs protection!" I heaved my tired body to its feet, frowned down at the girl. "Now threaten me again! This time you will not throw me by surprise!"

Her eyes grew large, she moved back a little. Howell shook his head, looked at Koko as she patted me on the shoulder. "Calm down, Whitey," soothed the gorilla, "nobody's going to hurt you."

"Look, Corporal, I was raised, with my sister, Ed-Wina, on the Confederate frontier—a place called the Venus Belt. I—" Lucille stopped suddenly. There was a lengthy silence, then more voices came to us from behind...

4

"But you cannot have it both ways, do you not see?"

The lieutenant was loud. Koko, Lucille turned in the direction of the words. Howell kept his eyes on Elsie, playing in the surf.

"Childish semantic games—of *course* the universe is determined, my good doctor; free will is an illusion!"

"Well"—the other voice chuckled—"you could have fooled me—but then, I suppose that's what illusions are all about. Hello, darling, hello, everybody! I'm trying to introduce Lieutenant Sermander to the wonders of praxeology, but he's resisting."

"Darling" turned out to be Koko. She reached a big hand upward to a bigger one, while the owner of the latter bent down, gave her a peck on the cheek. In the rapidly gathering darkness, it was difficult to see precisely who this friend of hers was—a gorilla, certainly, male to judge from his size. He wore a sleeveless short-pantsed outfit in pale green with a large red-circled cross on the left shoulder. He also wore wire-rimmed spectacles, held a small brown cigarillo in one hand.

He plumped down on the sand beside Koko.

"Francis," she began, "you know everybody except the corporal: Whitey O'Thraight. We went sailing this morning, while you were in surgery. Whitey, this is Francis W. Pololo, H.D., my husband."

I was suddenly glad they were gorillas, not human—then again, in a civilization that produced the likes of *Loose Lips*, who could tell what new, impossibly-compromising situations had been invented? Transferring the cigar to his left hand, he swallowed mine with his right. "Pleased to meet you, Corporal. Did you like sailing?"

I was also glad they could not see me blushing in the dark.

"Francis, you've made him blush! He did real well, for a first-timer. They haven't any open water at all, where he—"

How had she known that?

"Nor praxeologists, I gather," her husband interrupted politely, looking to me, then the lieutenant.

"*That's* obvious!" A sarcastic voice snorted on the other side of Koko.

"Hello, Lucille," Pololo responded. "Have you been teaching Corporal O'Thraight the finer points?"

"Only of feudin', fussin', and fightin'." Howell scratched himself with a back leg. "They hadn't got to praxeology."

"What in Ham's name *is* praxeology?" I demanded, exercising confused anger at Lucille upon a question I had been trying to get answered for days.

"Properly," the gorilla intoned, "the study of 'human action'—by extension..."—he brushed a hand over his pelt, patted Howell—"of the actions of *all* mindkind, taking in everything from ethics and epistemology, through sociology and anthropology, to politics and economics—"

"Are you a teacher of this subject?"

"Dear me," replied Pololo, "I'm a Healer, a physician—which is *not* a praxeological discipline, but a physiomechanical one. It's simply an interest of mine, as with many. Otherwise, soap operas would soon lose their lucrative appeal. I met Enson, here, while he was trying to find the captain." He grinned at his wife, who looked down at the sand, shaking her head. "I've been trying ever since to explain to him why that's so difficult."

Even in the dark, I could sense Sermander's exasperation. "He assures me that there *is* one—yet no one will conduct me to the bridge, the control room, even to the captain's cabin . . . I am told this personage may be found at unpredictable times in private quarters—which do not appear to exist—or in a certain forest. I wandered that forest for three hours this morning, witnessing nothing more than several groups of picnickers!—"

Koko laughed. "I know the forest. You might have seen me there, any other morning. I like picnics."

5

Before us on the beach, the fire burned low, no longer reflected by the glistening waves rolling up on the sand. One by one, the celebrators had departed, first the strangers who had built the fire, played games, eaten primitively cooked food, sung songs as we listened, then Koko, her husband, Sermander muttering about "getting an early start," finally the Nahautls.

The evening was warm, the off-water breezes moisture-laden. Even Lucille seemed not at all unpleasant, breathing beside me in the darkness. Eleva, Vespucci, duty, were far away. Thoughts of witchery, dangerous, often unbearable—but oh, so stirring—crowded my mind.

"What?" I asked, jolted out of my reverie.

She could not let things alone. "I said, 'a permanently powerless underclass'—why don't you pay attention? That's what you come from, Corporal, without hope, without a future—what's it like to spend your whole life, cradle to grave—in grade?"

"This is not strictly correct, Lucille. I am a corporal now, but we are all born privates."

"I'll refrain from the dirty double-entendre *that* inspires."

"That is uncommonly decent of you. Are you sure you feel all right?"

"Aha! The worm turns! You're learning bad habits with us here, Whitey: sassing back, disrespect for authority. I thought you were actually going to hit me, back there for a minute." Her tone had softened with the last few phrases, dropped half an octave. It was the first time she had ever called me by my given name.

I wondered what she wanted.

"I do not hit women. Not even small, nasty-tempered ones."

"I understand. That would be discourteous, unmilitary—or would it? 'Duty, Honor, Country'—is that all you *really* want, Corporal?"

Even in the dark, I could imagine the arching of her eyebrows. If anyone could have managed a provocative sneer, it would have been Lucille. I want to go home to Eleva, I thought. Now more than at any other moment, even in the dungeons of Sca, I wanted—needed—to go home to Eleva.

"Come on, Corporal, tell us what you really want. To save glorious Vespucci—what a name!—from the bad nasty anarchists? Is that what you want? Well, I've got news for you, it'll take a better man than you are to do it—and he won't want to! You'd have to do a heap of growing, all in the wrong direction, as far as your culture's concerned."

"What do you mean by that?" I snapped.

"Nothing much. Except—it's ironic, but far from surprising—at this moment, in order to serve the best interests of Vespucci, as you conceive them, you're going to have to overcome what it—Vespucci—has created in you: passivity, resignment, overawe for the high and mighty. To 'save' your precious culture, you've got to become what it least wants you to be."

"What is that? You are going to say 'a man.' are you not? Not very original, nor very true—although I do not expect you to see it. You do not see very much of anything, Lucille, except the mixed-up angry garbage inside your own head."

Craaack!

My mouth stung where she had backhanded it. I spat a drop of blood, grinning wolfishly. "What is the matter, little girl? You can ration it out, but you cannot take it yourself?"

She leaped up, turned to stamp away. In the dying firelight, I seized her by the ankle, twisted my wrist. She slammed back onto the ground, spitting sand as I had spat blood a moment before. In the moment's heat, she forgot what she knew of real combat, raining ineffectual blows on my shoulders as I crawled alongside her, holding her down. Finally, I grabbed her wrists, held them together with one hand. Her face was flushed, her breath came in harsh gasps.

Then she composed herself. "Let's do something military," she said sarcastically. "How about a little rape to round out the evening's—"

I laid my free hand over her mouth—her eyes were wild. "Lucille, with you, I suspect that would be impossible."

She would have hit me again, but by then I had her suit skinned down over her upper arms, pinning her. Another moment, she was free again, altogether, as was I. I entered her, her back arched, her arms went rigid around me, pulling me closer, deeper inside her.

Light flared in my brain, a brilliant, all-consuming white light that left little violet sparks behind.

Eventually, they faded, too.

For a moment, it had felt as if I knew the secrets of the universe, the answer to every problem men had ever confronted. As she lay in my arms, breathing hard, her voice, very low now, in my ear. "What took you so fucking long, Whitey?"

12

The Wrath of Koko

It was strange, waking up in a forest clearing. Breezes stirred the evergreens a hundred meters away, rippled uncut grass that lay between. The field was littered with upjutting boulders, covered in gray-yellow lichen, outcroppings of prickly pear whose blossoms were attended by flying insects. Our bed being circled, high above, by a broad-winged raptor passing overhead as if it could not see us—which it could not, since it was a recording, like everything else displayed on Lucille's apartment walls.

"More coffee, Corporal-darling?"

The swimming-pool session, the lieutenant's abstruse argument with Pololo, were neither the first educational experiences I was subject to aboard the *Tom Paine Maru* nor the last, but it was at all times difficult distinguishing teachers from students, schooltime from recess. Maybe that had something to do with the absence of books.

Recess had its moments. "Thanks, I think I will just lie here for a while—gathering my strength."

I leaned over, kissed Lucille in the hollow of her collarbone. She ducked her head—ticklish—grinned, then grabbed me around the neck, wrestling me down on my back.

"Well, you lazy bum, *I* do!"

"What? Oh—coffee—please go ahead without me."

One consistency remained: the focus of every conversation was Sodde Lydfe. Seminars on anthropology, I was pressed into attending by Howell, Elsie, or Lucille, psychology lectures, geography classes, economic dissertations, all aimed at analyzing cultures that, in turn, got compared to others I had never heard of: Nazi Germany, Stalinist Russia, Socialist England—a similar place called Denmark—Nortonian California, Occupied Hawaii.

Occupied by whom?

"Nazis are a local brand of fascist," she explained with ill-concealed impatience. Lucille tried to help. She rolled over on her side, ran a finger in a small circle over the middle of the bed. The surface firmed between us. She set her cup on the mattress, then reached back for the lit cigarette rising through the tabletop.

"I remember. Also that you called my uniform 'fascist modern.'" I thought back over history lessons inflicted on me over the last few days. "The Nazis were United Statesians, then?"

"Good memory, for a Kilroy, Whitey, but in that era, an entire world was controlled by fascism: Nazis in a nation-state called Germany, *Fascisti* in Italy, Shinto in Japan, the New Deal in the United States. Similar things elsewhere, though people didn't always realize which philosophy was in the driver's seat. Check into Zionism sometime."

I ignored the needle. "Is no one ever going to tell me what a Kilroy is?"

She laughed. "By coincidence, an expression from the period we're talking about, sort of a fragment of a joke. Millions of conscriptees battled all over the planet as politically identical nations struggled for control. Wherever soldiers went, they saw a chalked-up drawing of a little man—" She held the sheet up, fingers curled over the edge, her nose resting between them. "—and the legend 'Kilroy Was Here.' I always thought it was a pretty black piece of establishment humor: countless men and women bleeding and dying, thinking they were *fighting* the dragon, when, all the time..."

She trailed off a moment, then: "Anyway, when we Confederates finally had a reliable stardrive—as opposed to the engineering nightmare that got your ancestors into trouble—we burst into space expecting an endless, open frontier. Instead, you—the Vespuccians, the Scavians, the Obsidians, everybody else—were here first."

"Vespucii," I corrected, taking the cigarette from her hand. I drew on it experimentally, then made the mistake of inhaling. When I was through coughing, I said, "So we are all Kilroys—also fascists."

She nodded, dropped the sheet—I nearly forgot what the conversation was about. "You about through dogging it, Corporal-baby?"

My spirit was more than willing, but the flesh still needed time.

She lay back in one elbow, pulled my mouth down to hers. When I could breathe again, I shook my head. My debilitation was becoming an embarrassment. "So tell me something, something about yourself, Lucille."

She laughed again, bitterness touching the edge of her voice. "All right, then, I was born on Earth, though just barely: my folks had recently been to the Venus Belt and returned there shortly after I was born. I was raised on a homestead with my sister, we both grew up and studied praxeology."

"EdWina Olson-Bear? Somebody mentioned her as Chief Praxeologist."

"Whither thou goest." Lucille assumed a grim expression, replied enigmatically again. "As I was, once, before her. She taught at the same university we'd graduated from. I opted for field studies, aboard the original *Tom*

Sowell Maru. Somehow, we both wound up here..."

Abruptly, she set her cup back on the nightstand, re-softened the bed surface, got up with a graceful, unwinding motion. The outdoor scene vanished, replaced by white, sterile walls. "We're burning daylight."

"But Lucille, I thought—"

"You pissed it away. I'm not in the mood any more. Just like a man—all action and no traction. Get out of here, I want to dress."

2

I found Howell—or he found me—in the hall outside my compartment.

I had not been back for three days, not since a dreamlike evening on the beach that now seemed a century ago. I discovered with chagrin that I had not thought of him during that time, nor of anybody else—particularly Eleva, toward whom I was not only feeling guilty for what I had done, but for the very enthusiasm with which I had done it. In penance, every muscle ached, particularly my lower back. I desperately wanted a shower, despite the continuous cleansing action of my suit.

I also needed to talk: in a few well-chosen words—selected during the angry walk back to my room—I conveyed the difficulty I was having understanding a difficult subject. Women in general, Lucille in particular. Maybe the other way around.

"Well, I can tell you at least one part of her story," the coyote offered as I sagged into a chair. I did not even have the satisfaction of taking off my shoes—the damned things were part of my clothing, more comfortable than going barefoot. He hopped onto another seat, wrapped his bushy tail neatly about his hindquarters. "And explain one of her mysterious remarks. She can be quite annoying, can't she?"

Beyond a weary grunt, I did not bother to reply, but

simply sat there in the disgusted realization that I felt worse than I ever had, even in the dungeons of Sca.

"Naturally," Howell continued, once aware that silence was all he was going to get, "I would not reveal anything Lucille would not volunteer. I have known her a long time, watched her grow from a lovely child into a somewhat tragic young woman. But this much is public knowledge: she became head of praxeology aboard *Tom Paine Maru*, Whitey, and her sister's boss, not an arrangement contrived in any pleasant mythological realm: the sisters had never been on best terms."

"Howell," I said abruptly, "I want a straight answer. If you do not have it, I want to know who does. When can I go home?"

"Oho, a change of subject. Or is it? Whitey, I—"

"Do not string me, furry friend. I have been asking that question—among others—since I boarded the *Little Tom*. I have yet to receive an answer that satisfied me."

Howell sat thinking a moment, then: "You can't go home, poor fellow. Not yet. Events are about to culminate on Obsidia. We have stops to make at Hoand, Afdiar. There is, as you know, a major operation planned for Sodde Lydfe. We are sorely pressed for time and cannot afford a detour—"

"Howell, stop lying to me! I am not going to be deterred this time, not by you or anybody. This ship is *made* of smaller ships. Surely one—"

He raised a paw. "The truth, then, although I wish you'd waited until Obsidia. It might clarify matters. Still, no one ought to operate on faith. My boy, *Tom Paine Maru*, and all within her, rely upon a recent technological revolution so vast as to make the First Industrial Revolution, or what happened in electronics afterward, seem minuscule."

I snorted, "I am tired of being offered philosophy instead of substance. Lucille with her politics, Koko's husband with his nonsense about free will, chaos, or

determinism, your little girl with anthropological dissertations. Get on with it."

"Elsie's nine, it's true, small for her age, but a typical
Confederate in every other respect."

"Howell!"

"Very well. You are aware of the situation on Sodde
Lydfe. What do you suppose would happen if the Great
Fodduans or the Hegemony of Podfet got hold of even a
fraction of *TPM*'s capabilities?"

Those were states I had discussed with Lucille. Thinking about her—feeling the strange sensations it caused
me   made this all the more urgent. I had to get home, to
see Eleva. Yet, equally, I had to answer Howell truthfully,
as he seemed to be doing with me. "It would not be pretty."

"Now—and this is the touchy part—why should we of
the Confederacy more sanguinely convey such knowledge
to the government of Vespucci?"

It was what I had been expecting. "I suppose that
makes me—also Lieutenant Sermander—something of an
embarrassment, does it not?"

He laughed. "Only by demanding what is morally due
you. We are not kidnappers by choice. No policy has
been made concerning you—we don't know what policy
to make. Is it possible you owe us something—for the
rescue on Sca? Bear with us, then. When we have a little
breathing space—after Sodde Lydfe—we'll arrive at a solution mutually satisfying to all. That is the point of our
civilization, as you will learn with the passing of time."

3

Elsie offered to play mother, serving hot tea from an
insulated plastic baggie until the lieutenant, the last of us
she got to, held a hand up. She placed the "teapot" in the

center of a small table where it jiggled, climbed into her own chair.

"Now," Koko said, "as the saying goes, I suppose you all wonder why I called you here."

"Here" was the gorillas' apartment in an escarpment wall overlooking a dense tropical forest. Francis Pololo grimaced. "Don't keep them in suspense, dear, it's almost 0-hour. You'll wind up treading on the punchline."

The female shrugged. "Lieutenant Sermander, you've been looking all over for the captain. I understand you even rented a diving rig this morning and dropped down to the *orca* settlement at Seahunt. Well, I have a message from her—don't bother: she doesn't wield any power you'd be interested in."

"*She?*" Sermander's voice was a disappointed croak. "Satisfied?"

The lieutenant opened his mouth, a puzzled expression on his face, then shut it.

Koko continued, addressing me, "You've both been wondering about the mission of *Tom Paine Maru*. I wish I could say I've arranged events to show you Whitey. It's going to look fairly simple. But what we're about to witness has been under careful consideration for eighteen years. I did arrange this tea party, though. Will that do?"

Overhead, the ceiling starscape cleared.

"Obsidia," Howell announced, indicating the yellow-orange globe above our heads. "We share the viewpoint of a scoutship making her way toward the surface. Williamson's *Little Tom*, if I'm not mistaken."

It was a brilliant day, the sun baked down upon the dusty continent toward which the scout was falling. Suddenly, the viewpoint zoomed ahead to a city—primitive but impressive—made of huge stone pyramids. At the top of the tallest, a ceremony was in progress, witnessed by tens of thousands who stood on the stepped flanks of the building, looking upward.

"Here we go"—Koko chuckled—"I've been looking forward to this—"

A solitary individual, his humanity all but disguised in elaborate feather trappings, stood beside a bed-sized stone over which was stretched the supine naked form of a young man. In his hand, the gaudily dressed official held a huge black dagger raised above the youth's unprotected chest. It glinted as the sun caught its faceted glassy surface.

"Ev should be in range any moment now," Pololo said. Excitement was overpowering even the well-collected Healer. "We should—"

"—of the Sun who is the Sun, accept this unworthy offering from thy miserable and humble servants!"

There followed a lot of indistinguishable mumbling as the congregation made response. The priest held the knife high; its intended victim seemed unalarmed at the prospect of becoming an unworthy offering. Suddenly, a circular shadow dozens of meters in diameter—just right for a ship the size of Little Tom—fell across the flattened pryamid top.

"HEAR THOU THE WORD OF THE LORD, GOD!"

It was Elsie's voice. She grinned sheepishly at me across the room. "They offered: I just couldn't resist."

"THOU SHALT CEASE THIS ABOMINABLE PRAC-TICE IMMEDIATELY AND FROM THIS DAY FOR-WARD!"

The priest dropped his knife—it missed the reprieved victim by a millimeter, clattering on the altar beside him—and fell to his feather-draped knees, hands wringing together heavenward. Everybody else had eyes only for the scout-saucer.

"I TELL THEE THIS DAY THAT I AM GOING AWAY!" A low moan swept through the crowd, down the sides of the pyramid, dissipating along the ground. "FROM THIS DAY FORWARD SHALT THOU HELP THY-SELVES, NEITHER SHALT THOU WORSHIP ANY

GOD. INSTEAD SHALT THOU RESPECT MY LAW, THAT THOU MAYEST BE LIKE UNTO GODS THYSELVES. HEAR, NOW, THE LAW:

"THERE SHALL BE NO GOD BUT MAN.

"MAN HATH THE RIGHT TO LIVE BY HIS OWN LAW.

"MAN HATH THE RIGHT TO LIVE IN THE WAY THAT HE WILLETH TO LIVE.

"MAN HATH THE RIGHT TO DRESS AS HE WILLETH TO DRESS.

"MAN HATH THE RIGHT TO DWELL WHERE HE WILLETH TO DWELL.

"MAN HATH THE RIGHT TO MOVE AS HE WILLETH ON THE FACE OF THE PLANET.

"MAN HATH THE RIGHT TO EAT WHAT HE WILLETH.

"MAN HATH THE RIGHT TO DRINK WHAT HE WILLETH.

"MAN HATH THE RIGHT TO THINK WHAT HE WILLETH.

"MAN HATH THE RIGHT TO SPEAK AS HE WILLETH.

"MAN HATH THE RIGHT TO WRITE AS HE WILLETH.

"MAN HATH THE RIGHT TO MOLD AS HE WILLETH.

"MAN HATH THE RIGHT TO CARVE AS HE WILLETH.

"MAN HATH THE RIGHT TO WORK AS HE WILLETH.

"MAN HATH THE RIGHT TO REST AS HE WILLETH.

"MAN HATH THE RIGHT TO LOVE AS HE WILLETH, WHERE, WHEN, AND WHOM HE WILLETH.

"MAN HATH THE RIGHT TO KILL THOSE WHO WOULD THWART THESE RIGHTS."

4

"But this is anarchy!" Enson Sermander exclaimed. "It is a declaration of war against everything we know as civilization!"

"Exactly," Elsie said.

The picture in the camera-eye wheeled as the saucer banked, whirled heavenward toward its niche in the belly of the mother ship.

The Obsidians were on their own.

"Freely adapted from Aleister Crowley," Howell observed. He bent to lap at his drink. "And omitting—against my specific advice—the Nonaggression Principle, on the grounds that the Obsidians need to develop *that* for themselves."

"*You animals!*" the lieutenant cried. He dropped his cup, jumped from his chair. He stood rigid, his fists clenched at his sides. "You are nothing but criminals! I have watched! I know what you are doing! I see the revolts you are preparing to foment upon the governments of innocent nations! No wonder you have no captain—you probably murdered him in his—"

Howell yawned. "Well, at least he didn't say 'innocent governments.'"

"You're wrong, Lieutenant, we do have a captain." It was Koko speaking. "More of a manager, really. After all, this ship is a complex enterprise that she supervises on behalf of its owners. In some senses, they are everyone and anyone, here and there, on or off the ship. *TPM* is a corporation and the property of a corporation, actually run by the scientific staff who determine her course and—"

"The captain, a female!" The wounded disbelief was plain again in his voice.

"And a gorilla—me. It's a family illness. The uncle who raised me was the last President the North American Confederacy ever had."

13
The Purple Heart Approach

"Ungh!"

The front snap-kick was slow, aimed at my solar plexus. I swiveled my hips slightly, took the arch of Sermander's right foot on my elbow. Risky, but an effective maneuver when it works.

Hopping furiously on his left foot while cradling the insulted right, the lieutenant let a single tear of agony escape from beneath each eyelid. "Corporal O'Thraight! This is supposed to be practice!" He was so short of breath he could hardly get the words out.

I shook my head to clear away the angry fog. "Sorry. Guess I got a little too enthusiastic."

Taking deep breaths, I tried to relax, realizing I was taking out my frustration on the wrong person. It was idiocy to imagine that Lucille—

Baaapp!!

Knuckles seemed to come from nowhere, smashing the

side of my head above the right ear. I stumbled back, raising my guard as he whirled for a second turning back-fist. It glanced harmlessly along the diagonal of my fore-arm.

"Let that be a lesson, Corporal,". my superior snig-gered. He leaned on one of the hip-high mushroom protuberances extruded at random to make practice more demanding. "Proficiency is a virtue, but no substitute for remembering one's place. You grow lax in this undisci-plined environment—you will thank me for this once we return to Vespucci."

"No, sir."

Damn her, anyway.

"What is that, Corporal?"

"I mean, yes, sir." Threading around the obstructions, we stepped off the mat, heading across the gymnasium toward the showers. The place was like an aircraft hangar, dozens of others sparring, a complement for Sodde Lydfe in heavy desert gear. Lights flashed at random intervals, from random angles, simulating the confusion of combat amidst unpredictable explosions, blasts of recorded noise. Many here were practicing blindfolded, perhaps for night operations.

I weighed the advisability of following their example. Sudden flight might bring about the need at any time. I had begun to examine everything from a single viewpoint: how can this help us get home?

Apparently, the lieutenant had come to much the same conclusion. We stepped through a series of membranous cleansing-curtains on the way to the unnecessary but re-freshing showers. A hundred private cubicle doors faced us on the other side of the curtains. There was no familiar locker-room smell.

Sermander stopped short of the shower cabinets.

"I have been looking for a way off-ship," he stated flatly, in a half whisper. "All auxiliaries are privately owned, if you can credit that. What is more, they are residences, occupied continuously, jealously defended."

I could not think of anything I had seen that was not.
I said so.

"Er, yes," he answered in bad humor. "More to the
point, Corporal, none are for hire at any price *we* can
afford. Now, as I have told you, checking possible alternatives, I have determined, although not in any mortally
comprehensible terms, that there is no other point of vul-
nerability, no engine room, for example, that we might
occupy, threaten to destroy—"

"Nor even any *engines*." I was repeating something
Owen Rogers had told me earlier that morning. I was not
sure whether I believed it.

"Nor any engines. Corporal, if you are taking measures
of your own—"

"I—"

"No, do not tell me. If necessary, make your own way
back to Vespucci with what we know. In the meantime,
take comfort that I, too, am working toward our libera-
tion, the eventual salvation of our beloved planet."

"Sir?"

"I have arranged an appointment with the Chief Praxeologist, EdWina Olson-Bear. You will accompany me.
I have every confidence that subsequent, er . . . meetings
will afford me opportunity to learn *something* of use." He
leered suggestively. "If rumor is correct, considerably
more may be accomplished."

I had not the faintest idea what he was talking about,
but he was the lieutenant. "Yes, sir." We went to our
separate cubicles, agreeing to meet afterward.

My head still hurt when I was through in the shower.

2

Plastic 8-mm cartridges squeezed from the permeable
face of the fabricator into the covered hopper.

"One molecule at a time," Owen Rogers observed proprietarily. "If you could see inside, they start as a faint triangular—pardon me, trochoidal—streak in the matrix, building up in three dimensions, maintaining a perfect cross-section until closure at the end of the cartridge."

"But how does it work?"

"There are a hundred some-odd naturally occurring elements," said the gunsmith. "I lost track somewhere of exactly how many. From the dawn of time, mindkind has been limited to permutations and combinations of those to create his entire material civilization."

Some of the physics, I thought to myself, everybody said I needed. So be it, I would learn what I could, for the immediate project I had in mind, also out of longer-range considerations.

"Just as protons, electrons, and neutrons are the building blocks of atoms, *quarks* are the building blocks of the atomic nucleus. Electrons fill orbital positions around it, determining the chemical nature of any given element."

"I understand. What has this to do with your fabricator?"

"Everything. You see, we manipulate electron shells by—"

"Excuse me, Rog, but is this thing good for making ammunition only, or other things, as well?"

He blinked at the subject change. "Within limits. Like what?"

I had thought this through carefully, my first step in getting out of Confederate jurisdiction—with something to show for the adventure. Now, however, it began to feel like a betrayal of the generous people who—

—you cannot take a hamlet without breaking heads.

"Well...drawing, Rog. Paper to draw upon, something to draw with. I have noticed artists aboard, their sketches hang in meeting places, restaurants. I did some of that at home. I would like to take it up again."

There were no photographs aboard *Tom Paine Maru*, no writing, but there *were* paintings, other handicrafted graphics. It made me wonder. I reasoned that the only difference between the media was the intervention of the artist himself—but that was as far as I had gotten. Instead of simply wondering, instead of asking stupid questions, this time I had formed a plan on the basis of this peculiar knowledge. I was following it now.

I needed to make notes.

More, I needed to do it secretly. Each minute, I was being exposed to information of incredible value to my poverty-stricken culture. It was the very reason they would not let us go. This simply gave me greater impetus to escape. Lucille had been right: I was rapidly becoming an accomplished sociopath. From here on it would be a race: carrying out my self-imposed mission before the total disintegration of my character.

A long pause: "So that's it, is it? I warned Couper about this, too. Sorry, Whitey, I can't do it."

Shock: I had been anticipated. There were places on Vespucci one could not take a camera or recorder (plus the fact such devices were stricly licensed). Now I was forbidden to write down what I was learning. To be expected, nevertheless, the surprise was devastating.

Rogers went on without me: "I'm not set up to do obsolete organics. Shucks, any industrial-scale fabricator could turn out whatever you need, with little purple flags on every seventeenth item, if you ordered it. Being from a mass-production culture, you don't realize the difference that makes. But there are limits. You'd want wood or rag paper, and, let's see: graphite, clay, cedar, rubber—or were you planning to use ink?"

"What?"

"Guess I could order the software. But look, would plastic do, a nice matte that could hold an impression? And a smart pen to alter its molecular structure. We could make it erasable, even manage color, all from this little machine. What do you say?"

What I did *not* say was that I was confused. I simply thanked him profusely, agreed to stop by later to pick up what his wonderful machine created.

3

It was more like a real classroom than anything I had seen so far.

Forty assorted beings, at desks of appropriate design, sat in a room brightly decorated with paintings of what I assumed were scenes—cities, wildernesses—on various planets the starship had visited. Up front, a lecturer spoke on a definite topic in a linear manner. If you could ignore the pair of glass-fronted walls at the back, behind which various marine life witnessed the proceedings, it almost felt like home.

There was even something resembling a blackboard.

"We have many names and historical examples for each of the three possible political systems," stated the instructor, human, female, blonde, with a family resemblance to Lucille Olson-Bear.

"Each has revealing qualities." She turned: on the surface behind her, she sketched a triangle with her finger, pointed end up, indicating the lower right corner.

"All forms of authoritarianism are paternalistic in nature, usually oppressively religious, with emphasis on law, order, and swift, sure punishment for the miscreant. Majoritarianism, on the other hand—"

She swept to the lower left corner. "—is characteristically maternal, concerned with social welfare, the survival, above all, of the productively unfit at the expense of everybody else. Each system represents an essentially infantile 'adjustment' to cultural and economic reality preventing further development, either in the individual or society—a primary cause of the cyclic rise and fall we observe among the Kilroys."

Now she pointed toward the apex. "Individualism is *adult* in character, representing self-imposed responsibility, steady growth, individual and cultural maturity."

I watched the lieutenant watching EdWina Olson-Bear,

then caught G. Howell Nahautl watching me. Having brought us here on the pretext of introducing us to the praxeologist, I was certain the coyote was more interested in our reaction to the lecture than in any introductions he intended making. My thought was that a "paternalistic," disciplined society, or a "maternalistic" one taking care of its helpless in a responsible manner (both of which were the practice on Vespucci), represented greater maturity than the lawless hedonism advocated by Confederates, who often struck me as self-indulgently childish.

Striding across the room, she laid a hand alongside a representation of a mountain whose rocky face had been carved into the likenesses of men. "Thanks to the 'Rushmore Four'—Thomas Paine, Albert Gallatin, Thomas Jefferson, and Lysander Spooner—the North American revolution became worldwide. Peace, prosperity, and progress all grew from the concept of absolute individual rights, under a system of unanimous consent.

"Given the tragedy of human evolution—that, as defense against the agony of birth, the dangerous mechanism of *repression* developed, functioning both in mother and child, sabotaging while it soothed, like any powerful analgesic—that revolution looks more and more like a miracle."

I stirred uncomfortably in my comfortable seat. Despite the lecture, this was a class on neither history nor biology. The lieutenant was here to take advantage of an introduction wangled from Howell, I, as protective coloration—but also for a reason of my own. Only peripherally aware of the Obsidian operation until it was practically over with, now I was determined to watch what happened on the next stop closely. On a planet unattractively called Hoand, the warrior-praxeologists of *Tom Paine Maru* intended to pursue a method different from the one they employed on the previous world.

This session was supposed to explain it.

EdWina Olson-Bear went on to talk about three Hoandian nation-states. Uxos was a mass society where everything was done by the collective, for the collective, in the name of the collective; Obohalu, somewhat like the old Vespuccian Republic, made pretense at being a free country, was the most technologically progressive, likely the most powerful, but was currently on a steep decline; Houtty lacked the enormous regimented masses of Uxos, yet possessed much the same potential for mass destruction as Obohalu. All were on the verge of interplanetary travel, each at constant cold war with the other two, slowing progress, draining productivity. According to the lecture, in politics—unlike geometry or architecture—the triangle was the least stable of all forms. Something had to give, probably explosively, with lingering radiation.

I listened through detailed analysis of all three cultures, the teacher's questions, directed at students, regarding how things had gotten to be that way on Hoand, what could be done to change them.

Time passed.

"That will do for today," she said at last. "Be sure to review Wilson's *An Enemy of the State* and Kropotkin's *My Life with Pete*. You'll be asked to make comparisons among Hoand, Earth, and Sodde Lydfe, specifically Podfet, Nazi Germany, Stalinist Russia, and Houtty, as opposed to Great Foddu, England, Denmark, and Obohalu. Unlike Hoand, where a relative balance of terror has been achieved, the Sodde Lydfans are, after a long conventional war, about to use nuclear weapons. Employing proper praxeological notation, I want you to tell me why."

After a few informal questions about the next day's class assignment, the room emptied itself into the corridors. Through the walls, I could see the porpoises swim away.

4

"It's a break in my routine, Lientenant." EdWina nodded over her coffee cup. "I started as a lecturer, I like to stay in practice." Politely disguised annoyance tinged EdWina Olson-Bear's voice. Embarrassed, I could not have said exactly why. It had not been *my* stupid question.

The bizarre restaurant, not far from EdWina's classroom, was filled with the usual colorful, bewildering mixture of species, many wearing costumes I now recognized as native to Hoand or appropriate to Sodde Lydfe. An area large as the gymnasium had been filled, floor to ceiling, with man-high transparent plastic tubing, little bubble-alcoves every few meters for tables, the whole thing darkly lit by candles twinkling in their hundreds, refracted by the plastic, reflected from its twisted, curving walls. Howell called the place "Mr. Meep's In The Belly Of The Whale," a new establishment replacing one that, in the coyote's opinion, had been even stranger. The proprietor, apparently a friend of his, conducted us through the labyrinth. The chimpanzee-entrepreneur wore an ankle-length striped robe, a long false beard. Howell said the language he addressed us in was Yiddish.

Seen up close, EdWina was pleasant rather than pretty, with hazel eyes, a broad intelligent forehead, an upturned nose that, despite the description, was quite unlike her sister's. Where her sister was almost inhumanly slender without being skinny or fragile-looking, EdWina was rounded without being plump.

"After the accident, I replaced Lucille in praxeology." She looked from me, to the lieutenant, suppressed a scowl, smiled at the coyote. Candlelight at this time of day was a strange experience. Mr. Meep, it seemed, also proprietor of the *last* restaurant in this location, *specialized* in strange experiences. "Each of us, in turn, was the youngest Chief ever—"

"Accident?" I repeated.

Her glance at Howell stopped being a smile.

"They weren't told," The Coyote's electronic voice reflected oddly from the curved plastic wall. He turned to me. "During an initial planetary survey, some years ago, Lucille was 'killed'—injured so badly she could not be immediately reanimated. Yes, even by *our* medical technology, Whitey. Her remains were kept in stasis."

"Stasis?" Sermander paused to address Howell during a so-far uninterrupted campaign of patronizing glances toward the praxeologist. "Is that not the condition I—"

The coyote nodded, an oddly human gesture. "A state of suspension quite unlike refrigeration, sleep, or anything else you are familiar with, occurring at the subatomic—"

"Interesting," the lieutenant interrupted boredly, "I recall none of it." He rubbed the shoulder that had been nearly severed; I had seen him do this before—on Vespucci, calling modest attention to a wound suffered in the Final War—always in the presence of women. I privately dubbed it the Purple Heart Approach. "From the Scavian attack to my awaking aboard the *Little Tom*. From what the corporal says, it is just as well."

"That's the general idea," said Edwina, "although sometimes—in my sister's case—it doesn't always..."

"But tell me," the lieutenant interrupted a second time. He was getting as bad as the Confederates. "How it is an attractive, accomplished person such as yourself spends all her time amidst dry praxeology, wasting her femininity on graduate seminars more closely resembling military brief—"

EdWina laughed. "Howell, there's rather a good deal you didn't tell them. Lieutenant, what gave you the idea it was a graduate seminar—simply your august presence at it? Didn't you notice the visual aids, the—"

"EdWina," cautioned Howell, "I wouldn't—"

"Sorry. I *would* like to have him in a graduate seminar—as textbook example of the authoritarian personality!" She stopped to laugh again. The lieutenant's face grew purple. "That class is one of my charities, for retarded dependents and combat-damaged personnel. Brain injuries, mostly."

Before anyone could think of anything to say, the food arrived.

5

"Aborigines? Why, they're the original native inhabitants of Australia. Still are, for that matter. How'd something like that come up in idle conversation?"

Owen Rogers had brought me more than "paper" to take notes on. He'd arrived at my quarters that evening with a freshly fabricated notebook, the "pencil" he had promised, a load of ammunition I did not really need—it had merely been a pretext for the other items.

Also a mandolar.

If, indeed, there was no such thing as a free lunch, I was running up quite a tab.

I fingered the fret-buttons, idly fiddled with the vane adjustments. "Howell was telling me something about them I did not altogether understand, something about their not distinguishing, philosophically, time from space. What little I know about physics . . . well, on Vespucci, they are saying there *is* no such distinction. It is supposed to be the latest thing."

Rogers grinned. "That sort of depends on the context you're stuck with. What Howell meant, I suspect, is that the aborigines confused one with the other in an inappropriate context. They thought that, if you were from far away, you were also from the distant past. When the first explorers arrived in Australia, the aborigines thought the intruders were their own ancestors."

"That is almost an appropriate view, over interstellar distances, is it not?"

"Whitey, you don't know the half of it. But Howell was working toward a point. There are a number of different dimensions—directions—in the physical universe; there's back and forth, there's up and down, and there's side to side. Those are the three dimensions of space. There's also back and forth in time, the distance from the past to the future, with the present presumably somewhere in between."

"That seems simple enough."

"Yeah? Well, there's also side to side, timewise—"

"So I have been being told. Something about different history lines, different—"

"Probability. Look: no one knew about statistical probability—that's another way of looking at this sideways dimension—before Blaise Pascal. He was a mathematician, philosopher, and a gambler before he got religion, back in the—well, maybe four hundred years ago. It took even longer before anyone realized the importance of probability, that time is not only infinite *lengthwise*—the dimension of 'duration'—but *sideways*—in the dimension of probability, as well."

"What do you mean, infinite?"

"That there is an infinite number of universes, that every event which can happen in a number of different ways actually occurs every different way it *can* happen. That every human choice is actually made every way it *can* be made."

"Owen, there is something else I have to ask you."

The praxeologist stopped, blinked. "What's that, Whitey?"

"Well, when scientists dig in the sands of my home planet, they occasionally run across the remains of four-legged creatures very much like Howell. Apparently they were imported when our ancestors arrived on Vespucci, for food or for some other purpose. But they were obviously not intelligent. They were domestic animals of some kind, they lacked—as Howell must—the cranial capacity to *be* intelligent creatures. Yet Howell has mentioned several times in passing that he has 'circuits,' he not only never forgets anything, he seems to remember more than anyone else I have met on this ship—no offense intended, I mean." I flushed with embarrassment.

"None taken. And you're right, Howell began life as

a four-legged animal, not even a domestic one. He comes from a species of wild prairie rovers. But he's also different in that he carries several thousand megabytes of electronic supplementation—data storage and retrieval, speed and capacity boosters—attached to the surface of his brain. In a sense he's half dog and half robot. He'll gladly tell you all about it if you ask him. He's rather like the Patchwork Girl's glass cat in that regard—be prepared to stand around listening for several hours."

"Oh." It had been much as I expected. Trouble was, it led to a question I dare *not* ask, of Rogers, or of anyone else aboard this ship. I had figured Howell out myself, then made a leap: no one ever had to look up anything here, they all knew, at any moment, precisely what time it was, when the next auxiliary was arriving, what the temperature was, what the person in the next room was thinking. Were they *all* like Howell, with electronic brain implants, the slaves of some giant master computer?

They certainly believed the same things, acted cooperatively, accomplished great works, like *Tom Paine Maru* herself, without any visible institution to indoctrinate, direct, or coordinate their efforts. They all acted as if they were under the direction of a wise, powerful government somewhere. Trouble was, they did not have one.

Impossible!

The Patchwork Girl's glass cat?

14

Operation Klaatu

Hanging in the middle of the darkened room, I hooked my left arm underneath my right knee, folded myself into a sitting position. Holding the notebook against my naked thigh with the left hand, I twisted the business end of Rogers' pencil until it shed a soft light on the plastic pages:

Notes from the Asperance *Expedition*
Armorer/Corporal YD-038 recording

Page One:
Along the infinite dimension of "probability" are universes *existing side by side ("coextant" is the expression used aboard the* Tom Paine Maru*) in which, for example, the Big Bang never happened.*
Or happened differently.
Or where somebody in Earthian history named Albert Gallatin talked them out of the Whiskey Rebellion, instead of leading it to the anarchistic vic-

tory which Confederates hail as the beginning of their era.

The three principal developments that determine the history of that era, the 3rd Century A.L., *as they call it, were the perfection of fusion power production, improvements in the area of space travel, the discovery of parallel realities.*

While searching for a faster-than-light stardrive, Dora Jayne Thorens, with her partner, Ooloorie Eckickeck P'wheet (I render that last name phonetically as best I can—I will discuss the lack of written language among the Confederates later), stumbled upon another *Earth where their Rebellion had been lost, where the state grew instead of withering.*

The examples above are not chosen arbitrarily: the first, a somehow different beginning for the universe, made what they call the "Malaise Catastrophe" possible. The reference is obscure, yet this, almost as much as the Whiskey Rebellion, seems to be responsible for everything the Confederacy is doing now. It is the reason these enormous ships are exploring the galaxy. It forms the basis for their attitude toward "Kilroys."

The second produced the world we are standing in.

Inferences are impossible to resist. There are other universes where I was never forced to give up music, where I never met Eleva, where I never volunteered for the Asperance, *where I gave up in that dungeon on Sca, where I—*

I stopped, twisted the end of the pencil Rogers had given me to its ERASE mode, carefully rubbed out the last paragraph I had written. In its place, I wrote:

Each choice produces a new clutch of universes, entirely complete, perhaps differing only by a single

*human decision. According to Rogers (also others
I have begun talking to on this subject), this is not
a religious notion, but scientifically proven fact.*

*I have had many reasons in my life for feeling
insignificant, inefficacious. Yet, if each choice I
make, no matter how trivial, creates an entirely new
universe—an entirely new set of universes, what
does that say about the power of the human mind?
Any human mind?*

Even mine?

I stopped writing once again. Belatedly, it had occurred
to me that, if I were successful in my self-appointed spying
against the Confederates, it might advance me in rank,
help my chances with Eleva.

Now, more than ever, I must get home!

Oddly, that self-serving thought made me feel quite
guilty toward a dozen people at once. As time passed,
my friend, my nominal superior, Enson Sermander, looked
increasingly like . . . well, a rather stupid, boring individual in contrast to those I was meeting here. Yet he was
my lieutenant, lawful representative of the planet I had
been born on—which was, itself, looking a little stupidly
boring to me. As for Eleva—

A surge of guilt swept through me again, along with
the thought that a woman who needs something to stir
her like the promotion I aspired to does not deserve to
be stirred. I stifled the thought—immediately felt guilty
for repressing it, repression being the root of all evil to
my new-found friends.

Can you feel guilty about feeling guilty?

I had asked Howell about that. His answer had been
an enigmatic "Only in southern California."

"Writing in your little diary again?"

I jumped.

In free fall, this accomplished a slow rotation about
my own center of mass. Lucille's voice was sharp as she

reentered the room. Regaining proper attitude, along with
the remnants of my dignity, I irritably folded the notebook, tucked the pencil through its loop, tangled both in
the mesh along the wall I had kicked myself into.

She brushed at her freshly washed hair. "Don't worry,
Corporal-baby, I wouldn't peek if you paid me."

"I do not worry about that, Lucille." I looked around
for my suit. "I only worry whether I can get down my
impressions in a way that will make sense of them."

She could not know that the notebook was a weapon
for defense of my civilization. I would wrap up my dis-
sertation on metaphysical philosophy as soon as I had
provided enough background for Vespuccian Intelligence,
then begin on technological details. This might be useful
to our scientists even if I did not understand them myself.

"Okay, write *this* in your book."

The walls cleared. We were no longer in a warm cavern, but the upper section of a scoutship exactly like the
first I had ever ridden. Outside, stars—real stars—shone
as hard bright chips. The pearlescent disk of *Tom Paine
Maru* appeared like an oddly shaped moon. The brightest
object was the sun of Hoand, illuminating a half-dozen
planets, most of them out of sight, half a hundred natural
satellites. The planet itself hung before us, swirled white-
green marble with three pockmarked companions.

"Operation Klaatu" was about to begin.

Despite my annoyance, Lucille was another person I
felt guilty toward, possibly her more than anybody. We
were aboard a borrowed auxiliary, *John Thomas Maru*,
following the giant interstellar vessel that served as its
base. This was supposed to be a holiday excursion. She
had been working hard. Her compatriots had been working my head hard. It was time for a break.

It turned out to be another education, of sorts.

I had wondered what love in free fall would be like.
Aboard the *Asperance*, there had been no opportunity
(nor the room). Now I was finding out, as often as the
two of us could manage. It is messy, requires greater

energy than I expected, plus a modicum of equipment, but it is interesting, relaxing once you get used to it, oddly satisfying.

As usual, Lucille was irked with me. This time though she would never admit it, I had not tired as soon as she expected. She had that effect. We were an awkwardly met couple, our lovemaking invariably violent. Each seemed to have something the other needed powerfully. Almost against our wills, we had wound up together again, aboard this little ship. When it went well with us, I saw things more objectively, measured them less in terms of duty, more by what they had always demanded from me without offering any reward. I thought uncharitably about the lieutenant, even found myself considering that Eleva might be something of an—the proctological reference Lucille used we do not employ much in polite company on Vespucci.

She put her hair up now, snugging it into the hood of her suit—more as a safety precaution, since we would be docking with the mother vessel in the usual way. With her, however, this seemed to serve as punctuation, delineating business from pleasure, her ordinary toughness from the rare moments of softness that baffled me more than her habitual combat posture.

"I have to get back to the ship. There's a conference in an hour, over plans to discredit prowar politicians in Great Foddu. It's going to be a delicate job. War is always so popular with—"

I shook my head.

I threw up my hands. "Political lectures in bed, again."

"*After* bed; you started this one, don't complain. Look, stupid: there are three basic forms of majoritarianism, all of them represented on Sodde Lydfe: socialism, fascism, democracy. Understand that fascism is a majoritarian form—it relies as heavily on popular support as any democracy, look at the crowd scenes it's so fond of— and that democracy is just as rottenly dictatorial as the other two. Should half a dozen individuals tell a seventh what to do, just because they could beat him up if they wanted?"

This was insane. "Is voting not better than beating people up? Anyway, people need taking care of. Howell says your system is based on avarice."

She snorted with contempt. "A free market feeds more people more equitably than any other system. It's the only system capable of feeding nonproductive morons like you, and that's probably its undoing—you come to expect it, as a right. That it accomplishes this as a by-product of greed is irrelevant—unless you care more about motivations than results!"

Now she had raised her voice, centimeters from my face. Hers was flushed; fire crept up my cheeks, as well. Howell had told me something like this, more quietly. It was difficult, right enough, separating results from motivations. Right now, I was having trouble the other way around.

"Moron?" I asked at the top of my lungs, wishing she would just go back to being nice. "Stupid?"

"Moron! Stupid! And a military-industrial parasite on top of that!"

I had never hit a woman before. The slap echoed through the ship—outside, we were docking, though I did not consciously notice at the time—as did my voice a second later when she let me have a small, high-velocity fist in the pit of the stomach.

We stood, toe to toe, panting, speechless. Curiously, desire for her raced through my system. I could see it on her face, too, along with the embarrassment such spiritual nakedness left in its wake.

"All right"—she broke the spell—"that settles our account. Next time we run into one another, don't bother to speak. You'll never hear another word from me."

The floor rose beneath us, carrying us into the *Tom Paine Maru.*

2

Sermander was not home when I went looking. I could not have said exactly why I did it, except that, suddenly, I felt I had misjudged him. It was always like this: when things were not going well with Lucille, I grew homesick, overly forgiving, overcome by nostalgia. I was ashamed of letting interest in a woman distract me from loyalty to friends, duty to country. Returning to my stateroom, I found him waiting in the corridor.

"Corporal!" It was a hoarse noise, trying to be a shouted whisper, a whispered shout, all at once. He pranced nervously, wrung his hands, spread them, shook them, went back to wringing them as I approached.

"I have been looking all over for you! I have finally discovered the *truth* about this ship, the most startling information you possibly—"

"Sir?" Somehow, his face was pale, while the veins stood out on his forehead as if he were about to have a stroke.

"Let us go inside . . ." he said, craning his neck to make sure we were not being overheard, ". . . where there is less chance of being spied upon."

I could have told him there was *more* chance, but he was the lieutenant. I was suddenly tired, wanted to lie down. Entering, he threw himself on the bed, wiped a hand across his forehead. I sat in a chair, listening through depression.

"I have been speaking with that Nahuatl . . . person. You know him—do you think he is inclined to lie?"

"I think he is less inclined to lie than anybody else aboard this ship. Why?"

"Because if he tells the truth, we are in deep trouble. Do you know that he is half computer? He possesses a sophisticated implant within his skull—or it possesses him—which provides most of his intellect. We are speaking to a *device* when we are speaking to him, rather than an intelligent organism."

"Well, sir, I—"

"The truth is they are *all* like that! Nothing but walking computers, whales, chimpanzees, gorillas—Corporal, even human beings! Controlled by computers stitched in amongst their very brains! We are doomed!"

"Sir?" I was not feeling very articulate all of a sudden.

"I was offered hasty explanation by the creature, that *everybody* carries an independent multigigabyte computer in his head, that there *is* no master machine, no overall program. Laughable! What society would miss such a chance for control?"

"On the other hand, would the Confederates, with their fanatic devotion to individual liberty, tolerate such a thing? I find this highly confusing, sir."

"Not at all. Their desire for freedom, their very freedom itself, is an illusion fostered to maintain tranquility. Now that I know their secret—now that *we* know—they are certain to do us in! This society must have been taken over by artificial intelligence during a period not much greater advanced than our own—they are prisoners of their own *machines*! They will kill us before we let their secret out, I know it!"

3

The door said, "Corporal O'Thraight?"

I put my notebook away. The lieutenant had departed on some unnamed errand. As the door cleared, I saw EdWina Olson-Bear standing outside, her suit a plain, pale green. Noticing something in my movements that told her I had been busy, she began, "I'm sorry to disturb you—"

"That is all right, I was just finishing . . . come in, er—" I gestured clumsily, embarrassed by not knowing how to address her.

I was turning out to be a lousy spy.

She leaned on the frame. "EdWina. I've come to ask

if you want to see the first of our operations on Hoand. It'll only be another..." She rolled her eyes back, looked at me again. "...twenty-three minutes. We've just time to get there."

"Where?"

"You'll see—something I want to watch in person, rather than by 'Com, a pet project of mine. Hoand has been steeped in war for three thousand years. There's only one way to end it—all the organizing and demonstrating in the world never did a lick of good as long as taxation and conscription—"

"People like war." I defended cynicism grown hard inside me. "It is instinctive with them."

"Nonsense. War is the health of the state and nobody else. Put an end to the machinery of war—government—and you put an end to war. Simple, but most Kilroys are blind to it because, as much as they desire peace, they want the state around for other reasons."

I strapped on my gunbelt, joined her in the hall. After a transport patch, we were crossing a medium-sized park when the sky went abruptly from blue to starry black.

EdWina stopped me. "This isn't what I meant, but it'll be quite a show. Stay a moment, we'll watch it."

Hoand's outermost satellite was a worthless cinder several hundred klicks in diameter, reminiscent of everything that circled the sun of Vespucci.

Including Vespucci.

The Hoandians had reached their other moons via clumsy rockets, planted flags, made speeches, returned home when air or courage ran out. They had not yet come this far. Markers on the sky display showed where camera-landers sat in meteoric dust, one or two still operating. An orbiter relayed signals to the planet, five or six light-seconds away.

Motion in the park came to a halt. Confederates were standing around, sitting on benches, going places, as we were, or simply lying in the grass became statues as Koko's amplified voice was heard throughout the ship.

"Five, four, three, two, one, commence firing!"

From the broad underside of the mighty vessel came a blast twelve kilometers in diameter, so intense it looked like pieces could be cut off to build new starships. On the surface, an explosion to end explosions endowed that barren sphere, temporarily, with an atmosphere. Smoke cleared into the airless void, revealing a churning lava pool twice the size of *Tom Paine Maru*.

The beam winked off. People breathed again. There was a pause, then suddenly, a cheer went up, thundering through the ship, buffeting my ears.

"We'll give them an hour," said EdWina, resuming purposeful stride, "to hear from their tame scientists. This spot isn't visible from the planet. You need access to telemetered data."

I wanted badly to ask about her sister—*anything* to help me understand. I did not know how to begin. Howell had said Lucille's period of stasis had been intermittent, interrupted frequently for experimental treatment. Complete "regeneration"—whatever the tantalizing phrase meant—had been prevented for years by a genetic disorder inherited from her father. Finally cured, she emerged from her nightmarish ordeal a changed personality.

I started to speak, but we entered a room at the edge of the park. Koko, Howell, a few others—difficult to tell, as half the place was darkened. Lucille was there. The other half, separated from us by a transparency, contained four comfortable chairs, one occupied by Geoffrey Couper, freshly shaven from the blunt prow of his massive chin to the polished crest of his cranium.

The big man's smartsuit was adjusted to metallic reflectivity, the collar turned high, fastened in a crisp, military appearance—I wondered whether Lucille ever criticized *him*—on his feet were matching silvery boots. A pair of silver gauntlets rested in his lap. He turned toward the partitions, which EdWina said was a mirror on his side. "You people about ready?"

A pause I thought I was beginning to understand, then

"Fifteen seconds, Geoff," Koko said. "They're having trouble lining up on the premier."

"Okay. Sure wish I could have a smoke, but it would spoil the effect."

Across the room, I caught Lucille's eye. She glared at her sister, then gave me a rueful, appealing look. I was never going to figure the woman out.

A warning ping. Broach openings appeared over the unoccupied chairs, widened, deposited three human figures in varying attitudes of astonishment.

The first was neatly dressed for business, like Couper, a big man, fork in hand, chewing something. He looked up, his eyes widened. He looked at the fork in his hand, changed his grip to make it a weapon. Then glanced at Couper, whose rig included a plasma pistol, laid the fork on the arm of the chair.

At the same instant, there was a shout as a fat man in pajamas awoke in a sitting position in the next chair. He rubbed his eyes, snarled in a language I could not understand, started to get up. He could not—the chair was holding him fast—he slumped, staring about like a trapped animal. He did not notice Couper. He had eyes only for the man in the business suit.

"Get those translators on line, *stat!*" Couper barked. In the back of the darkened half of the room, someone scurried to comply.

The third man—the Premier of Uxos, my companion told me—was naked, a roll of toilet paper in his hand, the most surprised expression of the three upon his face. Couper tossed him a blanket, waited for them all to overcome their astonishment enough to listen.

"What we have here," Couper lectured, as he waited, to an unseen audience behind the transparency, "are the three most powerful individuals on the planet Hoand. Not terribly prepossessing, are they?" At mention of the planet's name, apparently the only word they understood, all three looked up.

EdWina whispered, "You're about to see what we call

the old Galactic Police gag. I wish he'd stop clowning, he could mess up the whole—"

"Greetings," Couper said suddenly, "from the Galactic Confederacy. As you have noticed, my speech is being translated into each of your languages. I need not introduce you to one another, nor apologize for the abruptness of our summons: the continued existence of your world hinges upon this event."

"What is the meaning of this outrage?" demanded the blanket-covered premier. The head of Obohalu, the fellow in pajamas, nodded belligerent agreement with his erstwhile enemy, glaring now at Couper.

When the others had finished, the Houttian chancellor said quietly, "I would like very much to know how this was done. The lunar explosion was spectacular, yet comprehensible. This, however, is magnificent. Will you tell me?"

"In due course, sir. That was but the smallest fraction of our available powers. But for now, we have other matters to discuss. Are you prepared?"

"Provided the premier and the president are likewise prepared."

"Gentlemen? We are perfectly willing to confer with members of your opposition, if necessary. Or go directly to the public."

More grudging assent I have not seen concentrated in a single room before or since. The chancellor alone seemed collected, the only sign he was alive, an occasional blink of the cool gray eyes.

"Very well: your planet, while well within our boundaries, was only recently discovered to be inhabited. I welcome you into the Confederacy, and advise that you are in violation—unknowingly, I am sure—of certain of its statutes." He pointed to a stack beside his knee, three massively thick aluminum-bound books, the first I had seen aboard the ship. "This must be repaired. These step-by-step instructions, carefully tailored for your individual nations, tell how to begin . . ."

15

Accountants
of the Soul

BLAAAMM!!

The Dardick bucked in my hand. The repulsive smelly thing attacking me disintegrated, but another one was right behind, its fangs dripping saliva.

BLAM! BLAM! BLAM! the rotor whirled; ivory-colored tround casings littered the ground at my feet. Claws extended, the monster lumbered closer, closer...

"Too bad, Whitey," a disembodied voice said. *"That one ate you."*

How had I gotten into *this* mess?

2

Arguing with Lucille, of course.

Yes, I was back with Lucille by that evening. We had dinner with Couper's team after the Hoandians were sent home, with promises that if they ran into trouble with

181

political opposition, those folks would be treated to the Galactic Police gag to insure cooperation.

Couper's metal-bound books were checklists, nothing more, for winding government down to total abolition. In one country, the first step was surrendering money production to private banks. In another, opening the arsenals. It hinged on local conditions, the exact steps, their number, the order they must be carried out in, requiring years of calculation by the praxeologists. The people of the planet might never know we had been there. Promising to let word out of an alien invasion had been Couper's best lever.

We made love again that night, the same violent, soul-shattering act that frightened us both, made us irresistible to one another. By morning, we had another screaming fight—this time about how bad conditions had really been on Hoand.

The way the Hoand dignitaries—rulers of an entire planet—had been treated like naughty children disgusted me. Naturally, I made the mistake of saying so.

Before my angry departure, after the short-lived passage-at-arms that preceded it—she hit me first, that time—two additional things happened: we made love again; she dared me to go see things planetside myself.

Which is how I found myself training for Afdiar.

I got back to my own compartment just in time to receive a wall-message from Howell.

The coyote's fur bristled in the display. "Whitey, get here quickly as you can. The lieutenant's quarters. He's collapsed—brain embolism, they're telling me—comatose. Unless you act immediately, he'll be dead in twenty minutes!"

3

Since I was nearest of kin within several hundred light-years, they wanted my consent before treating the lieutenant. That had been the only emergency. Once I had told them to go ahead, they simply popped him into paratronic stasis until the proper course of therapy could be figured out. Confederates were great for taking time to think things through.

They had the technology for it. Substituting quarks for electrons, they could selectively tailor billions of "elements," trillions of compounds, to suit whatever purpose struck their elaborate fancy. Fundamentally, that was all there was to apparent miracles such as the shower curtains or the selectively permeable floors. But that is a little like saying complicated proteins are all there is to human existence. The future was still unguessable. Already they were looking forward to what they might do with the building blocks of *quarks*!

Meanwhile, Francis Pololo had been in worried attendance upon the lieutenant all morning. Bad treatment on Sca, he had diagnosed; my superior was not a young man to begin with. At least not physiologically. The Healer tried very hard not to be insulting, yet he implied that we Vespuccians knew next to nothing about medicine, about nutrition, about extending human lifespan beyond the expectation of savages. As a consequence, the lieutenant was a much sicker fellow than he needed to be; it was too late now to do anything but attempt to repair the damage.

The gorilla/physician would not guarantee that could be done, fancy technology or not.

Nor was the fallen officer taken to anything resembling an infirmary. They seemed to set great store by being able to take care of him in his own quarters. Standing in the bedroom, over the tubular transparent coffin that housed the sleeping Enson Sermander, trying to make up my mind about something else entirely, I reflected that I had a couple of additional problems regarding the information I was storing up for Vespucci.

First, it was more important than ever that I do it

right—the lieutenant might not make it back to supplement what I was writing down. I had to consider what might be possible if *I* did not make it home, either. Probably nothing, but I felt stupid for not having thought of such a contingency before. My mind had obviously been elsewhere.

Second, everything I tried to set down was inextricably laced with sedition. Yet how was I to tell what lonely little datum might be crucial in the conflict presumably to come? Maybe some of it was garbage. But maybe it could make our generals—even our gunners—just a little smarter . . .

Even Confederate physics, claimed Howell, could arise only from a unique viewpoint he called "Discordian."

Was I qualified to separate technology from politics? I was not. Was anybody else available to attempt it? Would anything useful be left if I were successful? If Howell was right, there would not be. Yet, if I did not try, likely I would wind up stockaded upon returning home—or executed—rather than promoted.

That would not impress Eleva.

But I was stalling. The real burden of Pololo's diagnosis was that, after the stresses of our interstellar journey into barbaric captivity, Enson Sermander had collapsed primarily due to the absence of a cerebral implant to warn anyone about the impending embolism.

He must have the implant now, or remain "frozen" forever.

So where had loyal Corporal O'Thraight been when all this was going on? What had he been doing, instead of looking out for his lieutenant? He had been screwing his brains out with a female demon who did not care whether she herself lived or died, let alone anybody else. Now, if we were ever to get home, I must decide whether I trusted these people. Sermander greatly feared becoming the helpless slave of such "therapy," while the Confederates seemed to take its benign influences for granted.

4

Pololo finished inspecting the stasis cannister, wiped huge hands on his surgical greens, adjusted his wire-rimmed spectacles, extracted a small cigar from a flat plastic can. It had lit itself by the time it reached his lips.

"May he rest in peace—he won't age a nanosecond or change in any way we can measure, as long as the para-tronic field is up. A thousand years from now, he could be just like that."

The gorilla found a chair, dragged it over beside his charge, draped himself on it backward. I stood, hands in pockets, watching the lieutenant's immobile features, his unmoving chest. No mechanical equipment was in sight, the cannister was a simple crystalline cylinder. Nor was Sermander actually frozen: within the field, "tempera-ture" had no meaning. Even the light we were seeing him by was the product of very special manipulation at the subnucleonic level.

A thought struck me. "Lucille spent a long time, sus-pended like this?"

He nodded. "Off and on. I understand her case was pretty hairy, owing to an unexpected genetic twist. Long enough that, when she woke up, her little sister was a good deal older than she was."

For some reason, this touched me, perhaps because birth order can be very important; the tension between the two must have been unbearably complicated by this weird turn of events.

"Can they feel anything, Francis? Do they think while they are sleeping?

The gorilla shrugged. "That would require motion at the molecular and subatomic levels. I've always won-dered, though, if going under and coming back out doesn't have its effects, just as I've always wondered if the moment of death doesn't—for the dying, anyway—stretch into infinity. I've *been* in stasis—part of my medical education, just as I had to spend at least fifty hours in a hospital bed." He shuddered. "Makes you appreciate the things that made hospitals unnecessary. I wouldn't willingly do either again unless it was life and death."

I shuddered, too. If Vespuccian civilization were not to be casually subsumed by these kindly imperialistic destroyers, I must stop worrying about myself, stop fretting over Lucille or anything else. The whole thing was up to me.

Which is why I found it disturbing that, deep inside me, I detected a tiny wish that the son-of-a-bitch would solve everybody's problems by having the decency to die.

I shook my head, rapidly, as if to clear it of these unclean thoughts. Somehow, irrationally perhaps, I knew everything would be all right, if I could only get home!

5

Crawling from the gully, I spit sand, then jacked another loader into the Dardick. Somehow a small stone had worked its way into the footpiece of my smartsuit. Hiding down here had not done me any good; I had already been "killed" twice.

Nearby, a diamond-patterned legless reptile *whirr*ed its deadly frustration. Let it do its evil will; I was too tired to be frightened.

Staying low, I placed my back against a blackened stump, trying in vain to rest. The "sky" was overcast, yet it was very hot. I could not catch my breath. My suit was having trouble keeping up with the sweat pouring off my body. Excepting a few demented birds warbling nearby, not another thing moved on the scorched prairie, grass-covered between sparse clumps of dessicated trees. In the distance, a dust devil managed several turns before evaporating into the heat-shimmering silence.

The voice spoke again, from a resonator taped to my collarbone. It tickled. *"Only fifteen miles to go, Whitey. Better keep the pace, or we'll be here all night—and it gets* dangerous *at night!"*

"Captain Couper," I gasped exhaustedly, "is this really what Afdiar is like?" These were not the only second thoughts I was having: I had actually *volunteered* to assist in the Confederate domination of somebody else's world—

BLAM! BLAM!

Something covered with glistening barbed spikes had tried, in a blurry rush, to pin me to the stump. It lay thrashing in the long grass now, a few centimeters past my trembling toes. In the creature's death throes, the spines squirted vile-smelling liquid—where it fell, the grass began to smolder.

"Careful, Whitey, those things travel in pairs. No, this isn't anything like Afdiar. That isn't too bad a place: no native religion, for example. Afdiar is just preindustrial, has an undiscovered, uninhabited continent. The leading culture is a matriarchy. It rains all the time—consider yourself fortunate you aren't training for Sodde Lydfe, where we're really going to foul the weather up. You want to stop a war, make it harder for enemies to find one another. This is just for practice—or you can consider it a qualification course containing replicas of everything nasty and mean we've ever run across anywhere."

"A simulation?" I panted.

"Your funeral, if you like—that's real poison there. Give it a whiff. That thing would have paralyzed you, dissolved your flesh, and fed your gooey remains to its unborn young by sprinkling Whitey soup over its osmotically precocious eggs."

My eyes focused wearily against the noxious fumes. "What about the holos in the ditch?"

"To make you waste ammunition. Which you did. Get a move on!"

To this day I cannot explain how I got back on my feet, stumbling dully toward the next goal marker. Two freshly loaded pistols or not, I could have been captured alive by a squad of unarmed Vespuccian Young Patriots at that point, junior division, in wheelchairs.

The 'Com patch *was* a simulation, too—of the implants everybody else aboard this ship carried in their heads. Subject to demonstrating what I was made of on this do-or-die survival course (warm lime gelatin, I was discovering), I owed my highly probationary status on the operations team for Afdiar to the fact that I had no implant, nor would I willingly accept one.

It was a paradox. Maybe the lieutenant was right, Confederate freedom was an illusion, their rhetoric a sick joke. Maybe they were telling the truth: there was no central master computer. But it had occurrred to me that maybe it was the aggregate network that ran things, a sort of ultimate electronic democracy. The results would look much the same, the people would never know where "their" ideas were coming from.

The problem was not so much one of being free, but of knowing whether you were at any given moment or not. This made me think of Vespucci, but I shied away from the thought. I had other things to do right now.

Eventually, I finished the fifteen miles—miles are a *lot* longer than kilometers—only getting "killed" a couple of dozen times more. The sign over the gate said YOU ARE LEAVING HARRISON'S KIDDIE SURVIVAL PARK—COME BACK AGAIN. I had not been wearier, dirtier, or groggier since Sca.

Couper was there to meet me at the exit.

"Well, son." He leaned against the archway, pulling a cigarette from his pocket. His suit was camouflaged to match the hell I had just been through, but it was fresh, clean, unmarked. He had been sitting somewhere comfortable—probably with the parents of the other "kiddies"—directing me by remote while enjoying a tall cool drink. "You have an aptitude for massacre—your *own*. What kind of cannon fodder did they train you to *be* on that woebegone planet of yours?"

Oddly, I had not seen another soul in the park. Now children, every size, every shape, every gender, every species, were tramping through the gate, holstering their pistols, slipping outsize daggers into scabbards, their smartsuits scuffed or dusty, but with grimly satisfied expressions on their grimy little faces. Judging from their numbers, I ought to have seen at least a few inside the park. I wondered how much of that had been real, how much holographic illusion.

I planted my behind against the other gatepost, back bent, hands on thighs, trying desperately to blow some oxygen into my lungs.

"I was a musician, sir."

"You shoot like it. And your tactical sense leaves a lot to be desired. One thing I'll say for you, you learn fast—wound up right on the average-line for beginners, even counting early losses. Congratulations, son, today you are a five-year-old. Take fifteen minutes, and we'll crank you back through the course again—it's a little different every time, you know."

I stared helplessly at the waist-high warriors surrounding us. Running sweat still stung my eyes, making it hard to see. "God help me!"

"Somebody'd better, or you're going to wind up with your head sticking out of some Afdiarite hunter's trophy wall. I'd sure like to know how you took care of those troopies back on Sca."

I had been thinking the same thing, myself, all day. "Dumb luck."

"Horse manure, son. You've got a natural talent in there somewhere. We just have to find the right stresses to bring it out again."

"Gee, how can I ever thank you?"

"Think nothing of it, son, my pleasure—say, what's wrong with your suit?" He threw the cigarette aside, closed the distance between us in one long stride.

"Sir?" I said reflexively. Looking down at my left forearm, I saw that the small inset control panel was ablaze with lights. Red lights. They all had fuzzy haloes around them. The repeaters on the right arm were the same.

"Great Albert's ghost, boy, no *wonder* you look like something the government dragged in!"

He seized my arm, began pushing buttons. Abruptly, I began to cool off. My vision cleared. Breathing became easier. My fatigue started slipping away.

"This thing's supposed to *help* you, Corporal, not hinder you. How long's it been like this?"

"I do not know, sir—Coup. I did not notice it."

"You didn't?" He looked at me oddly. "Well, the blamed thing's an antique, probably been on the fritz all morning." He stood a moment, deep in thought, one hand still on my arm. "Guess I'll have to revise my estimate, if you fought your way through that course roasting alive and your body filling up with toxins. Whitey, a smartsuit's supposed to maintain correct temps, cleanse your system continuously, heal wounds, tend to half a hundred other things—but it can't do it right if you don't bother to look at the tell-tales, and it's a whole lot safer if the suit is simply allowed to communicate directly with your body."

My feet had begun swelling, almost at the beginning of the day, without my noticing. Now the pain, the feeling of an impending explosion in them, began ebbing away. My bladder filled, the suit went through its sanitary cycle without prompting.

I felt a hundred years younger. "Another commerical for brain implants?"

"Look, son, this suit you're wearing is half a century old. They hauled it out of mothballs for you, and that's about what it's worth. Like I said, it's your funeral, but I'd consider a plant. Think about your lieutenant. You'd never have to wonder what time it is, or use a calculator, or—"

I looked around at his oddly wordless world. Across from the park exit, a restaurant was filled with gaily chattering individuals—there were a dozen shopfronts in sight—nowhere a single sign or simple advertisement.

"Or see a billboard, or read a book," I answered. Or think for myself. I had been considering very little else. I opened my mouth.

"Nonsense, boy!" Couper interrupted. "I'm reading a book right now." He closed his eyes, recited: "... *night had already fallen. O was naked in her cell, and was waiting for them to come and take her to the refectory. As for her lover, he was dressed, as usual, in a—*" He stopped, reddened, started a cough that turned into a splutter. "Wrong file," he said sheepishly. "How the glitch did Pauline Réage get in there with ... ah, here we are—

"*... The best-explored alternatives pivot on Gallatin's decisions regarding the Rebellion—more correctly, on Jefferson's to include the word 'unanimous' in the Declaration. Outwardly similar, the two worlds are entirely different respecting their inhabitants' view of life ...*

"*Third-century interaction between North America and the United States had noteworthy consequences. Millions of refugees poured into the Confederacy, which began subverting other-world governments. Voltaire Malaise— incredibly, a Confederate native—constructed a 230-ship escape-fleet in 223 A.L., with Hamiltonian coconspirators kidnaping thousands of women for colonial breeding stock, controlled by primitive thought processors ...*"

He stopped. "From the introduction to Grossberg and Hummel's *History of the NeoImperialist party*. Never hurts to brush up on the classics."

Primitive thought processors. "You keep all that inside your head?"

"Just the introduction, which I wrote. You see, I *founded* the NeoImperialist faction of the Gallatinist party, very nearly a century ago. The idea was that government's a disease which nobody has the right to start or spread. We wanted to declare war on governments everywhere, wipe them off the face of the Earth. Don't think even I ever intended we'd be out *here* doing it.

"Just goes to show you: intentions count for nothing in the real world, it's only results that count. There was a fellow in the other universe—the United States—Henry Ford, who invented cheap, mass-produced automobiles and put everybody and his brother-in-law on wheels. He accomplished a lot of good, but the main thing was taking romance out of the front parlor, under the baleful gaze of Daddy Dearest, and putting it in the rumble seat of a Model A, giving sexual Victorianism the deep-six forever. He probably didn't *intend* for that to happen—shucks, he might have been *against* it happening. But it's results that count."

"In other words, the ends justify the means?"

"Non sequitur. Intentions are a third category, entirely separate from means *or* ends. And they usually don't have much at all to do with what eventually happens, anyway. Look at the market, for example. People seeking a profit help others because they inevitably must. Those with an altruistic bent invariably do enormous damage; their focus is on intentions, rather than results, a severe dissociation from reality which other people usually have to pay the consequences for."

I laughed. "You are out here curing governments. Trying to end wars. I have been to lectures on strategy, I have heard the plans for Sodde Lydfe—to pass government codes, other secrets between the two sides so that nothing is a surprise. Why are you doing all that, if not for altruistic motives?"

He started another cigarette, pointed me gently toward the watering hole across the street. "For profit. We figure private individuals are easier to do business with than governments, so we're liberating the former by eliminating the latter."

The idea of a light meal, a cold drink, had sudden irresistible appeal. "That is the *real* mission of *Tom Paine Maru*?"

He grinned, so that I did not know whether to take him seriously or not. "None other."

"I do not believe it." On the other side of the avenue, we entered the crowded restaurant. Approximately a hundred delicious smells hit me all at once. My mouth watered. I looked around for an empty table, paying half attention to the conversation with Couper.

"Then believe this—I just received a bulletin via my implant. The operations team is planning a twenty-mile orientation hike through jungle mud in a solid, typically Afdiarian downpour. They want you to join them in five minutes."

6

"Better have some coffee, Whitey. It hasn't been invented where you're going—it won't grow there, anyway—so you'd better stock up."

I rolled over on one elbow, waking slowly, with the feeling that this was where I had come in. "Sure. Thanks. Just, please, do not light a cigarette before I am in full control of my stomach, will you?" I squeezed my eyes shut, opened them, squeezed them shut again, then shook my head.

EdWina laughed. "I don't smoke, silly. No bad habits at all, except..."

"Except Kilroys. What time is it, anyway?"

"Does it matter? Here's the coffee, what do you want in it?"

I had not seen Lucille for several weeks. Someone told me she was keeping company with another man, perhaps that tall tanned one I had seen her with at the pool that day. Somehow it made me sad at the same time that it made me angry.

"Chocolatl, if it is not too much trouble."

Not that I had much right to feel angry. In the first place, there had been no words between us, no promises, no plans beyond an evening's dinner. After our last terrible fight, I had gotten to know Lucille's sister, attending some of her classes as part of preparation for Afdiar. I did not know what was wrong with her life, but what happened then was a warm but not particularly passionate matter involving mutual misery. I had established one important principle: kissing your girl friend's sister is fully as satisfying as kissing your own.

What I could not figure out is why that discovery made me feel so guilty.

EdWina handed me the cup, climbed back into the bed with her own. "Your mind is elsewhere, Corporal, isn't it? Don't worry, I'm not offended. Sis has the same effect on everybody. She drove off all her old friends after her experience with stasis. She also left praxeology forever, to join Security, of all things—though she's good at it, rising fast."

"Is that so?" I asked. "Well, I have the bruises to prove it." I shook my head, sipped the coffee, very much aware that we were in one lady's bed, discussing another. It did not seem to embarrass EdWina, but it did embarrass me.

"Look, Whitey, deep down, Lucille trusts no one. She won't listen to anyone who could help her to be happier. If you want my professional, praxeological opinion, she drove off any friends incapable of exercising the restraint—or tolerance—demonstrated by Howell and Koko, because she feels she doesn't *deserve* to be happy. She reacts with savage hostility to anyone—including her parents and her sister—who threatens to love her."

I turned, looked at EdWina. "What about Goeff Couper? What is he to her?"

She smiled. "Her new friend, her boss. He keeps a fatherly eye on her—but only from a respectful distance. He's too smart to get mauled."

"I wish to hell I had been, too."

"So do I, Whitey, so do I."

16

Afdiar

Notes from the Asperance *Expedition*
Armorer/Corporal YD-038 recording

Page Thirty-three:
Outline of History, continued. The Voltaire Ma-
laise escape plot was only discovered at the last
moment. Although not fully interrupted, the elec-
tronic slave controls it depended upon to pacify its
human breeding stock suffered destruction. The
crude stardrive operated with only partial success,
stranding 230 "authoritarian" starships in partial
feminist revolt throughout the stars, randomly dis-
tributed over ten centuries by time-displacement...

The Broach dilated upon a torrent.

Aboard *Tom Paine Maru*, in the comfortable, lounge-
like debarkation chamber, we could not see a meter past
the aperture, its rim a circle of azure brilliance against a

curtain of liquid steel gray, although a perfectly ordinary wooden-planked door—supposedly—lay not much farther away than that meter, just the other side of this tunnel-through-reality.

Like a billion tiny hammers on a billion tiny anvils, a relentless roar filled the chamber, broken by a flash, the roll of thunder scarcely louder. A moving wall of chilly dampness swept in upon us, dragging the odor of ancient mildew in its wake. An unusually dry summer morning on Afdiar: we had awaited this letup in the downpour for three hours. It had rained steadily on the planet for a million years. It would rain like this a million more.

So the geologists had maintained, orienting the team of which I became a part the next several days. The sun glared down upon Afdiar as mercilessly as that of Sca. The planet possessed a great deal more water. In consequence: eternal thunderstorms. Someday, nine tenths of the surface would be ocean. At present, half that moisture hung as vapor, continually fell as rain, usually evaporating before it hit the ground.

"No use postponing the inevitable!" I shouted against the hammering. I freed my shortsword from the tangle of my specially treated cloak, loosened it in its scabbard, gave it a hitch where the shoulder sling cut off my circulation.

Uncomfortable without a smartsuit I had never worn before a few weeks ago, I stepped through the Broach, groped blindly for the door. I dropped the knocker on the great green-tarnished plate bolted to the rough-hewn planking. The building, of gray stone equally rough-hewn, sat encrusted with a carpet of slimy moss. Others of the team guarded my back—that I had to take on faith; I could not see behind me. Water sluiced down my forehead, running into my eyes. Drenched fabric clung to my body, hampering movement. I banged again, not quite as happy with my status of "primitive expert" as I had been. It would have been helpful to know exactly what the title implied.

It would have been helpful to know a lot of things.

It had been suggested during training that I try one of the brain implants I worried about, on the same experimental basis as this mission, especially as we would have to struggle along without our accustomed suits—Afdiar was a "critical" planet where the betrayal of superior technology meant death in a number of particularly unpleasant ways. I had considered accepting: if I could overcome its presumed indoctrinatory influences, it would be better than the crude notes I had been making. Knowledge of the Confederate stardrive alone would be priceless.

But—the truth—I was afraid. By the time I really knew the facts about implants, it would be too late. Would I be a slave, sharing an illusion of freedom with the other slaves?

Circumstances had forced me, just before departure, to make the choice for the lieutenant. I could not let him die, even take the chance. He would have his implant. Or the implant would have him. It seemed prudent to preserve mental independence for one of us, at least.

Also cowardly.

I kept wondering why the Confederates dispensed information so freely. Did they plan to keep us prisoner forever? Subvert us? Kill us? Did they have even mightier secrets in reserve?

I wished for home, where everything seemed simple.

Also much, much drier.

The door swung open, hinges screaming. Even in the constant downpour, the musty smell took up more space than oxygen. A bear-shaped figure stood silhouetted in a rectangle of flickering yellow light.

I said, "Woodie Murphy?"

"Sure, an' if it ain't the blessed *Tommie* herself, come to rescue us from molderin' perdition. Dorrie, come a-runnin'—our day of deliverance is at hand!"

The secret word had been "*Tommie*." Close enough. I felt the others pile up behind me, drawn to the pitiable warmth inside.

Carlos Woodrow Murphy—alias Uberd Ubvriez b'Goverd—stood a couple of handspans short of two meters, constructed with a heavy globularity that made him linger in the memory as squat, even dwarflike. He had long hair in the back, no hair in the front at all, a dark full beard shot with gray. Behind the primitive spectacles, he possessed the soulful eyes of a dolphin. He wore the oiled, handwoven trousers, high boots, bloused shirt, waxed leather jerkin of an Afdiarite city-dweller. A soft, foreign lilt in his voice—interrupted by an occasional stammer—made me think back to the briefing I had been given.

Murphy, an "Irishman" from that *other* Earth Confederates spoke of, had fought a revolution in the cause of independence. When the opportunity arose, he had migrated to the Confederacy, convinced his comrades had forgotten the idea of freedom, degenerated into nihilistic murderers. Out here, he fought a revolution once again, though differently. He had surprisingly small hands, one of which he used to seize my own.

A voice, female, came from behind him. "Well, y'big lummox, don't stand there gawkin', ask 'em in! It ain't a fit night out for a magistrate!"

Confederates informally called the place we had arrived Mud City. I had expected any soil that once existed on the soggy, rain-beaten world to have long since washed into the sea. Now I faced scraping off a kilogram I had managed to accumulate in ten seconds' exposure to the outdoors.

The locals pronounced it Hobgidobolis, capital of the nation-state Udobia, also the site of Gabelod, queenly residence, as it had been for her predecessor, Jagelid XXIII, of Eleador XLIX, whose royal countenance, judging from holos, 'Commed to the mother ship, closely resembled those of the riding beasts of Sca. Not that we would be seeing it. Our assignment limited itself to picking up this strangely courageous deep agent, who had spent two decades "inventing" cheap mass-affc·dable flintlocks, introducing the concept of barrel-rifling, initiating mass production, while producing almanacs, newspapers, political handbills, that sort of item, for a living. By local standards, he had become wealthy doing it.

He had also managed to indoctrinate a promising Kilroy genius, one Johd-Beydard Geydes, himself an inventory, colleague/competitor in the printing trade, though of the upper classes, thus influential in his own right. Already Geydes had accepted the Nonaggression Principle that Confederates feel signifies an elementary understanding of ethical philosophy, had even written about it. Assured of other hands to carry the ball of social revolution, the phony b'Goverd looked forward now to "dying"—in order to move on to his next assignment.

"By all means! What can I be thinkin'? Dorrie, put a kettle on, darlin', these poor boyos're drenched!"

Murphy ushered us in: myself, Charlie Norris from the *Peter LaNague*, Owen Rogers, plus a big curly-headed martial-arts instructor, Redhawk Gonzales, who had shown me, during training, that the Confederacy had forgotten more about mayhem than Vespucci ever invented. We had rigged ourselves out as Udobian sailors.

Inside, a low, heavy-beamed ceiling flickered in the orange-yellow light from a huge fireplace set into each wall. "B'goverd," rich by local standards, could easily afford the tons of fast-growing vegetable matter this crude heating system consumed. In such a manner did Afdiarites measure their relative status. Even so, directly in the focus of the hearths, the chill dampness remained intolerable.

Rogers pushed past me, thrust a package into Murphy's hands. "Better take this, Woodie. You look like government warmed over."

In the light, I could see it, too. Murphy actually appeared old—the first Confederate I had met to do so—heavy lines in his face, silver splinters among the ebony. He moved stiffly, accepted the package, began to unwrap it, hands trembling slightly.

"Sure, an' it's the mold spores that've gotten me, after all this time, 'steada the Black an' Tan. Another year, I'll be subvertin' the Devil's bailiwick for him."

"Sixth months, more likely," Rogers contradicted, "unless you get back to the ship where they can take care of you." He indicated the half-opened package. "That'll help some."

"Indeed." Ignoring modesty, Murphy peeled off his Afdiarite clothing, slipped into the perfectly ordinary smartsuit with some help from Rogers, a look of benediction in his tortured eyes. "I'll be after lyin' down awhile, I think. Mind y'keep your Sassenach hands off me wife!"

"You slipped up, that time." Norris laughed. "Sassenach is *Scotch* Gaelic!"

"Shit!" Murphy answered, his accent mysteriously vanishing. "Any of you guys got a cigarette? Smoking hasn't been invented here."

2

It had come time for the "expert" to earn his passage.

Envious, I looked around at the other team members, each huddled less miserable than I would soon be, beside one of Murphy's cavernous fireplaces. I set my jaw, wrapped my sodden cloak about chilly shoulders to conceal the burden I had been entrusted with. The task ahead—a short walk in the rain through the streets of Hobgidobolis—seemed insurmountable.

Sprawled in a heavy wooden rocking chair, the still-unconscious secret agent snored, competing creditably with the thunderous downpour outside the thick windowless walls. His color was noticeably better already, Confederate technology was working its now-familiar miracle.

"Up the street this way," I repeated Dorrie Murphy's instructions, shivering with disbelief at the pale wrinkled skin of my pointing fingers, "then left for two blocks."

She nodded, lifting a scoopful of coals from one of the

hearths, to replenish the supply in a reservoir under the seat of her husband's chair. He mumbled, rolled over into what looked like an uncomfortable position, started snoring again.

I shivered again, shot a resentful glance at the others, nodded resignedly, lifted the latch, forced my way back into the eternal storm. I was soaked again instantly. So much for Confederate miracles. Shaking my head, I had to think hard to remember which way to turn up the street. The summery respite was over; visibility was down to centimeters.

Udobian streets were massively cobbled. There was no vehicle traffic; the downpour would drive hauling beasts insane. Heavily laden myself, I clambered from stone to rounded stone, trying to avoid a ruined ankle, ineffectively shielded by the broad overhanging roofs of buildings set apart by swiftly running gutters. It was impossible to hear anything but the rain, mingled with my own tortured gasping.

Suddenly: "What do ye think ye're doin' in this parta town, Jack Tar?"

The demand was shouted in my ear by a hulking shadow that barred my way. Instantly I regretted our choice of disguise. Apparently sailors were welcomed only at the port.

"Officer, I—"

He stepped back quietly. With a swish even louder than the rain, the constable's quarter-staff swung in a wide arc toward the side of my head, clanging off the forte of my hastily drawn shortsword, its tip still in the scabbard throat. My hip took most of the force, though my wrist tingled with its ferocity, as well.

"Resistin' arrest, is it?" Setting both hands on the staff, he raised it for a second swing. He never got the chance. Stepping inside his guard, I lifted my elbow, straightened my wrist, burying half a meter of quarkotopic steel in his throat. He went to his knees with a gurgle, blood blackening the runoff between paving blocks.

A *grit* of gravel on the stone behind me. I lurched as another wooden weapon sighed through the space I had just occupied. The staff end slammed on the ground. This policeman had a whistle at his lips. I saw him draw breath to summon help, wrenched the blade messily from his partner's neck, slashed it across his face. The whistle stub fell to the pavement, whirled away in the torrent along with most of his nose. The eyes above his ruined face were filled with surprise. He grunted with agony. I ended that with a thrust of short stiff blade through his solar plexus, finishing with a W-shaped pumping flex of the wrist.

The nightmare minutes stretched into hours. I tried dragging the bodies between two buildings, but they kept washing back into the street. Finally, I wedged the staves between a pair of walls, knotted their cloaks around them, left both dead men half floating, half hanging, the first policeman's limp arms making reproachful gestures as the moving waters waved them at me.

I staggered back into the street, shaking from much more than the cold. I resheathed my sword, glancing around for witnesses, thanking whatever waterlogged gods the planet possessed that buildings were constructed without windows for busybodies to peer from. Seeing no one, I reoriented myself with difficulty, resumed what was becoming an endless voyage to the house of Murphy's native friend, Johd-Beydard Geydes.

At the appropriate door, I unfastened the harness Murphy had given me. Attached was a fortune in gold, platinum, precious stones, practically everything the agent had accumulated here, plus a healthy portion of his original operating funds. Not surprisingly, the bulk of it was silica-gel crystals, another "invention" of B'goverd's, cornerstone of a coming industrial revolution. Geydes was rich, but would need more capital if the renaissance the little Irishman had started were to continue. Both men had spoken of an academy. This was the seed money, to be delivered with untaxable anonymity.

As quietly as possible, I lifted the slanted meter-square door of the delivery bin around back, accessible from the inside as well. I laid the bundle on the grill set in its bottom, then slowly lowered the cover again, ready to retreat back to Murphy's—not to mention his fireplaces.

A hand fell on my shoulder.

"Now, now, my dear fellow, that won't be necessary." A strong arm pressed my elbow, slowly forcing the blade back into its sheath. "I've an idea who you are and why you're here. Shall we make our way to Uberd's place, or stand here in the rain discussing it?"

I turned. In the rotten light, I saw the tall, distinguished form of "Johd-Beydard Geydes?"

He shook his head sadly. "If I were of Her Equality's Peace Police, you'd have given away the name of a fellow conspirator. Do not bother making up an amateur lie concerning your own identity. You're one of Woodie's mysterious friends who visit him from time to time, but this visit is the last, is it not?"

I shrugged.

"Let us be off, then. I'd have a word with him before he departs."

The journey back was easier, with two of us to hold each other up. Geydes paused momentarily at the alley where blood still ran into the street. "Bardin-Luther Garder and Jibby Ralv-Budge," he shouted into my ear. "They weren't such a bad sort. Pity you had to kill them."

I spat—the effect was lost in the storm—refused other comment. We trod onward to B'goverd's door.

Inside, the agent was sitting up, sharing a meal with the others.

"Johd-Beydard, ye rascal! Caught us up to it, did ye?"

The man nodded solemnly. "And now you're going away. It will be dull here without you, old friend."

"Ye'll find others to teach, Johd-Beydard. Young Walder Boddale Bagdabara is after inventin' repeatin' firearms already, an' a century ahead of schedule at that. Hedry Wallaz Keddedy's foolin' with magnetism. Just remember to avoid the likeliest pathways the comin' revolution'll want t'follow. Each of the major political systems has its own miserable methods of policy-makin'. Authoritarianism, such as ye have here, operates on whim, divine inspiration, stomach grumblin's of the monarch. All majoritarian systems appeal to the 'wisdom' of the masses. Usually a lot of votin' gets done, t'everybody's ruination. Real individualists, my friend, do '*none* of the above.'"

"I shall try to remember that—and to figure out what it means."

"It means that, no matter how pretty its promises, in order for government t'act humanely toward somebody, it must first act *inhumanely* toward somebody else, because it produces nothin' itself. Remember that—an' someday ye'll stop the rain."

"Someday," Geydes intoned, as if in ritual, "we'll stop the rain. Good-bye, Woodie Murphy. In any event, I shall never forget you."

"Nor I you, lad. Have a nice revolution." With that, he sighed, fell asleep again. His wife barely rescued the half full soup bowl in time to keep it from spilling.

3

Notes from the Asperance *Expedition
Armorer/Corporal YC-038 recording*

Page Thirty-nine

SHIPS OF THE CONFEDERATE FLEET

TOMFLEET:	BOBFLEET:	TRANS-UNIVERSE:
Tom Paine Maru	Bob Heinlein Maru	Ragnar Danneskold
Tom Jefferson Maru	Bob Wilson Maru	Hagbard Celine
Tom Szasz Maru	Bob Shea Maru	Captain Nemo
Tom Edison Maru	Bob LeFevre Maru	Peter LaNague
Tom Huxley Maru	Bob Poole Maru	Star Fox
Tom Sowell Maru	Bob Walpole Maru	Zorro

Some of Malaise's colony ships, in desperation, reworked their nearly exhausted drives, got back into the first universe. Thus two Confederate fleets exist. Tomfleet, Bobfleet, searching for lost colonies—plus a third, smaller cadre of vessels traveling between the universes.

Those notes I made by firelight, unable to sleep, the ghosts of two peacekeepers haunting me. Say their names: Bardin-Luther Garder, Jibby Ralv-Budge. A pair of human beings doing their jobs. Now they were butchered meat in a flooded alleyway. I had done it to them.

Going to see for myself, as Lucille had challenged me to do, had turned out a more complicated, less satisfactory experiment than I anticipated. I could approve—not that any of my teammates cared—that the Murphys had been trying to raise the living standard here for twenty years, struggling against a system deliberately built to prevent progress. Now he would die if he did not get back to the ship. I could approve of rescuing him, as I said, not that anybody cared whether I approved or not.

Around me, Gonzales, Rogers, Norris, were sleeping noisily beside their personal fireplaces, wary even in sleep, hands upon their weapons. The Murphys were in another, smaller room with even bigger fireplaces. I rolled over to warm my other side, tucked the notebook away, quietly unsheathed my shortsword. Despite its sophisticated alloy, its sheen seemed dulled by the use I had put it to. For the dozenth time that evening, I tried to wipe it clean. Perhaps the tarnish was inside me, rather than upon the blade.

It had been child's play, murdering the two policemen.

On the other hand, hypocrite that I was becoming, I had been shocked to learn during the evening's conversation that elsewhere—on Sodde Lydfe—relations among the allies of the Hegemony of Podfet would be systematically sabotaged by means of dirty tricks openly discussed, laughed about, while simultaneously communications were opened between various warring states. Woodie Murphy looked forward to being "plugged into the program" if he could recover his health quickly enough. Dorrie asked about the technical details; she supplied the praxeological expertise on Afdiar.

A long time ago—what seemed an eternity—I had asked "Who are these people?" The more I learned in answer to that question, the less I liked it. Worse, they were dragging me into their machinations. Surely, I had killed on Sca, in defense of my life, of my comrades. I had killed before that, in the Final War. Somehow, tonight seemed different. I said nothing about it to the others, who would simply have talked me out of my depression. I did not want to be talked out of that difference I felt, at least not until I could examine it, determine whether it was real, significant.

17

The Misplaced
Continent

"In any uncoerced transaction, 'tis impossible t'distinguish between buyer an'seller, because 'money' is a myth. *All* transactions're barter, no matter what you're after callin' the commodities bein' swapped."

Returning good health seemed to have an unfortunate effect on Woodie Murphy. As we trudged through the unceasing rain, he took the opportunity to give me a lecture on economics. I could hardly wait until the lieutenant was feeling better.

It had begun that morning, as soon as Murphy had discovered I was a Kilroy, continuing as we took what he insisted on calling a "bus" to the waterfront main street of Hobgidobolis.

The bus "drivers," each bearing a pole supporting the leather canopy over our heads, looked at Murphy oddly as he lectured on oblivious to the fact that I was no longer listening. My head was filled with other, less lofty thoughts. Something was missing—there was no *magic* with EdWina the way there had been, occasionally, with her sister. I determined to be honest with her myself, to break things off as soon as I got back to *TPM*.

And absolutely *never* to fall in love again.

Rain fell, making noise like a ripping sheet.

Dorrie walked beside me, speaking whenever her husband fell silent. Redhawk Gonzales walked behind, his eyes never resting on any single object, his hand never leaving the curved grip of a gigantic muzzle-loading pistol thrust through the belt beneath his cloak. Rogers walked with Norris, at the front, conversing with Johd-Beydard Geydes. Between us, other passengers got on or off at intersections in the steeply sloping streets, handing the drivers a few coins as they did so.

"No such thing as money?" I shook my head. "Try telling them that where we are going!"

"The *Elephant & Donkey*, me bhoy—though personally I prefer the *Porcupine*, 'tis nearer home—they're the principal reason I'm tryin' t'bring enlightenment t'this heathenish balla mud—a free market'll increase hilk production an' lower prices—simple as that—or me name ain't Uberd Ubvriez B'goverd!"

He winked at Geydes.

Hilk was the native high-potency brew that Murphy favored. Dorrie suggested it was how he had contracted the mold. The waterfront hilk-hole he had mentioned was the reason we were dressed as sailors. Frequented by seapersons, among them Captain Ugeed B'garthy, half pirate, half merchantman, half explorer—Murphy insisted I write it that way, adding that B'Garthy was half-again the man any other native of the planet was. One task was left before we Broached up to the *Tom Paine Maru*; it could not be performed by the agent or his praxeologist wife alone. We had come to bring *hope* to this miserable planet.

Murphy needed no disguise, being a familiar figure there. For twenty years he had pestered ocean voyagers, exerting that microscopic pressure—a tankard of hilk was all it usually required—necessary to get sailors to tell stories. Always he listened for news about Tissathi, the Misplaced Continent. Always he was disappointed.

He would not be disappointed tonight.

"The *Elephant & Donkey*!" he repeated as we neared the tavern. Except for the dirty gray waves lapping at its foundation, it looked to me like any other pile of slimy stone the planet had to offer. The agent paid our fare, we leaped from the leaking canopy into the dripping shadows of the tavern's eaves, then went inside.

The aristocratic Geydes was definitely out of place. Noise of the rain was suddenly replaced by shouting, laughing men, the roar of a dozen fires, the clash of a thousand (or so it sounded) tankards of dark, evil-smelling hilk. In one corner sat a sailor, a rag wrapped about his eyes, torturing a musical contraption that was half bellows, half keyboard.

Beneath our feet was a floor of heavy metal grating. I suppose it saved the management the trouble of cleaning up after spilled drinks or customers who had one hilk too many. From the looks of the place, the owners invested what they saved elsewhere. Below, waves rolled from one end of the crowded room to the other. Scattered about, men gambled, drank, sang along with the blind musician, paid their disrespects to the wenches bringing drinks. The smells of tar, of hilk, mingled with that of the sea.

Captain B'garthy was unmistakable, a tall, trimly built individual with close-cropped gray hair, the look of a middle-age athlete. He held court at a corner table strewn with maps, weapons, tankards of hilk, a scattering of coins. A woman sat on each of his knees, skirts hitched up to show their legs. B'garthy paid his real attention, however, to the miserable little fellow standing opposite the table.

"An' what have ye t'say fer yerself, young Chrissie Hockins?"

Hockins twisted his knitted cap in nervous hands, shifting from one foot to the other.

"I didn't mean nothin' by it, Cap'n, I swear!"

A roar went up from B'garthy's tablemates, a mean-looking collection of peg-legs, eye-patches, hooks in place of hands.

"He didn't mean nothin' by it, says he! Hawr! Hawr! Hawr!"

"Calm yerselves, bhoys," replied an unruffled B'garthy, once the laughter had died a bit. "We'll hear him out."

"An' *then* we'll keel-haul the little bilge rat, right, Cap'n? Hawr! Hawr! Hawr!"

Hockins' features did, indeed, remind one of a sneaky little rodent. He had a ratty moustache; his pointed nose quivered. He twisted his cap again, a tear squeezing from beneath each eyelid.

"Awrr, Cap'n, these be only landlubbers I was kypin' from. That don't hardly count, do it?"

No immediate reply. B'garthy's sudden silence was contagious. The blind accordian player stopped, conversation ceased. There was no braying chorus from the captain's table.

Then: "By the saints, you little barnacle, I orta let the landsmen hang ye after all! Theft is theft, Chrissie Hockins, be it from lubbers or yer mates. Fer that matter, ye *were* stealin' from yer mates in a manner of speakin'— now the lubbers'll have yet another reason t'be seein' us as untrustworthy dogs, a'n every bit it's yer fault. What have ye t'say t'that?"

Hockins stood straighter, a defiant look on his weasel face. "Cap'n, I was not alone, pinchin' them chickens, 'twas the Edwards twins helped me out. If I hang, they orta hang, too!"

B'garthy snorted. "Misery loves company. All right, here's punishment—an' the same fer Glarg an' Graid Edwards, *if* they confess. If not, then the townies can have 'em, draw, quarter, hang, stab, shoot, an' burn 'em, an' Afdiar hisself have mercy on their nonexistent souls!"

The captain took a swig of hilk, cleared his throat judicially. "Ye shall go about the town, Christopher Hockins, in every street an' alleyway. There shall ye shout twice in every block 'I am a liar an' a thief an' a betrayer of me friends,' an' this ye shall do until we raise anchor from this port, pausin' only for bread an' water an' two hours' sleep each night. In addition, ye shall pay back the chickens ye stole, an' at the rate we been takin' loot lately, ye'll be at it till ye've a long gray beard. I'll not ask ye what ye say t'that, for ye know the alternative. Can ye read an' write?"

"Aye, Cap'n, after a fashion." Confusion flitted across Hockins' face, mixed with the first touches of hope.

"Very well: *four* hours' sleep shall ye have, an' a spare hour t'write *'I shall never initiate force again'* a thousand an' one times. The chickens'll come outa ship's expenses. Dismissed. See to 'im, Sharkey!"

A grim-looking figure rose from the table, possessing as many missing parts as the rest of the captain's mess-mates combined. "Aye, Cap'n-darlin', I'd be delighted. Come, lad, ye've yer work cut out."

Caught in the middle of thanking B'garthy profusely, Hockins cringed, was taken by the collar, led away.

Music started again. Soon the room was back to its familiar uproar. "Uberd! Uberd B'goverd! An' Johd-Bey-dard Geydes hisself, slummin'! Come here, ye old philosophizers! What think ye of the disgustin'ly enlightened sentence just passed?"

We squeezed through to B'garthy's table. Murphy shook the gray Captain's hand. "'Twas a fine upstandin' thing ye did, Ugeed, a fine upstandin' thing. Sounds like ye been listenin' t'somebody we know."

B'garthy winked at Geydes. "Aye, we've both accepted yer damnable Nonaggression Principle—'tis no man's right to *initiate* force against another human bein' fer any reason—though it's cut *that* deep into me priva-teerin' income. Ah, but 'tis the only code fittin' t'sea rovers, an' 'twill add to our wealth immeasurably in the long run, I trow."

"That it will, virtue bein' its own punishment to the

contrary notwithstandin'. An' I'm here to add a pinch more, if ye be willin'.' "

Murphy removed a rolled-up piece of parchment from his cloak, added it to the pile on the table. "'Tis a map, my friend, of the Misplaced Continent, Tissathi."

Raucous laughter circled round the table. B'garthy slapped the other parchments with a hard hand. Flagons jumped, slopping hilk over the scrolls. "Scrounge around in these, old dog, ye'll find another dozen claimin' the same. Hilk for me mates!" he shouted at the air. "Ye never outgrow yer need for hilk!"

A woman brought drinks to the table. Murphy took a long draught, looked at me expectantly. I gulped, but had thought in advance to disguise it with a swallow of brew.

"Ye will find no such a map in yon haystack, Yer Worship," I said as I had been coached. I still had not gotten the hang of the accent. Now I had to control my stomach as I spoke: the drink did not agree with me.

"It is of the Misplaced Continent—though she be misplaced no longer—I should know, for I have been there myself."

There were only two decent-sized landmasses on the planet, both straddling the equator, at opposite ends of the globe. We had examined the ancient spherical vessel left in orbit, identical to that which circled Vespucci. The first colonial arrivals had mapped the world, intending to land in the more hospitable place. Something had gone wrong. They had sunk into a barbarism they were only now climbing out of. Their Misplaced Continent, Where It Only Rained Occasionally, had become a fantastic legend.

B'garthy laughed. "The land of hilk an' money, is it? Well, say on, lad, I'm in need of a tall tale."

Tall was the word: the map was hand drawn from an orbital photo of the other side of Afdiar, provided details of closer islands already half explored that only a sailor would know.

The pirate was impressed.

"Ugeed, I've a plan," B'goverd offered. "Ye say yerself yer privateerin' days're over: explore these coasts, take only those as accept the Principle. John-Beydard'll sign on. Build a city, a nation, free of queens an' rules an' regulations—an' repel all boarders!"

"A dream." Ugeed B'garthy sighed. "An impossible dream."

"More than that, my friend." He looked directly at me. "There are cures, me bhoy, individual an' otherwise, for the authoritarian personality. None simple or easy."

B'garthy smiled at me as if he was perfectly used to outbursts like this from his old friend. All this talk about ethics bothered me. Aboard ship, I had seen people practicing jailbreaks for Sodde Lydfe, rehearsing assassinations, preparing bombs, planning to wreck monetary systems, to encourage the growth of black markets. The object, I had been told, was to *minimize* disorder or loss of life, leave surviving *real* economics intact, while utterly destroying governments. This was supposed to be good, the right of any being anywhere to undertake. I wondered if B'garthy would still be smiling if *he* knew.

"What we're tryin' to'do here," said Murphy, "is simply abolish the opportunity t'gain power an' circumstances where folks seek others t'rule 'em."

He hefted a pouch, the remainder of the fortune he had not given Geydes. "This'll outfit the voyage, Ugeed."

Geydes raised the ante, plopping another bag on the table.

B'garthy's eyes lit. "An' will ye an' Dorrie be comin'?"

Murphy shook his head. "Ye'll need fresh recruits. I'll stay here, teachin' an' writin' till they cast me out."

"Or hang ye, more likely. All right, by Afdiar's two-wheeled chariot, I'll think on it, my—"

"Whaddyou shay aboud Afdiar anna Gweed?"

A drunken man in uniform had passed by the table several times, the last nearly stumbling across it. Now he planted both hands on his hips, challenging anyone to speak.

I looked at Geydes. "Your noble friends, the police."

Geydes looked up, opened his mouth. "Officer—"

Casually, the cop backhanded the aristocrat across the mouth, then raised his staff, brandishing it at the rest of us. "Thaddle do it, resistin' arrest—I'm running the lotta you in!"

Geydes hit him in his swollen stomach with a tankard.

Snatching up the precious map, the money that went with it, Murphy rose while B'garthy overturned the table. Wishing for the pistol I had not brought, my hand went for my sword hilt.

Another hand fell over mine.

"That won't be necessary, son," the priate said, "just go an' have yerself a grand time."

He smacked another constable over the head with his own flagon, ducked a flying chair, then plunged with a *whoop!* into the melee that had spread away from us in circles. The accordion player did not miss a beat, simply speeded up the tempo, getting into the spirit.

I felt another hand, this time on my shoulder, turned—

Whaaaack!

—wound up on the floor, rubbing my jaw. A huge civilian stood over me, his fists raised.

"Hey, get up an' fight like a man!"

I kicked him in the kneecap, heard cartilage crumble. When he had sunk to my level, I let him have a straight shot with my hardest knuckles, right in the nose. He fell over on his face. I stood, trod over his body, found another person sneaking up on Geydes—who was punching the bartender—from behind. Picking up a chair, I lifted it over my head, took aim—

"Hey!"

—it was snatched out of my hands. I whirled. There stood another policeman, hanging onto my chair.

"Naughty, naughty, little bhoy. That's Councilman G'neezovig, don't you know. Now come along quiet— Ungh!"

I hit him in the nose, too, while his hands were full.

It felt good, so I did it again. He fell backward, over someone crawling on the floor. I repossessed the chair, but Geydes had finished his debate with the councilman using a broken bottle. I used the chair instead to hold off a trio of Udobian Navy men who had joined the fun while I watched Redhawk Gonzales.

Gonzales stood at the center of a ring of fallen bodies, back to back with Charlie Norris. The two of them—I could not decide whether they were an irresistible force or an unmovable object—were the center of considerable attention.

Occasionally one or more men would step into the circle. Gonzales would kick, Norris would punch, they would both whirl about; before you could tell what had happened, the wall of unconscious idiots around them would be a few bodies higher.

But it could not go on forever.

There was a shout, a whistle. Suddenly uniforms were pouring in from every door, from every window. While busy with half a dozen sailors, Norris took a sharp crack on the arm that had just healed. I heard it break from across the room. He sank to his knees. Someone hit Gonzales from behind. Eyes crossed, he joined Norris on the floor.

I used my chair, unable to see my comrades in the crowd, smashing it over the heads of two policemen who were kicking someone. Someone else jumped on my back. I turned around, smashed that person into the bar, but another pair of hands seized my throat.

I began to suffocate, the light in the room growing dimmer, dimmer. I thought I was beginning to hallucinate. The burning blue razor-line of a Broach appeared on one wall.

Lucille Olson-Bear stepped out of it.

In her upraised hand, she held an object like a grenade. Taking deliberate aim, she threw it at my feet.

Catching in the grating, it went off.

2

Notes from the Asperance *Expedition*
Armorer/Corporal YD-038 recording

Page Forty-seven:
   *The Confederacy developed a reliable stardrive
circa* A.L. *250 (I have yet to reconcile the dates to
our Vespuccian calendar—they make mention of
another reckoning,* A.D. *2026), began exploring among
the stars. They worried that "degenerate" colonies
might make use of the new technologies (inertialess
tachyon drive, quarkotopics) to plunge the galaxy
into eternal warfare. A minor "party" in the N.A.C.,
the neoImperialists insisted that the revolution must
be* completed, *systematically destroying every post-
Malaise government as it was discovered.*
   *Two huge fleets were constructed to accomplish
that task ...*

   Lucille was still there when I regained consciousness,
a surprisingly genuine look of concern on her pretty face.
I was lying uncomfortably on the gridded floor, its pattern
printing itself into my back. She knelt—probably even
more uncomfortably—slapping me in the face with a greasy
bar towel.
   "Whitey, speak to me! Say something intelligent!"
   "Something intelligent." I groaned.
   Some tidying-up had been done. Someone—the rescue
team from the ship, apparently—had sorted out the bodies. Policemen were stacked like cordwood over *here*.
Navy personnel were lying in a corner over *there*. There
was a pile for civilians, another for bar employees. Somehow, they were being kept unconscious while Confederates were being brought around.
   "That one's an informer," Woodie Murphy sneered

from the chair he was reclining in. "Put 'im over with the police."

Laughter I recognized. Geoff Couper said, "That should cause some raised eyebrows when everybody wakes up."

"Oh, yeah? Well, the other one there—that's right, the little one with all the face-fur an' the naked scalp—he's Navy Intelligence, such as they have ... put *him* with the cops, and the street-snitch with the Navy. Confusion to the enemy!"

I sat up. "Your accent is slipping again, Woodie."

"An' what of it, me bhoy? I'm retirin' from this mud-ball, about t'be listed as the only fatality of an otherwise lovely bar fight. Me grief-stricken wife'll be after dyin' of the shock. You people *did* bring those silicone corpses with you? That orta keep 'em from makin' me a plaster saint like every other conveniently deceased dissenter in Afdiarite history!"

"Well, we'd better be quick about it," Couper suggested. "We've got to get back upstairs, and fast. You'd all have been recalled, within the hour, fight or not. There's an emergency."

I looked at Lucille. She nodded. "Message from Bobfleet, via *Zorro*: a planet over on their side it's too late to save—now a ball of radioactive lava."

A premonitory chill ran down my spine. "Sodde Lydfe?"

Couper nodded. "Our own mission's been accelerated. We may be just in time to save their counterparts in *this* stretch of reality—if we hurry."

"Counterparts?" I echoed stupidly.

"And our first alien race," Lucille admitted, "the lam-viin. Nine legs, three sexes. Pretty weird. We didn't know whether to tell you or not. Weren't sure how you'd take it."

I struggled to my feet, the realization dawning that the actions of a starship twelve kilometers in diameter, possibly the fate of everyone within, were suddenly in the hands of a nine-year-old child simply because she had once been the only one interested enough to think about a particular topic. Elsie would be ecstatic.

"Aliens," I repeated, "All right, let us go, then."

Lucille asked, "You're sure you feel up to it?"

"Just fine," I lied.

"Good—"

Lucille kicked with all her strength, at the precise point where my legs joined my torso. Red haze filling my head, I went straight to my knees.

"That's for fucking around with somebody else, Corporal, *especially* my little sister! *Now* we can go home."

PART THREE

The
Lamviin

Wings of an Angel

Notes from the Asperance *Expedition
Armorer/Corporal YD-038 recording*

Page Fifty:
*From Afdiar to Sodde Lydfe is about nine hours,
an uncounted number of parsecs, also perhaps a
lifetime—if I choose to believe people can change,
I am writing this—though I will surely have to erase
it eventually—in order to decide. The necessity arose
before we reached the planet of the lamviin, just
after we were whisked up from the bar in Udobia . . .*

"I've been briefed." Lucille grabbed my arm as we
reached the debarkation lounge. Others of the team dispersed to various quarters of the ship. I wanted to go
three rounds with a shower curtain, get back into my
smartsuit.

"There'll be nothing but wheel-spinning the next few

hours, and we've got important matters to settle," she said.

I tried to conceal the limp she had given me. "That sounds ominous."

"You should hear it from this side." Was that a tremor I heard in her voice? Whatever it was, she passed it by with a rush, pulling me along in her wake.

Leaving the lounge, we toothpasted ourselves through a dizzying series of transport patches, finally arriving at the beach where we had first . . . gotten to know each other better. This time, no one else was there. It was very hot. I shed my Afdiarite cloak, the swordbelt, stripped down to the trousers, pulled the boots off. The entire ship seemed busy, almost at battle stations. We stopped, sat down, leaning against a weed-topped dune.

High above us, white birds soared.

Folding her legs under her, she produced a cigarette, inhaled deeply. I envied her the habit, not knowing what to do with my hands. I wrapped them around my knees, watched the surf.

She said, "Whitey, how old are you?"

Strange way to begin a conversation. Keeping my eyes on the water, I replied, "I am thirty-seven Vespuccian—"

"That would make you"—she paused to consult her damnable implant—"twenty-eight Terran years old. Do you like older women?"

I swiveled to face her. "Look, if this is about EdWina again—"

"No, you moron, it's about *me*." She buried the end of her cigarette in the sand, her face beginning to screw up in a manner I had never seen before. "I was born in A.L. 224. That's the year 2000, by the old reckoning. This would be 2052."

I did not see what she was getting at. I brushed a few sand grains off the hilt of my shortsword where it lay beside me. "Which would make you—"

"Fifty-two, Whitey. I spent twenty-three years in stasis!"

Suddenly tears were streaming down her cheeks. She hid her face in her hands while her shoulders shook. Tentatively—odd, since we had been to bed together so many times—I laid a gentle hand on her. She turned, leaned against me, cried a little more, then, nose running, stifled her sobs, sat up stiffly as if awaiting something from me.

I did not know exactly what. I did not have a tissue. Far, far away, the brightly colored triangle of a sail skimmed across the horizon.

"Constitution, Lucille." It was the first time I had sworn in Confederate. "If I understood what happened to Voltaire Malaise's fleet, you are fifteen hundred years older than I am. So is everybody else aboard this ship."

I put a hand on her silver-colored knee.

"Do a few centuries matter, between *us*?"

The crying really started then, choked laughter wedged into the spaces between gasps for breath. "Whitey, if you really meant that, I ... but it's so hard, trusting ..."

She stopped, then: "I did once. All it got me—"

Lucille, having difficulty trusting *me*? Momentarily scandalized, I folded my arms across my chest, looked away. Then I realized I was a stranger to her, for all our passionate intimacy, just as she was to me. Even with the computer pasted on her cortex, she could not read my thoughts, know how I really felt, understand how much I had come to ...

But she was looking out to sea, as well, going on:

"It was the 'accident,' of course, the one that got me 'killed.'"

She turned to face me. "You know, I've thought of it that way so long, it's hard remembering it was an attack by stone-age natives ... not even *proper* Kilroys, during an initial planetary survey.

"I was with Praxeology then." She produced another cigarette, "So was my ... my *husband*, whose—whose stupidity and cowardice precipitated the attack. Who abandoned me to whatever perversities those savages wanted to commit, using me as the centerpiece.

"Security didn't believe I was dead, but there were delays locating me. Coup arrived just minutes too late. I don't remember very much of the really rough stuff— enough of the preliminaries, believe me—but they tell me I was...that I was *tortured* to death over a period of several days."

That is not exactly how she told it. It took a little longer. She smoked, she wept. We talked, we touched. We did not make love. That would be for another time.

The husband, she never said his name, subsequently took their only child while Lucille was in stasis, leaving *TPM* under a cloud.

"I had words with Mac," she said at last. "He insisted I tell you this, told me I'd treated you rotten. He said I'd better—"

"Wait a minute: Mac?" I asked, jealousy creeping in around the edges. "Mac who? You lost me at the last turn, Lucille."

"You've seen him around, darling, I'm sure of it. We had only just found each other, after all these years. The tall, blond, very tanned young man?"

"Oh. Yes. The tall, blond, very tanned young man."

"You idiot." She laughed. "He's my *son*, MacDougall Bear. He's twenty-nine, the same age I am, physiologically. That's why I asked how you felt about older—"

"My god." Relief coursed through every capillary. "Anything else?"

She looked up at me, her eyes very big. "One more thing. An explanation, not an excuse. Whitey, I've had one particular ordeal to face ever since I came out of stasis. Unfinished business. I was all braced for it, every emotion I possessed shut down in preparation...and now this...*you*. I was ready to go back, really I was, ready to...the place where it all happened, where I was left for dead—"

"Sodde Lydfe. Of course. Just because there is civilization there does not mean there cannot be savages as well. Also, you make the same practice we tried on Sca—

landing in the hinterlands. Forgive me, Lucille, I should
have known."

"That's right, Whitey, you should. Now let's talk about
this Eleva...person, shall we?"

2

Notes from the Asperance *Expedition*
Armorer/Corporal YD-038 recording

Page Sixty-nine:
It has been argued that, while you sweat your
brain over personal choices, other "yous," sweating
over them equally in alternative universes, make
them differently. They cancel out; therefore every-
thing is stupidly futile. The Confederates call this
Niven's Fallacy, pointing out that you are the only
one you have—only your choices count, since you
can only live in one universe at a time.

Now Howell informs me that Confederate phy-
sicists are playing with the idea of a third time di-
mension, completing symmetry with the dimensions
of space. They do not know what it is, any more
than aborigines saw that time is different from space,
or people knew about statistical probability before
Pascal (or that it was a fundamental pillar of reality
before P'wheet-Thorens). But it will likely be some-
thing we knew about all along, in an entirely dif-
ferent context. After all, people gambled long before
Pascal.

It might simply be the way time flies when you
are having fun!

"Whitey!" Owen Rogers hissed at me. *"Come here a*
minute!"

His sibilant crackle in my helmet-phones threatened
the well-being of my eardrums. I shrugged, levered around

to face the praxeologist where he lay like a beached porpoise beneath a porous, wind-weathered overhang. The
sun broiled straight into my face. As long as I kept my
eyes closed, that unmerciful orb shut out of my consciousness, I was comfortable. My suit was more than
adequate to the task this planet set for it.

It was only my mind that threatened to bake me to a
cinder.

Below, the quarried fortress squatted in a low, marshy
depression, a long-extinct caldera atop the isolated mon-
olith locals called Zeam Island. We were just off the south
coast of the nation-state of Great Foddu, seat of the worldwide Fodduan Empire. Triangular in floorplan (like most
buildings on the overheated planet), the keep was a low-
security prison, reserved for high-ranking clientele. It was
three stories tall—yet broad enough to appear low, for-
bidding, dangerous.

My thoughts took me unwillingly to Sca, full circle,
dungeon to dungeon. Not a comfortable feeling.

Elbow-crawling toward Rogers, I kept low as possible
behind meager cover, wary of the soldiers below. Six of
us—me, Rog, Couper, Lucille, Howell, along with little
Elsie—plus the alien who acted as our guide lay concealed by an outcrop, the Gulf of Dybod behind us at the
foot of a sheer, cruel cliff face. The soggy meadow with
its sprinkling of wildflowers, guarded jealously by heavily
armed beings of the same species as our guide, lay before
us.

Everything looked *wrong*.

The sky overhead glowed custardy yellow, cloudlessly
clear, the sun on the horizon the color of dried blood.
This would brighten to dull orange as it rose, bringing
temperatures even higher than the hundred thirty-five degrees my instruments attested. Water all around, an extension, according to my suit-map, of the Rommish Ocean,
was brilliant crimson, owing to a variety of algae with a
high red-chlorophyll content. This far from the mainland,
dense growths of equally red higher-order plants thrust

through the water's surface, their stalks calming the waves to oily languor. It got on my nerves as much as the color of the sky, which on my homeworld would have been a warning of destructive twist-storms.

Pink surf pounded on the white sand cliff base.

The meadow itself was a riot of reds, oranges, yellows. Anything that offered cover lay in a charred heap to one side of the building, but fresh grass, or something like it, a few low shrubs, told a tale of garrison troops grown lax. Overhead, one of the creatures Elsie had dubbed "whirlybirds" circled, looking for something helpless to pounce on.

Like every other advanced organism on Sodde Lydfe, it was constructed on trilateral symmetry, boasting three large wings, three eyes, even three *sexes*, exactly as promised. Sculling itself around it own axis to obtain lift, how it saw where it was going was anybody's guess. *Tom Paine Maru*'s biologists would be scrabbling gleefully over the planet for three centuries asking themselves similar questions.

Provided the natives did not reduce it to cinders first.

Settling beside Rogers, I realized my inquiring expression was not being conveyed by a smartsuit-face camouflaged to resemble rock-grown cactus. Apparently he needed help adjusting a setting-dial on the fist-sized piece of machinery he had brought with him through the down-Broach. It was identical to the one Lucille had thrown at my feet in the bar. I held it while he tightened a screw.

Elsie, lying on her stomach, conversed in low tones with Coüper, who was interrogating the native while Howell looked on. As she talked, she played with a small, double-edged knife. Lucille sat up a little higher, keeping watch, a plasma pistol in each hand. I was amazed the way my attitude had changed toward her. Lucille's personal problems were fairly easily understood, after all— though not so easily dealt with.

Somehow, the alien had contrived to meet us in exactly the correct place when we dilated down from orbit. It was my first chance to see one of the lamviin up close. The thing stood a meter tall, wider than a human, covered with thick, coarse, blondish fur, shading darker at the extremities. Its pelt rippled as it spoke, making me suspect the movement was not an effect of the offshore breeze. Each of its eyes, a trio evenly distributed around the inverted-bowl-shaped body, was the size of my hand, dark-irised, protected by a heavy ridge of bone. It gazed from beneath a fringe of furry lashes with calm, unnerving wisdom. An obscenely hairless hemisphere, divided into three saw-toothed sections, formed a mouth atop the creature.

Even more disturbing were its limbs. At the rim of its carapace, spaced between the huge eyes, three heavy "legs" emerged, covered with a camouflage fabric spanning the underside of its body. About halfway down, at the cuff of the garment, each limb split into three more-delicate extremities, heavily furred like the rest of the alien, terminating in strong, slim, three-fingered "hands"— or "feet": it walked on six, holding the remaining three upward.

Carrying a large valise made of the same brush-colored fabric, it wore a large gun in leather harness strapped to the underside of its carapace. Rogers itched to get hold of the weapon. I will admit to some curiosity myself, not only about the gun, but about the fact that the creature was not an "it" at all, nor he or she, but a third sex human beings do not have. I wondered what pronoun to call it by, what its biological function was.

It answered to the name of *Mymysiir* Offe Woom, "Mymy" to its friends. We were here to rescue its husband.

As the conference broke up, Couper slid over where we were finishing adjustments on the bomblike object. Behind him, Lucille was examining Mymy's gun, a big-cylindered three-shot revolver, gray with long use, hard wear. It looked as if it might use blackpowder cartridges.

"Here's the situation," Cooper began. "Our pigeon's cooped up down there on the top floor—V.I.P.—in a cor-

ner cell. Luxury quarters, considering circumstances, lots
of light, good view, dry and warm the way people here
like it. The catch is, he can be reached only through a
guardroom, and we have to get past the guards. How are
you coming on that stasis bomb, Rog?"

The gunsmith looked up. "You know this is a proto-
type, Coup. There were only two, Lucille used one on
Afdiar, and I'm not sure this one's going to work. The
Heller Effect is iffy."

Couper assumed the grim expression he felt most comfortable with. "I want to avoid hurting people if we can.
We're here to stop the killing. Mymy tells us rher husband
is something of a celebrity down there. The guards treat
him like royalty."

"A policeman's lot." Howell trotted up beside Couper.
He wore a close-fitting smartsuit of his own, a pair of
remote-controlled pistols affixed to the helmet.

"'Rher'?" I asked. "Is that the proper word for this
whatchamacallit?"

"Careful, old fellow," Howell admonished. "The lamviin have excellent hearing, albeit the atmosphere is rather
thin. They evolved in it, after all, and I suspect Mymy's
beginning to pick up a smattering of English. Rhe's ex-
ceptionally bright. "Rhe, rher, rhers', those are the pro-
nouns. Mymy's a *nidfemo*, 'surmale,' the weakest and
smallest of three sexes, although if that's true, I dread
the coming confrontation. Rhe's quite a formidable being.
Rhe's also a physician, and has explained to me how the
biology works."

"Oh?" Rogers asked at the same time I did.

"No time now," Howell replied, a malicious expression
on the face-piece of his helmet. He turned to look at
Couper. "Have we a plan?"

The big man returned the coyote's gaze, unrolled the
blueprint—ochre, actually, with reddish ink—the alien had
given him.

"If you want to call it that. The only way is through
that ground-floor arch, with a portcullis either end of the

passage. Mymy's been allowed to visit Mav. He's been in a couple of years, local time, since the war started heating up, so rhe knows the layout."

The others joined us.

"I don't know what you got me down here for," said the diminuitive xenopsychologist, tucking her dagger away. She patted Mymy between the eyes. "They may look a little strange, but in here, they're just like us."

"Why, thank you, Elsie," said the alien. I jumped, started at her—*rher*—"command" of the language until I realized it was only our suits translating. Had I dared strip off my helmet, I would have heard the creature speaking Fodduan. "You look a little strange, yourself. And you say Howell, here, is your father?"

"More so than most fathers." The little girl nodded proudly. "I was a contract baby, constructed especially to order."

"I think that is illegal in Great Foddu." Rhe glanced at the map, pointed to the center. "That is the courtyard. In fact, the place is little more than three walls about an exercise yard. Round the inside, as you may observe on the outside, as well, there is provided a walkway upon each floor, the salient difference being that, inside, these are connected by flights of stairs."

Mymy's real voice seemed to emanate from little dilating orifices either side of rher leg where it joined the dome-shaped body. I could hear rher breathe between phrases.

"We have two choices: entering the arch, passing through both iron gates, up two flights to the second floor, through the guardroom, and into my husband's cell—or scaling the outer wall and passing through the same guardpost.

"In any event, we shall have to contend with at least an octary of guards assigned to supervise scarcely half again that number of prisoners." Rhe shook rher carpetbag in emphasis, laid another hand on rher revolver. This left a third, with which rhe pointed to the fortress angrily. "Scandalous, that's what it is!"

"What is an octary?" I asked, watching the alien in amazement.

"Eighty-one," Lucille answered. "Nine times nine. It's one hundred in their base-nine system. Any more stupid questions?"

"Sure. We are supposed to get in there past eighty-one guards (or is it a hundred?), climb three floors past professional opposition, *without hurting anybody*? Why did we bother coming at all?"

Couper laid a hand on my shoulder. "Just do your best. I never said you couldn't defend yourself. We've got the stasis bomb, and that's what we'll use in the courtyard. What radius have you set it for, Rog?"

The gunsmith looked disgusted. "The marks on the case say a hundred yards. I haven't any idea how truthful they are. How're we going to play this?"

Couper gathered us all around, even laying a brotherly hand on Mymy's furry carapace. "Well, here's my plan . . ."

3

There had not been any point waiting until sundown, after all. Three moons rose, almost simultaneously, flooding the marshy meadow with reddish reflected light. Each of us lay, face down, at the edge of the field, our suits telling lies to any eyes that happened to wander this direction.

Suddenly Howell jumped up, his suit turning—at Mymy's suggestion—a bright green, a hue that never occurred in nature on this planet. At forty kilometers an hour, he rushed, yapping loudly in the evening stillness, toward the open portcullis of the prison archway. Couper followed, more slowly, the Heller-Effect bomb in one hand, ready to throw.

Mymy ran with Rogers, behind Couper, while I followed Lucille, with a different task, angling off toward another wall, hoping the diversion would distract attention from us. The idea was to keep Elsie from getting shot at, not because she was only nine years old—Confederates do not look at things that way—but because she was physically little, could not run as fast as the rest of us. Also, despite her disclaimer, because she was the only expert we had on alien psychology.

From the corner of my eye, I watched the other group converge on the entrance, Howell already inside, making noise to raise the dead. The guards would be shocked, never having seen anything like the coyote before. No one on the planet knew we were here except Mymy, plus whoever rhe talked to via underground radio. It was that station—plus half a hundred more like it, planetwide—that had called Confederate attention to the enormous antiwar movement we were now attempting to aid. Not even Agot Edmoot *Mav*, rher husband, suspected he was about to be rescued, by aliens, at that. Life on other planets was still a speculative concept here, the subject of fiction or fairy tales.

Wait till they saw a killer whale.

Lucille reached the wall ahead of me, began to climb the rough stone toward the catwalk overhead. She would likely reach Mav's cell ahead of everybody else. Responsible for Elsie's safety, I certainly could not climb that way. I started the little girl up, began following, when a bullet zinged past us, striking the stone wall. I glanced up, flattening myself against the triangular stones, saw a lamviin armed with a large automatic pistol taking aim again from the guardpost corner. I drew my own gun, fired three shots. The arm withdrew.

More gunshots rang out, most of them from overhead.

"Whitey!" Lucille shouted.

She had slipped, a leg thrusting down between the widely spaced slats of the second-floor catwalk. I could see their purpose now: They allowed plenty of room for

the guards to shoot through. They were almost unnego-
tiable by human feet. Still at ground level, shielding
Elsie's body with my own, I returned fire to the second-
floor corner guardpost, nearly got myself caught in
crossfire between two posts on the ground-level corners.

"Keep climbing!" I shouted at Lucille. "I have an idea!"

Tucking our xenopsychologist behind me, I stepped to
the door of the nearest cell, fired point blank at the clumsy
brass padlock keeping it shut. The metal bent, shattered.
I threw the door open, gesturing at the blinking creature
inside.

"Come on out, friend, you are free to go!"

I was shocked when the lamviin picked up what looked
like a wooden stool. I was shocked even more when he
(she, rhe) threw it at me. I could see why Fodduan prisoners were constructed differently from Vespuccian ones:
nobody wanted to escape. Ducking, I ran to the next cell,
blew the lock off the door.

Before I could open it, hot lead came whisking through
the air from the corner. Elsie suddenly fired three or four
shots, I heard an alien scream—she must have connected
with a careless trio of fingers—then kicked the cell door
in. Its occupant, a small non-Fodduan lamviin, to judge
from the reddish-black color of his fur, dashed outside,
nearly knocking me over, began running across the
meadow.

That was more like it!

The next cell I opened was empty. Next after that was
occupied by a pair of individuals. "You are free!" I shouted.
"We have come to rescue you! Get out of—*hey!*"

"We may be criminals," one of the lamviin said, grabbing at my gun, "but we are not traitors! Get it, Byv!"
The second lamviin joined the fray.

"I'm trying, Toym! It won't hold still! What is it, anyway? It's certainly ugly!"

"So are you!" I yelled, forgetting interspecies civility.
Hard as I could, I punched the first creature between the
eyes, only my smartsuit saving me from a broken hand.

Crowded, hurried, I pulled the trigger when the second prisoner rushed me. It staggered back, only stunned, then came for me again. I fired again—this time it ignored the bullet, began grabbing at me with all three hands.

I shot it in the foot.

The lamviin began hopping around, cursing like any human being, trying to hold its injured foot, yelling at its cellmate to do something. I waved my Dardick at him in warning, deflecting the muzzle toward his toes. "Get out of here, both of you. Right now!" I fired a shot into the floor. It ricocheted once off the flagging, then fell silent.

"We're going! We're going!" He helped his companion out the door.

By now, the guards seemed to have lost interest in the outside of the fortress. My idea of diverting them with escaping prisoners was failing. Elsie and her smoking pistol in tow, I rushed around the corner to see Couper, Rogers, still outside with Mymy, the bomb in Couper's big hand.

The portcullis was closed.

Howell, apparently, was still inside, trapped.

The plan was not working: he had been supposed to attract guards into a bunch so Cooper, once the coyote had dashed out of range, could knock them all out—in theory without hurting them—with the stasis bomb. They were not cooperating. I ran back, let more equally uncooperative prisoners loose on the remaining two sides of the prison. They ran into the field, then stopped some distance away to watch what was going on.

We were not impressing them, either.

Leaving the little girl with Mymy, I climbed to the second level, tiptoed gingerly along the widely spaced slats in the catwalk, opened more cells, skipping the ones without locks.

More gunfire.

I holstered my first gun, drew the second, shot back, wounding at least one more guard. Completing another circuit of the building, I looked down to see the outer portcullis had been torched open, probably with a plasma gun. As I watched, there was an explosion from within the archway. Elsie, Couper, then Rogers stumbled out, cursing, followed by the surmale lamviin—

—then Howell!

His suit was torn, the muzzles of his pistols glowed in the twilight. Couper cocked an arm, ducked a big-caliber bullet winging toward him on a cloud of blackpowder smoke, then threw.

There was a thump, then—silence.

I climbed to the next level, made it over the catwalk rail just in time to catch a lead ball, right in the chest. Pain became my whole world for a moment. I nearly slipped as I passed the rail going the wrong way, but grabbed, hung on, pulled myself back up. I could not see Lucille, but a huge lamviin with a gun in each of his three hands was charging directly at me. I took careful aim, remembered the hardness of the carapace on these creatures, shot him right in the eye.

Boom of gun, slap of recoil. The ruined eye spurted green goo.

The lamviin pitched over the side with a smashing sound where he landed on the cement sidewalk at ground level. Surprised I was still alive, I glanced at my chest—not even a hole, but it felt like I would have to have my ribs taped. I hopped from rung to rung until I drew even with a guardpost door, not remembering where I was or where this Mav character was supposed to be. There was gunfire *inside* the large triangular room. Peeking around the corner, I ran smack into another lamviin, grabbed his outstretched hand, pulled in the direction he had been running. He fell headlong over the rail. I did not hear this one hit.

Inside, across the room, Lucille was hiding behind an upturned table of heavy wood, trading shots with three guards. Their soft lead slugs stopped in the table or passed over her head harmlessly to splatter on the wall behind her. She could hardly get a shot in, her small gun against nine, but when she did, she kept her fire high, showering her adversaries with hot flakes of stone that her plasma gun exploded from the wall. Smoke came from more than one carapace, along with the suit-relayed smell of singed fur—plus more cursing.

I picked a victim, shot him in the foot—that seemed to work downstairs. He screamed something impolite that my suit refused to translate, turned all three pistols my direction. I shot him in another foot. He lost interest in me, falling into a toe-massaging heap.

Lucille took this opportunity to set a wall hanging on fire. Huge flaky ashes drifted in the air, settling on the two remaining guards. One of them threw his guns away with a sudden gesture, slapped at his fur, then put his hands up.

"I give up! I give up! Peace, in the name of—"

"Shut up, Viideto, you craven weakling!" His companion beat him about the eyebrows with a pistol butt. "Just because you've gotten a little singed..."

I shot this one in what I think was a knee, just as the entire wall hanging fell over him. There was a muffled screaming as the creature began running blindly about the room.

Lucille flung herself on him, brought him to the floor, flipped off the covering, slapped out the coals with her gloved fingers. Viideto rushed to his side, did the same thing with his bare hands.

"Zimo! Zimo! Are you all right?"

"Of course I'm not all right, you *vesa*! Who *are* you people? What do you want?"

Zimo seemed to have gotten used to the human appearance almost instantly. I could see what Howell had meant by formidable.

"And by the way, thank you for saving what little pelt I have left."

I stepped forward. "I want your prisoner. Is he in there?"

I gestured toward the heavy metal triangular door set in the wall. There were three locks on it. The barred three-cornered window through it had been covered.

Couper, Howell, Rogers, Mymy, also Elsie, rushed in through the door opposite me.

"Missur Mymy!" shouted Viideto. "So *you* have engineered this breakout. What a mistake you're making! Mav is safe here, and there's a war on. I—"

"I am sorry, Viid," Mymy said, not in an unkindly voice. Rher fur lay smoothly flat, which I took for some kind of calm expression. My own heart was racing. "You must release my husband. We are going to end this horrible war, right now."

Couper bent, took a ring of keys from Zimo who was lying on the floor, a little smoke still issuing from his hair. "Be good, now, and you won't get hurt."

To me: "The stasis bomb worked all right, once we got a chance to use it. There are about seventy unconscious lamviin down there—more, if you count cells within the radius of the bomb—who'll be awake and hopping mad in a few minutes. We'd better skedaddle."

He reached to unlock the brass padlocks. Only two yielded to the keys on the ring. He turned to look at the two guards. They looked at him. Lucille hefted her pistol. I holstered mine, reloaded the first with a *clack!*, raised it toward them.

"Oh, for Trine's sake," said Zimo finally, "give it the key. They've saved my life, they're friends of Mav's—and I'm about ready to give up and become a Mavist myself—I don't think I can take another philosophy lecture!"

Reluctantly, the unwounded guard gave Couper an extra key. He turned it in the upper lock. It clicked open. Releasing the hasp, he swung the huge iron door aside.

Inside the next room, moonlight flooded in through curtained windows. Some kind of incense burned in a brazier on a table.

On a bed of sand in one corner, the wood of its edges decoratively carved, an elderly lamviin glanced up from the scroll he was reading, set the reading material aside,

glanced from Mymy to Howell to Couper to Lucille to
Rogers to Elsie to me. Then he took what looked like a
long cigarette holder from a pocket on the leg of his jacket,
dribbled a little clear liquid into it from a silver flask,
thrust it in a nostril.

He rose with an outstretched hand.

"I say, aliens from the stars at *last*—hullo, Mymy my
dear—Agot Edmoot *Mav* at your service."

He removed the monocle from the eye that was facing
us.

"What the devil *took* you so long?"

19

"My Friends and
Gaolers"

"What I should like to understand"—Agot Edmoot Mav
gazed out the window at the scurrying nine-legged soldiers
below—"is why you did not employ this wondrous
'Broach' to bring you directly to these chambers. Thus
we should have been able to avoid all this noise and blood-
shed."

The elderly detective cast his third eye on Geoffrey
Couper, who was examining the *kood* service on the low
table in the center of the room. It had not been incense,
as it appeared, but was used socially, like tea. The furry
pseudocrustaceans never took liquid directly, thinking
water deadly poison, although Mymy maintained it was
required by their metabolisms. "I should like very much
to examine your wound, O'Thraight." Rhe wagged rher
carpet bag at me.

Elsie had explained that Fodduans bore three names,
one for each of their parents. Mine, so Mymy thought,

was Corporal-Whitey-*O'Thraight*. Since I was male, I got called by the last third of it. It could have been worse: rhe was calling Lucille "Olson."

Couper thrust gloved hands into pockets programmed in his suit. "For a variety of reasons, sir, the first thing being that the other end is in orbit. You understand what that—of course you do. In any event, there are limits to precision. A minor fluctuation in the mass-average under the ship might have opened a Broach within the walls of this place—messy. Now that we have coordinates, we'll be leaving that way, however."

"I see," the alien said thoughtfully. "Mymy, my love, *do* stop fluttering about! I'm sure the corporal would be better off in the hands of his own people—what do you know of his physiology?"

His surwife—surhusband—whatever, stepped back from me, rher fur crinkling in an odd way.

"Husband, I am well aware of my ignorance—which I had hoped to rectify while rendering aid to a fellow being. My, but you are difficult for one so recently rescued."

Rhe turned to me. "It is obvious something troubles him, yet he will not admit it forthrightly, male that he is, however sage. He would rather bite my jaws off and those of your companions."

Mav's fur rolled into tight curls. "Guilty as charged, dear lurry. I throw myself—wholeheartedly, I might add, it has been a long time—upon the mercy of the court. Were that Vyssu had come with you. I suppose her *mifkepa* precluded such a journey?"

Mymy snorted. "Since when would even so serious a malady keep either of us from your side? We should have broken you out of this abominable place *ourselves* had you not forbidden—"

He strode across the room, six walking legs clattering along the stone floor, to embrace the surmale physician.

"Nor do I recall lifting that prohibition even now—do

not misapprehend: I am grateful. This life was beginning to pall. Where, pray tell me, is she?"

"I cannot truly say at the moment, my dear."

Mymy made another halfhearted attempt to practice rher arts on me, picking at the front of my suit, then gave it up, closed rher bag, threw it on the "bed"—the sandbox in the corner of the room.

"She and her old fellow-conspirator, Fatpa, have smuggled themselves out of the country. She said she'd an idea, but refused me any—"

"Fatpa the tax collector? Dear me, what subversives we have all become! Ah well, what you do not know, you cannot tell, even under the most stringent of duress, correct?"

Scandal filled rher tone, even through the translation: "Mav, I cannot believe that *our* government—"

"If the first casualty of war be truth, my overly patriotic paracauterist, then the second, scarcely moments afterward, is decent, civilized behavior."

He paused. "But I am remiss—I cannot offer *kood*, your environmental suits prevent its use. Nor, do I suspect, would you find my inhaling fluid to your liking. It is scarcely tolerable to my surwife. Do you relish juicing?"

"Juicing?"

Owen Rogers had finished taking Mymy's revolver apart, putting it back together. It used cartridges of brass, bullets of lead, some unidentifiable white propellant. Now he looked up from his tinkering with interest.

"What's juicing?"

"Why, second to inhaling the foul vapors of petroleum distillates," Mymy volunteered, a disapproving crinkle in rher fur, "it is the nastiest habit in . . . in . . . it is the imbibing of magneto-generated current through the digital extremities. The habit leads to—"

"Shocking!" interrupted Howell to the groans of everyone present. Rogers handed the gun back to Mymy, who slipped it into rher holster.

Standing beside her father, Elsie had been watching both Fodduans with silent interest. Her smartsuit was a perfect miniature of everybody else's, complete to belted pistol that she had used to good effect in the assault. The small dagger hung at her waist opposite the gun. Now she spoke:

"Mav, how come none of those people outside are trying to do anything about us? Shouldn't we be getting ready for a counterattack of some kind?"

The philosopher stepped to the balcony, shaded his eyes against the moonlight glare, then returned, rummaged through his belongings for an enormous brass telescope. Elsie peeked over the railing to see what he had been looking at.

"I believe they are preoccupied, young human, although by what—"

I squeezed into the window beside the two of them, activating buttons on my arm. Within my field of view, the nighttime darkness vanished, the horizon zoomed nearer—with it, an ominous circle, growing closer.

"What is black, divided into segments, with a—?"

"A riddle!" Mav exclaimed. "I haven't the mistiest, old fellow, but coming from that direction it will have been observed first at the other end of the island and its approach reported telephonically. Which accounts for the disinterest of our—I see it now . . . it's . . . good heavens, I should say we are being invaded!"

The window suddenly became very crowded.

Extracting Rogers' elbow from my armpit, Lucille's gun butt from my ribs, I noticed the soldiers below had lined up in orderly ranks, rifles pointed upward toward the object that continued to loom closer.

"What is it?"

"Indubitably an airship of Podfettian manufacture," Mav answered, "possibly the *Onwodetsa* rherself—ironically enough, that means 'word of hope' in Podfettian, perhaps a salubrious omen. However, such a warcraft is capable of transporting octaries of troops and a great deal in the way of ordnance. I'm afraid that our escape is about to be interrupted by the very war we had hoped to prevent."

Words of hope. *Asperance*. Dungeon to dungeon. A chill went down my spine that the smartsuit could do nothing for.

"Or accelerated," Lucille said grimly, checking her pistols. "This would make a terrific time to get the congress out of here!"

Shots rang from the rifleman below. Unperturbed, the airship continued on course, its gondola visible now as were the engine pods braced on stanchions away from the black fuselage.

Those aboard were not returning fire.

Closer came the *Onwodetsa*, closer, closer...

Even for those accustomed to the Confederate scale of doing things, the airship was huge. Its shadow in the triple moonlight cast a pall over the entire building. Its engines, driving many-bladed propellors the size of the room we stood in, filled the island with their roaring. Bullets whistled toward it, whizzing harmlessly off its sides. Mav began to say something about fiberglass resins. There was a *clank!* the engine noise died off, something began lowering from underneath.

"*Attention, soldiers of Great Foddu!*" shouted an amplified voice from the airship. "This bomb contains more high explosives than any other ever assembled. It is capable of blasting this end of the island and everything upon it down to sea level! Throw down your weapons!"

Smoke began to issue from one end of the bomb.

I do not know how the Fodduans took it; *I* was frightened. Progress seemed to have taken a somewhat different path on Sodde Lydfe. In many ways, their culture seemed old-fashioned, but their electrical sciences were far ahead of what they ought to be judging from other artifacts scattered about. I wondered about their explosives technology.

There was some milling about. Then, one by one, we

heard the clatter of rifles on hard pavement. The airship
approached the prison. A door popped open, a figure
leaped—

—swinging as the slack in its rope was spent. In a clean
arc, a lamviin figure sailed to the balcony, seized the rail,
climbed over, cast the rope away.

"I will be triple-damped!" the detective exclaimed.
"Also highly delighted.

"Gentlebeings of the starship *Tom Paine Maru*, permit
me to introduce our wife, Vyssu!"

2

All the lamviin looked alike to me.

"Seven octaries, you say? I'm afraid this complicates
matters a bit."

Mav had resumed his pacing. The Fodduan...
triple... had greeted each other with a characteristically
reserved enthusiasm.

Vyssu had brought news.

One item was that the combat dirigible outside had
been stolen from the Podfettian Navy by its own officers.
It was full of Mavist refugees, underground radio person-
alities, armed "to the jaws."

Another was that the terrible bomb suspended beneath
the *Onwodetsa*, keeping the Fodduan troops on their best
behavior, was a fraud.

"We could never have made the voyage with that much
extra weight, my dear," the female observed.

She was bigger than Mymy, smaller than Mav. Any
other differences were concealed by her clothing, basically a pair—trio—of elbow-length trousers, the legs (or
sleeves) of which were connected by a span of fabric that
concealed the underside of the carapace. Mymy had been
dressed similarly, as had Mav, although the texture of the
fabric varied.

"We needed the extra lift across the Arms of Pah—the range of mountains that embraces Foddu to the north and west, dear humans—so we emptied the bomb casing and stored food in it."

"You know," Rogers offered, "we could transport the Fodduan soldiers upstairs and turn this island over to the refugees."

"Who would starve within a trinight," Mav countered. "The supply-boat arrives daily, a service, I greatly fear, that would be shut off in the circumstances you describe."

"Well, it was the only idea I had, at the moment."

"Not a very good one." Couper snorted. "I guess that takes care of Broaching up from this room, anyway. We'd need an enormous cargo aperture, and for that, the court-yard or the grounds outside the prison. Try that, and somebody down there'll make a heroic move, discover the bomb's a hoax, and that'll take care of emigration policy."

Mav puffed on his inhaler. "Are you actually capable of swallowing the entire *Onwodetsa* in a gulp like that?"

Rogers waited a while before speaking, consulting the computer in his head. "*Tom Paine Maru* is a little under ten *fymon* in diameter, a hemisphere, perhaps a third that height."

"My word. Very well, then, I shall try my own idea."

With that, he stepped out on the balcony, raised three hands in salutation.

One of the soldiers picked up a rifle, threw it to what served as his shoulder. There was a report. A bullet spanged off the stone above the philosopher's head. Someone else grabbed the weapon, thumped the shooter across the jaws with it, then threw it down.

Except for the throb of idling airship motors, silence fell across the island.

"My friends and gaolers," Mav began.

The crowd below stirred a little, grew silent again.

"It is time for leave-taking. I know you must prevent

this, though I contemplate harm to no living being.

"I have been with you because I endeavored to stop a conflagration that rages even now around our globe. That it was in concert with similarly minded Podfettians proved intolerable to Their Majesties, who maintain it their prerogative to choose our enemies for us."

He laid two hands on the balcony, gestured with the middle one. "I tell you we must choose our *own* enemies—and allies. Our commerce with others must be solely on the basis of unanimous consent. No nation, no king, no group of *any* composition is entitled to anything that any individual among their number objects to.

"That constitutes the sum of what friends and enemies alike are calling 'Mavism.'"

At the same time that I was horrified, I was fascinated. It was as if this Agot Edmoot *Mav* had been a Confederate all his life. Apparently all by himself, he had reinvented everything the Confederates had taken hundreds of years to learn. I came closer in that moment than any before to wondering if there might really be something to it, after all.

He was going on. "Rather than prodigious bodies of law, the only value necessary for us all to share proposes that no one may obtain his satisfaction by initiating violence against another. Our new acquaintances from the stars—for that is who they be—having made this discovery independently, call it 'Non Aggression.' In terms of evolutionary history, we are both predators. This Principle is the only way predators may relate with one another safely."

There was murmuring below at that, though whether in approval or disapproval, I could not tell.

"I hear it argued that unanimous consent, a positive expression of this Principle, engenders inaction or bland mediocrity. I assert this can only occur in the *opposite* circumstance, where no individual may act without the group's consent—this is the threadbare 'reform' that had brought us from absolute monarchy to absolute majoritarianism. It is no improvement.

"Unanimous consent does not require everyone be constrained to mindless uniformity, or that nothing ever get done, simply that no one be forced against his will. No more natural, lamviinitarian system may be devised.

"In history, its first expression was economic, the free market that made Foddu the mighty empire it became. But there are parallel social forms whose absence point us even now toward disaster. Social order and cooperation arise neither from princes nor politicians, even from advances in the technology of communication, but out of the aggregate of voluntary exchanges, whose driving force consists of a desire to better oneself. Elementary greed, my dear listeners. There exists no 'invisible hand,' an unfortunate turn of phrase: simply millions of highly visible *fingers*, doing—for gain—what others are freely willing to barter for.

"We defy the ordinances of nature at our peril. Taxation, no less than conscription, both in contravention to the Principle, are the very fuel of war. No one who favors them, whatever his intent, can end that tragic institution however pious his claims to a desire for peace.

"Are we become so uncertain of our prowess we must steal, or force what we create upon others at swordpoint? Yet that is the nature of the law, which I depart now to combat. I beg you, release me, refrain from injury to others, from bringing injury upon yourselves. Destructive engines are about to be employed that will end life upon our planet.

"In the name of decency, help me to prevent that."

Lucille was weeping openly, as was, to my astonishment, Geoffrey Couper. Mymy's fur drooped, the lamviin equivalent, apparently, of tears. Without opposition, the *Onwodetsa* lowered rher guide-ropes, was pulled down to a mooring on the island by the Fodduans. Someone thought to throw a bucket of sand over the still-smoldering fuse of the phony bomb. Rhe disgorged rher passengers, who mingled indiscriminately with their former enemies.

Mav turned to us. "I think that we should be about our business. There is a war to stop. Tell me, does this Broach contrivance *hurt* ?"

20
The Prime Directive

*Lieutenant Enson Sermander lay on the bed in his state-*room, sipping nutrient fluid through a plastic tube from a green small-waisted bottle held in his free hand. The disgusting-looking dark-brown liquid fizzed as it was shaken. A very good month, the waiter had said, long ago.

"Whitey!" Sermander nearly shouted at me as I entered. "Come in, come in!"

My own minor injuries had just had time to stiffen. Back aboard *TPM*, I was attending to a pair of errands at once, visiting a sick friend, seeing the doctor myself, while he was handy. There was not much time: things were shaping up "downstairs" for a final, deadly battle.

Sermander's voice jiggled as he rhythmically squeezed the plastic ball he had been given. "I understand I have you to thank for my health!"

He wore the bottom half of a smartsuit, the rest of the

garment lying draped across the foot of the bed. A small round bandage—more of a sticking-plaster, really, was visible at his left temple. I swung my gunbelt with its double burden from around my waist, tossed it in a chair, sagging wearily into another at the lieutenant's one-handed gesture.

Francis Pololo released Sermander's other wrist—odd to see a doctor taking someone's pulse with his eyes closed—turned to his patient. He wiped broad hands down his pale-green tunic. There was a circled red cross on its left shoulder.

"Your bad shoulder's bad no longer. It'll take several days to get used to your new implant, Enson, several weeks to master it completely."

The ape removed his wire-rimmed glasses, polished them thoughtfully, arranged them atop his flat black muzzle again.

"Meantime, take it easy, don't overdo things, and get lots of rest."

"You medicos are all alike." The lieutenant grinned. "Are they not, Corporal? Very well, sir, I shall give your advice the conscientious attention it merits. Will you see to my associate before you go? He appears a bit out of sorts."

The gorilla examined the indicators on my suit-sleeve, unzipped the seam to finger the painful, slowly spreading bruise on my chest.

"Blue today, black tonight," he muttered as if delivering an incantation, "green tomorrow, yellow the day after that. You'll live, Whitey. But have your suit looked at—it absorbed a lot of punishment."

"Gee, thanks a trillion, Doc, I will try taking better care of it."

"Don't mention it, I'll bill you. Have a nice day." He gave us a big-fanged gorilla smile. "And next time somebody shoots at you—duck. I've already had a report from Howell, he says you saved his little girl's life a couple of times. Are you a hero, or simply accident-prone?—don't answer, we need all the help we can collect on Sodde Lydfe."

Lighting one of his small brown cigars, Pololo left the apartment.

The occasion called for a change of subject. "How are you feeling, sir?" He certainly did not look like someone who had just come out of surgery. His color was excellent, his movements energetic. There was a light in his eyes that had never been there before.

"Much better—almost by the passing minute." He frowned briefly, then smiled. "There are no words for how I feel, Whitey. This is amazing, virtually a religious experience. I wish I had realized before . . . look, if I want to know what time it is, almost before I consciously wonder about it, I see a display in my mind, superimposed over the visual field, that tells me. If I wish to know where the bathroom is, a voice whispers in my ear, or words appear, scrolling across the bottom of—"

He tossed the plastic ball through the doorway, striking the bathroom sink precisely, then laughed. "I do not know how to say it, but you get my meaning, do you not?" He was ecstatic—feverishly so—exactly like somebody full of drugs. My earlier misgivings flared to full life. What had I done to my lieutenant?

"Yes, sir, I believe so. Sir?"

"Yes, Whitey?" He rose from the bed, put his feet on the floor, picked up the smartsuit top to shove his arms into the sleeves, his voice benevolent, friendly.

"Sir, I have to ask you a question . . ."

Sealing the seam, he replied, "Well, ask it—if I can possibly answer it, my boy, I will."

"Uh, how do you feel about the Confederacy, sir, I mean, about the fact that it is likely to try influencing Vespucci the same way it has other planets we've—"

Pausing he burst into deep-throated laughter. "There is nothing to worry about, Whitey, I *know* these people now. They will do no mischief on Vespucci."

He stood.

"Sir?" It was exactly what I had been afraid of. He had been *had* by the implant they placed on his brain. I was alone, against a mighty stellar empire.

"That is right, Corporal, because we will not permit them to." He took a few paces, bent his knees, flexed his arms, his fists. "They have made a serious mistake, giving me this device. Every secret of the ship is open to me, every facet of their history." He turned, looked straight at me. "I now know enough to stop them, *whatever* they have in mind."

"Sir?" Confusion, embarrassment, dawning hope, where only despair had been.

He thrust his hands in his pockets. "Did anyone ever tell you that you are a monotonous conversationalist?"

"Uh, no, sir—I mean, yes, sir, that is, I—"

"Nor a particularly intelligible one. I fear your little, how shall I say, that little *convenience* of yours has had a distressing effect upon the workings of your mind."

Red heat rushed into my face. "Sir, I—"

"Do not look at me like that, Corporal! Perfectly normal—that is why the Navy gives hygiene lectures." The gunbelt in the other chair caught his eye. "By the way, I *will* have one of those pistols now—no, do not bother with the holster, I will just carry it in a pocket of my own devising."

I got up, unsnapped the flap of one of the holsters, handed him the weapon, which he tucked away under his arm. I started to ask him if he wanted a spare loader, but he spoke first.

"At that, she looks a palatable little receptacle. Is she any good? Never fear, I do not begrudge you—we shall simply acquire one like her for me, before we leave this ship. Keep an eye out, will you? Dear me, sixteen hundred hours already—we must get moving, or you will be compelled to perform an enlisted man's unpleasant duty. It must be the implant; I am feeling the first animal stirrings I have had in a long, long time."

2

Imagine the sound of three hands clapping—multiplied by half a dozen octaries. Such a noise enveloped Mav as he stood atop a large stump, attempting to introduce Koko Featherstone-Haugh to the group that he refused to call his followers.

A thing with poison-dripping spines had tried to kill me on that stump not too many days before. Now I hoped the rattlesnakes could take care of themselves. To the lamviin, the artificial desert was an overhumid, temporary billet—the only place they were even moderately comfortable aboard ship.

"It isn't our custom," Koko was saying, "to welcome anybody in the name of the Confederacy or any other collective. But I think you're nice, those I've met of you, and I'm very happy you're here."

For some idiotic reason, I had been asked to stand beside the pair. Mymy was off being fitted for a nine-legged smartsuit so that rhe could see the rest of the ship without drowning in the attempt to breathe. I looked forward to seeing rher dressed in the height of Confederate fashion.

3

The great ship hesitated, then tipped into the atmosphere. Twelve kilometers in diameter, over seven miles across, a world with her own mountains, deserts, prairie, she had never been constructed for such a mission. Inertialess, suspended only by the glare of tachyons from her underside, she skipped, skidded, glowing along her leading edge until she was a starship no longer, but an improbable gigantic flying thing, high above the scarlet Sodde Lydfan ocean.

In an otherwise comfortable living-room chair, Koko Featherstone-Haugh gripped the arms in grim concentration. I wondered whether, under their fur, gorillas could sweat. *Tom Paine Maru* had no control room—rather, the control room was inside the captain's head, wherever that happened to be at the moment. I heard the structure of the chair-arms fracture with the stress that she put on them, in counterpoint to a low moaning in the ship's tortured structure.

From the ceiling, strangely enough, music: some hoarse-voiced woman shouting about "The Wrecking Ball." I certainly hoped not. Beneath us, visible through a floor that had become a window, pink foam frothed over the shallow seas of a dry planet. The wakes of two mighty fleets pointed straight at one another, steaming to keep an appointment with racial death.

We were trying not to be late for the occasion, ourselves.

"There she is!" Couper shouted, pointing like an excited child at the giant flagship in the center of the Podfettian fleet.

"Rhe," corrected Mav, "the *Wemafe*. It means 'bird of peace.' Rhe's the largest warship ever constructed in the history of civilization."

He looked out a real window—at least I thought it was a real window—at a bright blue ocean where I had been sailing with the captain not very long ago. "*Our* civilization, that is. I am still having difficulty absorbing the magnitude of—"

"*Tom Paine Maru* is not a warship," insisted Pololo.

For the first time, Koko opened her eyes, looked up fiercely at us. "Yes, she is, dear. We go now to make war on war itself!"

"The *Effulgence!*" Mymy's voice was louder than Couper's; rhe had grown up in a thinner atmosphere than rhe was breathing now, also had six orifices to speak through. Rhe pointed to the middle of the Fodduan fleet. "Oh, Mav, we've got to *stop* this!"

"I am afraid, my dear," Vyssu replied, reflecting her husband's calm demeanor, "that it is in the hands, as few as they may be per individual, of our new friends. May I have some more tea, Francis?"

"Certainly." The gorilla poured a few drops onto a silvery rubber pad on the floor beside the alien. It would transmit the sensation to Vyssu without necessitating the ingestion of fluids.

The giant ship soared lower.

"Well, I'll be a politician's nephew—it's the battle of Midway with helicopters and dirigibles," Couper observed professionally. Having only Sodde Lydfe's whirlybirds for example, the lamviin had never invented fixed-wing aircraft. "This would almost be interesting, if they were playing with anything but atomics down there."

"Nasty ones"—Rogers grimaced—"with cobalt jackets."

"I do not believe that was malicious," the Fodduan detective offered. "It is a commonly employed metal in our civilization. I, myself, did not realize what effect—"

"Even so, it was a near thing." Lucille toyed with a *kood* stick. "We have a specific mission out here, to clean up our own trash. There was a lot of debate over interfering with a totally different species. If those had been plain, old-fashioned low-yield nukes..."

Mav laughed. "Then perhaps we should be glad they were not. Thousands of years, you say?"

She nodded. "Base nine *or* ten. My mother's culture never invented them, not for warfare, anyway. But my father's did; we've seen a lot of them out here. Or their leavings: millions of minds, and everything else on the planet, dead above the evolutionary level of a—"

"Des," all three lamviin supplied at once.

"I'll bet that's Fodduan," Owen Rogers suggested, "for senator."

"Here we go!" said Koko between her teeth.

The mighty vessel banked, bringing us out of the sun from the point of view of the two fleets. They were too far apart to see one another—although their aircraft had begun to engage—but they could see us. The shadow cast by the starship was dozens of kilometers in extent, a giant ominous footprint, precisely as her captain had intended it should be. Smoke poured from boiling places in the sea where otherwise intelligent beings had died for their countries.

Fire lashed from *Tom Paine Maru*'s underside, a column of raw searing energy meters in diameter.

"They were just about to throw out the first ball of the season," Koko explained, "using the biggest artillery I think I've ever seen."

Koko's Podfettian victim began to settle slowly, rher bow burnt off where a cannon loaded with a nuclear bomb had been. We were low enough now to see crew-beings scrambling over the side into the hated sea.

Instantly, another burst of energy: a Fodduan dirigible flashed out of existence.

"Gas-bags to deliver nukes?" Couper shook his head sadly.

"Maybe that's the last," Koko said. "I'm hearing from the Broach crews now."

The tidy patterns of each fleet had begun to disintegrate as commanders realized the new threat they were facing. Despite the gorilla's words, there was a third flash, within a kilometer of the starship.

"Whew! That was close. One of those would've ruined our whole day!"

Personally, I could not help admiring the courage, Fodduan or Podfettian, that had launched that weapon against what must have seemed an invincible new enemy.

"*Attention!*" Koko demanded suddenly. I looked up, wondering what was going on, only to realize her eyes were still closed, concentrating on her implant readings. "*Attention ships of the fleet! The war is over! Cease hostilities immediately! This is the Solar Confederacy's starship* Tom Paine Maru *ordering you to cease hostilities or perish! The war is over! The war is over!*"

Another *flash!* as a Podfettian cruiser emptied its artillery at us.

The war might be over, but it was going to be a long, noisy peace.

4

The decoratively enameled deck pitched slowly in a languid swell that was all the thick, blood-colored seas of Sodde Lydfe were capable of. Given the lamviin attitude toward water, it may have seemed a sizable storm to frightened sailors forced to abandon their vessel at the height of an engagement that had turned, for them, into a nightmarish fantasy.

Adjusting the soles of my feet for medium adhesion, I looked aft, through the haze of battle. *Tom Paine Maru*'s tachyon cannon had burned a blackened pit three meters across, straight through the *Amybo Kiidetz* from rher ornately decorated upper deck to rher specially stiffened keel. Rhe was a comparatively new vessel, crisply painted where the fire had not blistered the shocking pink that, on this planet, served for naval camouflage. Smoke drifted from the cauterized hole that had been rher death-wound. From time to time, the muffled sound of a small explosion was heard. Only rher richly carved water-tight doors had kept rher afloat this long.

Lucille stepped through the Broach behind me.

"Wow, art deco *militaire*! Too bad about this, she's beautiful, isn't she, Whitey?"

"Rhe," I corrected automatically.

But she was right. From downswept ramming prow, embellished with scrolls ground deeply out of living stainless, to the upswept highly figured cowling wrapped around the gigantic pusher-fan, rhe was some three-eyed architect's vision of harmony. Even the gun turrets flowed into the structure of the ship without interrupting those graceful lines.

Somewhere below, I knew, were a massively shielded fission powerplant to drive the fan, crew quarters, officers' country, galleys, messrooms, communications shacks, every one of them alien in design, yet recognizable, admirable.

I was finding that I liked the lamviin, Fodduan *or* Podfettian. Maybe saving them from their ultimate fate was a presumptuous intrusion, as the lieutenant had said, but I was glad we were doing it.

Time enough later for feeling guilty.

Lucille consulted her implant. "Through this door, across to the other side of the deck, down three flights, and a left turn. Why do you suppose they bolted the bomb so firmly into the ribs of the ship?"

That, of course, was why we were here.

"Upstairs," a dozen busy technical squads were confiscating nuclear weapons via Broach—slapping them into stasis until somebody figured out what to do with them—those that had not been vaporized hastily because they had been armed. This particular bomb was presenting problems that called for a "primitive expert" once again.

One with training in dismantling the things.

Poking the muzzle of my Dardick through the rainbow-enameled hatchway, I bent halfway over, followed it into a deserted low-ceilinged cross-corridor. The colors *really* got bright, once you were inside.

"My first theory is no good, that rhe was intended as a giant manned—make that 'lammed'—torpedo . . ."

"Fire-ship, Koko said."

Lucille was right behind me, suit-top brushing the overhead. I was having second thoughts about that pair of plasma guns at my back. They did not have a line of fire, they had a *field*, a broad one, at that.

"Fire-ship, then," I said. "Rhe is too new, too pretty. Also, it is too early in the war. Later, when one side or another gets desperate . . . Look how clean rhe is. Rher crew took pride in rher, Lucille. I feel awful about having done this to them. This is an absolutely gorgeous machine."

Traversing the corridor, we passed several doorways. Bending forward, I could make out an auxiliary bridge: three massively ornate wheels, a clever periscope, binnacles for navigation in the shapes of mythical characters, radar set in expensive-looking framing, etched embellishments encompassing the telecommunications screens.

Aft, across the corridor, was a chart room.

"It's a murdering-machine, Whitey, however well gilded. What do you think, then, that it's a self-destruct mechanism?"

"Not with that yield, the biggest fission bomb I ever heard of, enough to vaporize a dozen ships this size along with a major city for dessert. Darling, a bomb like that could turn even *TPM* into junk."

"I wouldn't have known. I'll try to remember once we get the thing aboard."

"Do that—also, in case you forget, I will disarm it here."

Stepping cautiously over the doorsill, we found the ladder, a broad-treaded affair with low risers, followed it through the smoke down into the bowels of the vessel. Visibility was getting worse, even with contrast-enhancement from our suits. Occasionally, we passed a video unit, its screen still ablaze with the bright-green Fodduan characters for "abandon ship."

The lamviin really knew their electronics—yet still mixed animal-powered vehicles with motor carriages in their city streets. The sugar-based equivalent of black powder still found favor in their small arms, although the ship's artillery ran on natural gas. They had not yet invented surgical anesthesia. Progress in different fields proceeds at different rates, I guessed, depending on the interests of the culture making it.

Rounding the corner, we discovered the remains of a crew-being, its carapace perforated. leaking copper-color ichor onto the decking. We stepped around it, to negotiate the next set of uncomfortably proportioned stairs.

WHAAANG!

What must have been a thirty-gram projectile dashed itself to fragments on the bulkhead next to my shoulder. I ducked back, stomping Lucille's feet, peered out from behind the doorway's protective steel in time to see a pair of lamviin wearing battledress peering out at us from the next doorway.

One of them had a weapon with a bore the size of my fist.

So did the other one.

"Surrender, monster, or die! Your Podfettian masters will pay for this!"

Before I could answer, there was a roar beside my ear. A ball of fusion-fire streaked toward the Fodduans. One stood up, firing at Lucille. I heard her scream, looked back in time to see her slam against the opposite wall. I snapped a shot at the rifle-barrel, getting a slug down the center of the enormous bore. It was not difficult. The weapon exploded in its user's hands, killing him instantly.

His partner retreated. Keeping an eye behind me, I knelt beside Lucille where she lay crumpled against the wall not a meter away from the first dead Fodduan we had found.

"I'll be okay, Whitey, it just knocked the wind out of me."

Her suit-arms shrieked with blinking scarlet lights.

"Call the ship, Lucille! Bomb or not, we are getting you back upstairs!"

There was a long pause. "I can't raise them. Some-things happened to my—Whitey, look out!"

Blam! Blam! Blam!

I had learned by now to aim for the few vulnerable places a lamviin possessed. He dropped his bigbore weapon, pitched over onto the edge of his carapace. His legs crumpled. He was still. I felt terrible. I liked these people, had no desire to kill them.

Stabbing buttons on my own suit-arms, I found I could not reach *Tom Paine Maru*, either. Probably too much metal wrapped around us this deep in the ship.

"We must disarm the bomb, sweetheart," I told the girl. I could not even strip her helmet away. The atmosphere had plenty of oxygen, but it would suck the moisture from her tissues in minutes, even so far out to sea. Instead, I used the manual controls of her suit to produce a true image of what lay under the silvery rubber. Her face was deathly pale.

"I must go disarm the bomb, Lucille. It is being watched on instruments. They will know to haul us in, then."

She put a weak hand on my arm. "Don't leave me... I—"

I nodded, understanding. "Do not worry, I will not leave you."

If I could believe it, her suit was telling me she had no serious internal injuries, no broken bones. Whatever the damage, it would be nothing compared to being abandoned again. I collected her pistols. She would not want them left there. Tucking an arm between her legs, I grabbed the back of her neck, stooped even further, levered her onto my shoulders. I then gathered ankle to wrist together in my left hand. That would leave me one hand free for fighting.

I stood up, only halfway, as the ceiling was too low. Pointing my gun ahead of me, I trudged to the stairs, began to take them one by one. At the foot, I stood for a moment, catching my breath.

"Lucille?"

No answer.

One more flight, if I could find where it began. I cast around in the smoky darkness, wishing now I had undergone the implant. As light as Lucille was—not more than forty-five kilos—strain was beginning to hurt me in my cramped, bent-over position. I kept imagining nine-legged things with guns coming out of the blackness at me.

Instead, I saw an angel.

With a blue halo: the Broach-circle opened, its edges like neon in the dim light. Out stepped Elsie Nahautl, suited up, pistol in one hand, dagger in the other. The Broach snapped closed behind her with an explosive *pop!*

She sheathed her knife, but kept her pistol handy. "I thought I'd find you here. How come you haven't disarmed the bomb ye—oh, boy, are we ever in a mess."

That was how long it took her to see Lucille's condition.

"Are you in communication with the ship, Elsie?"

"Not exactly, see, I—"

"Get that way, now! Tell them to get us out of here. Lucille's been shot!"

"Whitey, they're all busy up there now and nobody's listening. Besides, I can't communicate through all this metal! I came to tell you that they're going to Broach the whole *Amybo Kiidetz* up. The only thing we can do—"

WHIRRINGGG!

A heavy-caliber bullet ricocheted off the bulkhead from behind us. I fired half a dozen random shots in that direction, grabbed Elsie, found the stairs. At the bottom, a door opened onto a large, high-ceilinged hangarlike hold where I could stand up. The smoke was even thicker in here than above.

THUMP!

The blow took me full in the face. There was a sickening, disorienting sensation as the ship lurched. I fell atop Lucille—who only managed a moan at the impact—felt Elsie's hand wrenched from mine. Her gun clattered to the floor. She screamed.

The hold filled with the sound of tearing metal as a shaft of light burst in upon us. Through a brand-new hole in the hull, I could make out the outline of a helmeted head. The smoke was emptying rapidly.

"Whitey! It's Owen Rogers! Have you seen Elsie? We think she came to find you. Have you wrecked that bomb yet? Where's Lucille?"

I opened my mouth to speak—

BLAM! BLAM! BLAM!

It was a Dardick pistol, I knew by the sound. Rogers

ducked as the bullets flattened on the metal plating around his head.

At the other end of the hold, Lieutenant Enson Sermander stood straddling a bulge in the floor where the atomic bomb had been welded. In front of him he held little Elsie. She struggled. He slapped her on the side of the head with his pistol. She stopped struggling.

"Hold still! It will not be much longer. Corporal, get on your feet. Come over here. We are going to blow this starship, with everyone aboard it, to kingdom come!"

21

The Teddy Bears' Picnic

Slowly gathering my feet beneath me, I stood. Lucille still lay unconscious on the floor.

"That is right, Corporal," Sermander soothed. Tightly holding the little girl's neck, he reached up with his gun hand, peeled his suit mask down to his chest.

"Come join me. There is no responsible alternative. I have discovered, with the startling powers these people have been naive enough to bestow upon me, that they have not felt it necessary to notify the rest of their fleet about Vespucci."

Elsie squirmed, "Let me go, you mammoth-turd!"

He looked down at her almost benevolently. "Is that any way for a child to talk? At home, we would teach you better manners, would we not, Whitey?" He shook his head. "Indiscipline is chronic among these people. It deserves only death."

He looked up again at me. "We cannot send a warning

home, but we can buy our nation time. What do you say, Corporal?"

"I say that they need more than time, sir. They need that warning—all the information you alone can give them, now."

Glancing sideways at the hole that had been cut in the ship's hull, I could just make out the motion of fingertips clinging to the ragged lower edge. Someone had adjusted his suit to give visual impressions from the ends of those digits, a sort of periscopic effect.

"It is we who have no time left, Whitey. It is required of both of us that we give our lives, unremembered, unsung—the ultimate sacrifice for which our beings were shaped at their incep—"

"Let me go!"

Renewing her struggles, Elsie flailed her arms at the waist as Sermander held her by the rubbery nape. Almost negligently, he slapped her head a second time with his heavy military pistol.

A third.

The little girl went limp.

"At long last"—Sermander sighed—"blessed silence."

I drew my own gun, pointed it directly at his face. "If you have hurt her...Let her go, Lieutenant, there is something wrong about your implant. This insanity has gone far enough if it means hurting little girls."

Big ones, too. I did not know if Lucille was still alive.

He laughed. "So they have gotten to you after all. I thought so. How many little girls, do you suppose, perished in the Final War? Yet can you deny it was a war which had to be fought? Sentimentalism will not alter what has to be done, even now, Corporal."

He transferred his weapon to the hand that also held the now-unconscious little girl. Stooping, he reached to the glowing control panel of the bomb between his knees.

"Enough debate. So long, Corporal, it has been—"

Firming my two-handed grip on the Dardick, I shouted,

"I am not fooling with you, Sermander, let her go! Get away from there!"

Chuckling, he lifted Elsie until her unmoving form shielded his body from head to knees.

"Do you know how foolish you look, using a mere pistol to threaten a man prepared to blow himself up with—

"*AAAGHHH!*"

Elsie twisted the dagger she had slid beneath his kneecap. In an agonized reflex, he tossed her savagely away. Her tiny body crashed among a mountain of stowage—a barrel exploded around her with the impact. Sermander plucked feebly at the knife-hilt where it projected from his ruined joint, looked up at me, a sickly smile on his face, then reached down for the bomb.

I pulled the trigger. The hold lit briefly with the muzzle-flash.

Sermander's headless body pitched forward, spewing. Owen Rogers' shot roared through the space where it had been a fraction of a second earlier. His bolt of plasma blew yet another hole, in the opposite side-wall of the *Amybo Kiidetz.*

Unconcerned about anything else, I whirled, knelt, gathered Lucille in my arms.

I was cradling her motionless body when they found me.

2

The people of *Tom Paine Maru* filled Lucille's place with flowers.

MacDougall Olson-Bear turned out to be a decent-enough fellow. Much taller than I was—perhaps two meters—he possessed a thick mop of reddish-blond hair, his mother's sea-green eyes, muscles on his muscles on his muscles.

Under the circumstances, I did not think to ask him

very much about himself. A fighter pilot, someone had said. Whatever it might have been, it had given his clean-shaven face a weathered reddish-pink finish typical of people who spend a lot of time outdoors but do not tan well. It looked as if his chin had never seen a razor—or needed to.

I met him in Lucille's quarters where he was filling cartons with belongings. The place smelled cloyingly sweet with murdered foliage.

"It wasn't really like having a mother," he admitted, continuing our awkward conversation while attempting to control his expression as each item that he packed evoked a long-buried memory.

Earlier, he had told me he had grown up aboard the *Tom Jefferson Maru*, had never gotten along particularly well with his father, from whom he had sought something like a divorce at an early age. He had pursued an adventurous life since then, still using his father's name, unaware of his mother's or even that she was still—

They had found each other years later through a fleet-wide survey for people who had blood like hers, rare blood that had been needed after her eventual revival. How ironic life could be. How stupidly ironic.

"It was more like having a sister I had never met until it was almost too late."

I was having trouble with emotions, too, especially when he found a bedraggled teddy bear in the closet. Peculiar, how similar the customs of two civilizations, separated so long. There had been a toy like that for me once, back home...

"This was mine!" he said with a catch in his voice. "She must have kept it all these..." He cleared his throat violently, wiped a broad freckled hand across his eyes. "Whitey, I've no need of this where I'm going. Neither has Lucille...anymore. Can you think of anyone who'd like it?"

Elsie was recovering from minor injuries at Howell's. She had fetched up against a barrel of spike-nails aboard the Fodduan warship when Sermander had thrown her. When I could speak, I said, "Yes, Mac, if you are absolutely sure. I will take care of it."

"Thank you very much, Whitey." He walked around the bed where he had placed the cartons, handed me the bear, hesitated, then: "I'm very glad that you and Lucille met each other—"

I shook my head. "You need not to say anything, Mac. I, er...your mother...we—"

He grinned ruefully. "I understand, and I hope—"

"You two about through with man-talk?"

Looking ten years younger than the giant she had given birth to, Lucille came in from the spare bedroom, another carton of her son's belongings in her arms. There was a pained expression on her face. She set her burden on the bed—like me, Mac had known better than to offer to carry it for her—rubbed her sternum where the Fodduan sailor's heavy, slow-moving bullet had been stopped by her smartsuit. Looking at both of us guiltily, she slipped her left arm back into the sling Pololo had insisted she wear about her neck.

"Mac, I'm awfully sorry to pitch you out like this, just when we'd started getting comfortable with each other, but..."

He laughed. I do not believe I have ever seen a human being more relaxed, so completely self-confident. "Don't mention it, *Mumsie*, I have parsecs to go and promises to keep, myself. Besides, I wouldn't want to interfere with your, er, honeymoon."

She blushed.

So did I.

"And since you're running off again so soon, before you give this away," she said, "you might ask me." She took the bear from me, plumped up its slightly leaking body, squeezed it in her good arm. "What's so all-fired important that you'd leave your poor old mother and her—"

"Gigolo," I offered.

"I kind of like that—'gigolo'—to go running off for?"

"There's an alarm of some kind in *THM*'s investigation sector, something about one of Voltaire Malaise's colony ships that's only just now arriving, thanks to time displacement, and with its mind-control system still operating. Maybe the old son-of-a-bureaucrat himself is aboard. I want to be there when the plug gets pulled."

"Tom Huxley Maru?" Lucille consulted the ceiling for data, then blinked. "Why, that's Brion Bayard's new command. Mac, I hate to disappoint you, but we're beginning to think Voltaire Malaise wound up on Whitey's world, isn't that right, Corporal-darling? Nevertheless, I wouldn't mind being there, myself. Think of it: tens of thousand of freshly kidnapped women, free to do whatever they want with their kidnappers!"

She held the bear out at arms' length, then sat it on the bed, leaning against one of Mac's plastic cartons. "Well, if you have to go, you have to go. About this . . ."

"I think Whitey was going to give it to Elsie Nahuatl."

She grinned, looked at me. "My daddy gave it to me when I was laid up with a bad appendix. Good therapy. You'll probably need it yourself, after *your* operation this afternoon."

The animal stared at me dementedly with its scratched plastic eyes, but refused to offer any comfort or advice.

3

Nahuatl, Elsa Lysandra: hd. of xenopsych. dept., prax. div., Tom Paine Maru; b.Cody, Wyoming, Solar Confed., 5/23/267, Aust. aborigine lineage, [ident. of bio. parents under privacy-protect except in certifiably appropriate emergency]; adopt. parent G. Howell Nahuatl, ops div., Tom Paine Maru; ht.37in., wt.53 lbs., hr.blond, complex.d.brown, eyes blue.

More info? [Y/N]

Her likeless, in full color stereo, hung before my eyes. Curious, I nodded microscopically. Before long, I had been told a little while ago, the subliminal muscular traces of my *intention* to nod would be sufficient to cue the implant correctly. Until then, it would take a little practice to get to know one another.

Through the ID holo, I could see another Elsie, chatting with her friends. We were attending something like a wake, except that the nine-year-old guest of honor was sitting up in bed, cleaning her dagger. Her tiny automatic pistol lay in neatly ordered pieces on a cloth on the end-table, ready for reassembly after Owen Rogers had thrust them through the shower curtain three or four more times.

She was a tough customer to satisfy, apparently. On Sodde Lydfe, she had confided in me that she wanted to be just like Lucille when she grew up. God help the galaxy!

> *Assoc. ref.: Nahuatl, G. Howell, ops div.*, Tom Paine Maru. *Further info under discretionary privacy-protect at subj.'s specification.*
> *Contact subj. for info release? [Y/N]*

With a shake of my head, I suppressed any further retrieval from the implant. It was the first thing I had been shown how to do, by the implant itself. The arduous "operation" I had dreaded for so long had taken all of three minutes, most of it to dab a little alcohol on the site before injection, a useless procedure medically, but some rituals survive everything. It seemed to make the nurse feel better.

The bright-green letters vanished from the bottom edge of my field of vision, along with the picture of the coyote.

Howell, of course, was there, curled up on one corner of the bed, also Francis W. Pololo—along with Mymysiir, who was listening to the gorilla lecture rher on the subject of human anatomy. In the corner, Vyssu was showing

EdWina how to knit using three needles. My freshly inserted computer likely would have stripped its gears supplying information on this crowd.

"They're fragile," Pololo was telling the lamviin paracauterist, "unlike you or me, yet somehow very tough. This rugged individual, despite a fractured vertebra, a punctured lung, and three broken ribs, wanted to get up and stomp on what was left of Serman—oh, hello, Whitey! I didn't see you come in. Lucille, how are you feeling, dear?"

She gulped. "A lot better before I walked into this room! I had no idea little Elsie had been hurt so badly."

Neither had I.

"Little Elsie's gonna hurt you badly, Lucille Olson-Bear, unless you stop talking about her in the diminuitive third person! Hi, Corporal-darling, what did you bring me?"

I held up the tattered toy with a fresh red ribbon around its neck. "This, sweetheart, it is really from Lucille, here— also Mac."

"MacBear? He 'Commed to say good-bye, but I didn't know he was going to send me any—a teddy! An *old* one! Oh, Lucille, he must have been yours!"

My warrior-maiden nodded. The little girl peered thoughtfully at the gunsmith as she supervised his reassembly of her pistol, teddy bear clutched to her chest.

"Wanna know what I'm gonna call him?"

He smiled, shook his head—*cursed* as the end of a coil-spring gouged him under the thumbnail.

Elsie giggled. "I'm gonna call him Owen!"

Mymy examined the bedraggled stuffed animal closely. Howell sniffed at it. The gorilla physician closed up his case, extracted a cigar from his pocket, drew smoke as the smelly thing lighted itself.

"I'll be going, now. Koko's calling. She's arranging a tea for the royal trines of Podfet and Foddu, and the pleasure of my company's requested. We're going to show them holos of the ruined Sodde Lydfe on the other side, so they may not have much of an appetite. Thanks for the smelling-salts, Mymy. Now a question of protocol: how are they likely to react when they find out we won't call people by their authoritarian titles aboard this ship?"

Mymy stirred a manipulatory limb, gave the teddy bear an affectionate stroke. "I don't know about the Podfettians, but the surprince will be delighted. Rhe's just finished preparatory school—the first surmale of the royal family ever to do so—and wants everyone to call rher 'Vuffi'!"

I do not know exactly when I made up my mind about Vespucci. Perhaps in the hold with Sermander, perhaps on Afdiar somewhere. It is not the kind of conclusion one comes to overnight or all in one piece. I simply began operating on the assumption—before I knew I had come to it—that I would be acting as *TPM*'s "primitive expert" on my native planet, that Afdiar or Sodde Lydfe were merely practice for what would be to me the main event.

Perhaps it was at the same time I made up my mind about Eleva.

For Lucille, the main event was over. I planned to begin training, right alongside her, so that, together, we could make sure no demons would ever begin haunting her again. I thought my being beside her from now on would make a lot of difference. At least I hoped it would.

The trouble with being free is that it funnels a lot of decisions your way that you were used to having made by someone else. Mav had made a decision I learned about when he joined his mates in Elsie's room:

"I say, old armorer, this is a bit of all right, what?"

"What?" His breathing orifices had not moved a centimeter. He was "speaking" to me over the implant link. *"Mav, you have had an—!"*

As silently as the "priests" who had rescued me on Sca: *"Too right, my dear fellow. I loathed and detested growing old, although I attempted to make the best of it.*

Now I find it won't be necessary. This niggling little operation is the first step. The Healing staff informs me that, with Mymy's assistance, there will soon be a cure for aging among lamviin much as there are for the various species of the Confederacy. I shall await it with as much patience as I can muster."

I laughed out loud, then: *"I take it, then, that one of our ships will be returning to Sodde Lydfe in the not-too-distant future."*

"You take it wrong. Actually, I haven't the foggiest—you see, we're going with you."

"But Mav," I said aloud, "Your planet is undergoing a revolution. Everything is going to change. Your people will be needing you. There will be peace, freedom, prosperity—"

"And no heroes and no gurus, not if I can help it. Whitey, I am going to be yong again and see more of the universe than I had ever imagined possible. My people? They need only themselves. And besides, these"—he gestured with his middle hand at everyone in the room—*"these are my people—what they call mindkind. I am content."*

I put my arms around Lucille. She looked up at me. I winked. She went back to watching Elsie playing with the bear.

"Yes, Mav, so am I."

About the Author

Self-defense consultant and former police reservist, L. Neil Smith has also worked as a gunsmith and a professional musician. Born in Denver in 1946, he traveled widely as an Air Force "brat," growing up in a dozen regions of the United States and Canada. In 1964, he returned home to study philosophy, psychology, and anthropology, and wound up with what he refers to as perhaps the lowest grade-point average in the history of Colorado State University.